COLLECTED NOVELLAS

OTHER BOOKS BY GABRIEL GARCÍA MÁRQUEZ

One Hundred Years of Solitude

The Autumn of the Patriarch

Innocent Eréndira and Other Stories

In Evil Hour

Collected Stories

The Story of a Shipwrecked Sailor

Clandestine in Chile: The Adventures of Miguel Littín

Love in the Time of Cholera

The General in His Labyrinth

GABRIEL GARCÍA MÁRQUEZ

COLLECTED NOVELLAS

Leaf Storm

No One Writes to the Colonel

Chronicle of a Death Foretold

Translated from the Spanish by
Gregory Rabassa and J. S. Bernstein

HarperPerennial
A Division of HarperCollins*Publishers*

First HarperPerennial edition published 1991.

Designed by Cassandra J. Pappas

The Library of Congress has catalogued the hardcover edition as follows:

García Márquez, Gabriel, 1928–
    [Novellas. English]
    Collected novellas / Gabriel García Márquez.
      p. cm.
    Contents: Leaf storm — No one writes to the colonel — Chronicle of a death foretold.
    ISBN 0-06-016384-4
    I. Title.
PQ8180.17.A73A6 1990   89-46106
863—dcc20

ISBN 0-06-092128-5 (pbk.)
    94 95 MV/RRD 10 9 8 7 6 5

Contents

Leaf Storm

translated from the Spanish by Gregory Rabassa

—SUDDENLY, AS IF A WHIRLWIND HAD SET DOWN ROOTS IN THE center of the town, the banana company arrived, pursued by the leaf storm. A whirling leaf storm had been stirred up, formed out of the human and material dregs of other towns, the chaff of a civil war that seemed ever more remote and unlikely. The whirlwind was implacable. It contaminated everything with its swirling crowd smell, the smell of skin secretion and hidden death. In less than a year it sowed over the town the rubble of many catastrophes that had come before it, scattering its mixed cargo of rubbish in the streets. And all of a sudden that rubbish, in time to the mad and unpredicted rhythm of the storm, was being sorted out, individualized, until what had been a narrow street with a river at one end and a corral for the dead at the other was changed into a different and more complex town, created out of the rubbish of other towns.

Arriving there, mingled with the human leaf storm, dragged along by its impetuous force, came the dregs of warehouses, hospitals, amusements parlors, electric plants; the dregs made up of single women and men who tied their mules to hitching posts by the hotel, carrying their single piece of baggage, a wooden trunk or a bundle of clothing, and in a few months each had his own house, two mistresses, and the military title that was due him for having arrived late for the war.

Even the dregs of the cities' sad love came to us in the whirlwind and built small wooden houses where at first a corner and a half-cot were a dismal home for one night, and then a noisy clandestine street, and then a whole inner village of tolerance within the town.

In the midst of that blizzard, that tempest of unknown faces, of awnings along the public way, of men changing clothes in the street, of women with open parasols sitting on trunks, and of mule after abandoned mule dying of hunger on the block by the hotel, the first of us came to be the last; we were the outsiders, the newcomers.

After the war, when we came to Macondo and appreciated the good quality of its soil, we knew that the leaf storm was sure to come someday, but we did not count on its drive. So when we felt the avalanche arrive, the only thing we could do was set a plate with a knife and fork behind the door and sit patiently waiting for the newcomers to get to know us. Then the train whistled for the first time. The leaf storm turned about and went out to greet it, and by turning it lost its drive. But it developed unity and mass; and it underwent the natural process of fermentation, becoming incorporated into the germination of the earth.

Macondo, 1909

1

I'VE SEEN A CORPSE FOR THE FIRST TIME. IT'S WEDNESDAY BUT I
feel as if it was Sunday because I didn't go to school and they
dressed me up in a green corduroy suit that's tight in some
places. Holding Mama's hand, following my grandfather, who
feels his way along with a cane with every step he takes so he
won't bump into things (he doesn't see well in the dark and
he limps), I went past the mirror in the living room and saw
myself full length, dressed in green and with this white starched
collar that pinches me on one side of the neck. I saw myself
in the round mottled looking glass and I thought: *That's me, as
if today was Sunday.*

We've come to the house where the dead man is.

The heat won't let you breathe in the closed room. You
can hear the sun buzzing in the streets, but that's all. The air
is stagnant, like concrete; you get the feeling that it could get
all twisted like a sheet of steel. In the room where they've laid
out the corpse there's a smell of trunks, but I can't see any
anywhere. There's a hammock in the corner hanging by one
end from a ring. There's a smell of trash. And I think that the
things around us, broken down and almost falling apart, have
the look of things that ought to smell like trash even though
they smell like something else.

I always thought that dead people should have hats on. Now I can see that they shouldn't. I can see that they have a head like wax and a handkerchief tied around their jawbone. I can see that they have their mouth open a little and that behind the purple lips you can see the stained and irregular teeth. I can see that they keep their tongue bitten over to one side, thick and sticky, a little darker than the color of their face, which is like the color of fingers clutching a stick. I can see that they have their eyes open much wider than a man's, anxious and wild, and that their skin seems to be made of tight damp earth. I thought that a dead man would look like somebody quiet and asleep and now I can see that it's just the opposite. I can see that he looks like someone awake and in a rage after a fight.

Mama is dressed up as if it was Sunday too. She put on the old straw hat that comes down over her ears and a black dress closed at the neck and with sleeves that come down to her wrists. Since today is Wednesday she looks to me like someone far away, a stranger, and I get the feeling that she wants to tell me something when my grandfather gets up to receive the men who've brought the coffin. Mama is sitting beside me with her back to the closed door. She's breathing heavily and she keeps pushing back the strands of hair that fall out from under the hat that she put on in a hurry. My grandfather has told the men to put the coffin down next to the bed. Only then did I realize that the dead man could really fit into it. When the men brought in the box I had the impression that it was too small for a body that took up the whole length of the bed.

I don't know why they brought me along. I've never been in this house before and I even thought that nobody lived here. It's a big house, on the corner, and I don't think the door has ever been opened. I always thought that nobody lived in the house. Only now, after my mother told me, "You won't be going to school this afternoon," and I didn't feel glad because she said it with a serious and reserved voice, and I saw her come back with my corduroy suit and she put it on me without saying a word and we went to the door to join my grandfather, and we walked past the three houses that separated this one from ours, only now do I realize that someone lived on the corner. Someone who died and who must be the man my mother was talking about when she said: "You have to behave yourself at the doctor's funeral."

When we went in I didn't see the dead man. I saw my grandfather at the door talking to the men, and then I saw him telling us to go on in. I thought then that there was somebody in the room, but when I went in I felt it was dark and empty. The heat beat on my face from the very first minute and I got that trash smell that was solid and permanent at first and now, like the heat, comes in slow-spaced waves and disappears. Mama led me through the dark room by the hand and seated me next to her in a corner. Only after a moment could I begin to make things out. I saw my grandfather trying to open a window that seemed stuck to its frame, glued to the wood around it, and I saw him hitting his cane against the latches, his coat covered with the dust that came off with every blow. I turned my head to where my grandfather was moving as he said he couldn't open the window and only then did I see there was someone on the bed. There was a dark man stretched out, motionless. Then I spun my head to my mother's side where she sat serious and without moving, looking off somewhere else in the room. Since my feet don't touch the floor and hang in the air half a foot away, I put my hands under my thighs, placing the palms on the chair, and I began to swing my legs, not thinking about anything until I remembered that Mama had told me: "You have to behave yourself at the doctor's funeral." Then I felt something cold behind me. I turned to look and I only saw the wall of dry and pitted wood. But it was as if someone had said to me from the wall: *Don't move your legs. The man on the bed is the doctor and he's dead.* And when I looked toward the bed I didn't see him the way I had before. I didn't see him lying down, I saw him dead.

From then on, as much as I try not to look, I feel as if someone is forcing my face in that direction. And even if I make an effort to look at other places in the room, I see him just the same, everywhere, with his bulging eyes and his green, dead face in the shadows.

I don't know why no one has come to the wake. The ones who came are us, my grandfather, Mama, and the four Guajiro Indians who work for my grandfather. The men brought a sack of lime and emptied it inside the coffin. If my mother hadn't been strange and far away I would have asked her why they did it. I don't understand why they have to sprinkle lime inside the box. When the bag was empty one of the men shook it over the coffin and a few last flakes fell out, looking more like sawdust than lime. They lifted the dead man by the shoulders and feet. He's wearing a pair of cheap pants tied at the waist by a wide black cord, and a gray shirt. He only has his left shoe on. As Ada says, he's got one foot a king and the other one a slave. The right shoe is at one end of the bed. On the bed the dead man seemed to be having trouble. In the coffin he looks more comfortable, more peaceful, and his face, which had been like the face of a man who was alive and awake after a fight, has taken on a restful and secure look. His profile is softer. It's as if in the box there he now felt he was in his proper place as a dead man.

My grandfather's been moving around the room. He's picked up some things and put them in the box. I look at Mama again hoping that she'll tell me why my grandfather is tossing things into the coffin. But my mother is unmoved in her black dress and she seems to be making an effort not to look where the dead man is. I try to do the same thing but I can't. I stare at him. I examine him. My grandfather throws a book inside the coffin, signals the men, and three of them put the lid over the corpse. Only then do I feel free of the hands that were holding my head toward that side and I begin to look the room over.

I look at my mother again. For the first time since we

came to the house she looks at me and smiles with a forced smile, with nothing inside; and in the distance I can hear the train whistle as it disappears around the last bend. I hear a sound from the corner where the corpse is. I see one of the men lift one edge of the lid and my grandfather puts the dead man's shoe into the coffin, the shoe they had forgotten on the bed. The train whistles again, farther off, and suddenly I think: *It's two-thirty.* I remember that it's the time (when the train whistles at the last bend in town) when the boys line up at school to go in for the first class in the afternoon.

Abraham, I think.

I shouldn't have brought the child. A spectacle like this isn't proper for him. Even for myself, turning thirty, this atmosphere thinned out by the presence of the corpse is harmful. We could leave now. We could tell Papa that we don't feel well in a room where the remains of a man cut off from everything that could be considered affection or thanks have been accumulating for seventeen years. My father may be the only one who's ever shown any feeling for him. An inexplicable feeling that's been of use to him now so he won't rot away inside these four walls.

I'm bothered by how ridiculous all of this is. I'm upset by the idea that in a moment we'll be going out into the street following a coffin that won't inspire any feeling except pleasure in anyone. I can imagine the expression on the faces of the women in the windows, watching my father go by, watching me go by with the child behind a casket inside of which the only person the town has wanted to see that way is rotting away, on his way to the cemetery in the midst of unyielding abandonment, followed by three people who decided to perform a work of charity that's been the beginning of his own vengeance. It could be that this decision of Papa's could mean that tomorrow there won't be anyone prepared to walk behind our funeral processions.

Maybe that's why I brought the child along. When Papa

told me a moment ago: "You have to go with me," the first thing that occurred to me was to bring the child so that I would feel protected. Now here we are on this suffocating September afternoon, feeling that the things around us are the pitiless agents of our enemies. Papa's got no reason to worry. Actually, he's spent his whole life doing things like this; giving the town stones to chew on, keeping his most insignificant promises with his back turned to all convention. Since that time twenty-five years ago when this man came to our house, Papa must have imagined (when he noticed the visitor's absurd manners) that today there wouldn't be a single person in the whole town prepared even to throw his body to the buzzards. Maybe Papa foresaw all the obstacles and measured and calculated the possible inconveniences. And now, twenty-five years later, he must feel that this is just the fulfillment of a chore he's thought about for a long time, one which had to be carried out in any case, since he would have had to haul the corpse through the streets of Macondo by himself.

Still, when the time came, he didn't have the courage to do it alone and he made me take part in that intolerable promise that he must have made long before I even had the use of reason. When he told me: "You have to go with me," he didn't give me time to think about how far his words went; I couldn't calculate how much shame and ridicule there would be in burying this man whom everyone had hoped to see turn to dust inside his lair. Because people hadn't just expected that, they'd prepared themselves for things to happen that way and they'd hoped for it from the bottom of their hearts, without remorse, and even with the anticipated satisfaction of someday smelling the pleasant odor of his decomposition floating through the town without anyone's feeling moved, alarmed, or scandalized, satisfied rather at seeing the longed-for hour come, wanting the situation to go on and on until the twirling smell of the dead man would satisfy even the most hidden resentments.

Now we're going to deprive Macondo of its long-desired

pleasure. I feel as if in a certain way this determination of ours has given birth in the hearts of the people not to a melancholy feeling of frustration but to one of postponement.

That's another reason why I should have left the child at home; so as not to get him mixed up in this conspiracy which will center on us now the way it did on the doctor for ten years. The child should have been left on the sidelines of this promise. He doesn't even know why he's here, why we've brought him to this room full of rubbish. He doesn't say anything, sitting, swinging his legs with his hands resting on the chair, waiting for someone to decipher this frightful riddle for him. I want to be sure that nobody will, that no one will open that invisible door that prevents him from going beyond the reach of his senses.

He's looked at me several times and I know that he finds me strange, somebody he doesn't know, with this stiff dress and this old hat that I've put on so that I won't be identified even by my own forebodings.

If Meme were alive, here in the house, maybe it would have been different. They might have thought I came because of her. They might have thought I came to share in a grief that she probably wouldn't have felt, but which she would have been able to pretend and which the town could have explained. Meme disappeared about eleven years ago. The doctor's death has ended any possibility of finding out where she is or, at least, where her bones are. Meme isn't here, but it's most likely that if she were—if what happened and was never cleared up hadn't happened—she would have taken the side of the town against the man who warmed her bed for six years with as much love and humanity as a mule might have had.

I can hear the train whistling at the last bend. *It's two-thirty,* I think; and I can't get rid of the idea that at this moment all of Macondo is wondering what we're doing in this house. I think about Señora Rebeca, thin and looking like parchment, with the touch of a family ghost in her look and dress, sitting beside her electric fan, her face shaded by the screens in her windows. As she hears the train disappearing around the last bend Señora Rebeca leans her head toward the fan, tormented by the heat and her resentment, the blades in her heart spinning like those on the fan (but in an opposite direction), and she murmurs: "The devil has a hand in all of this," and she shudders, fastened to life by the tiny roots of everyday things.

And Águeda, the cripple, seeing Solita coming back from the station after seeing her boyfriend off; seeing her open her parasol as she turns the deserted corner; hearing her approach with the sexual rejoicing that she herself once had and which changed inside her into that patient religious sickness that makes her say: "You'll wallow in your bed like a pig in its sty."

I can't get rid of that idea. Stop thinking that it's two-thirty; that the mule with the mail is going by cloaked in a burning cloud of dust and followed by the men who have interrupted their Wednesday siesta to pick up the bundles of newspapers. Father Ángel is dozing, sitting in the sacristy with an open breviary on his greasy stomach, listening to the mule pass and shooting away the flies that are bothering his sleep, belching, saying: "You poisoned me with your meatballs."

Papa's cold-blooded about all this. Even to the point of telling them to open the coffin so they could put in the shoe that was left on the bed. Only he could have taken an interest in that man's meanness. I wouldn't be surprised if when we leave with the corpse the crowd will be waiting for us with all the excrement they could get together overnight and will give us a shower of filth for going against the will of the town. Maybe they won't do it because of Papa. Maybe they will do it because it's something as terrible as frustrating a pleasure the town had longed for over so many years, thought about on stifling afternoons whenever men and women passed this house and said to themselves: "Sooner or later we'll lunch on that smell." Because that's what they all said, from the first to the last.

It'll be three o'clock in a little while. The Señorita already knows it. Señora Rebeca saw her pass and called her, invisible behind the screen, and she came out from the orbit of the fan for a moment and said to her: "Señorita, it's the devil, you know." And tomorrow it won't be my son who goes to school but some other, completely different child; a child who will grow, reproduce, and die in the end with no one paying him the debt of gratitude which would give him Christian burial.

I'd probably be peacefully at home right now if twenty-five years ago that man hadn't come to my father's home with a letter of recommendation (no one ever knew where he came from), if he hadn't stayed with us, eating grass and looking at women with those eyes of a lustful dog that popped out of their sockets. But my punishment was written down from before my birth and it stayed hidden, repressed, until that fateful leap year when I would turn thirty and my father would tell me: "You have to go with me." And then, before I had time to ask anything, he pounded the floor with his cane: "We have to go through with this just the way it is, daughter. The doctor hanged himself this morning."

The men left and came back to the room with a hammer and a box of nails. But they hadn't nailed up the coffin. They laid the things on the table and they sat on the bed where the dead man had been. My grandfather seems calm, but his calmness is imperfect and desperate. It's not the calmness of the corpse in the coffin, it's the calmness of an impatient man making an effort not to show how he feels. It's a rebellious and anxious calm, the kind my grandfather has, walking back and forth across the room, limping, picking up the clustered objects.

When I discover that there are flies in the room I begin to be tortured by the idea that the coffin's become full of flies. They still haven't nailed it shut, but it seems to me that the buzzing I thought at first was an electric fan in the neighborhood is the swarm of flies beating blindly against the sides of the coffin and the face of the dead man. I shake my head; I close my eyes; I see my grandfather open a trunk and take out some things and I can't tell what they are; on the bed I can see the four embers but not the people with the lighted cigars. Trapped by the suffocating heat, by the minute that doesn't pass, by the buzzing of the flies, I feel as if someone is telling me: *That's the way you'll be. You'll be inside a coffin filled with flies. You're only a little under eleven years old, but someday you'll be like that, left to the flies inside of a closed box.* And I stretch my legs out side by side and look at my own black and shiny boots. *One of my laces is untied,* I think and I look at Mama again. She looks at me too and leans over to tie my shoelace.

The vapor that rises up from Mama's head, warm and smelling like a cupboard, smelling of sleeping wood, reminds me of the closed-in coffin again. It becomes hard for me to breathe, I want to get out of here; I want to breathe in the burning street air, and I use my last resort. When Mama gets up I say to her in a low voice: "Mama!" She smiles, says: "Umm?" And I lean toward her, toward her raw and shining face, trembling. "I feel like going out back."

Mama calls my grandfather, tells him something. I watch his narrow, motionless eyes behind his glasses when he comes over and tells me: "That's impossible right now." I stretch and then remain quiet, indifferent to my failure. But things start to pass too slowly again. There's a rapid movement, another, and another. And then Mama leans over my shoulder again, saying: "Did it go away yet?" And she says it with a serious and solid voice, as if it was a scolding more than a question. My stomach is tight and hard, but Mama's question softens it, leaves it full and relaxed, and then everything, even her seriousness, becomes aggressive and challenging to me. "No," I tell her. "It still hasn't gone away." I squeeze in my stomach and try to beat the floor with my feet (another last resort), but I only find empty space below, the distance separating me from the floor.

Someone comes into the room. It's one of my grandfather's men, followed by a policeman and a man who is wearing green denim pants. He has a belt with a revolver on it and in his hand he's holding a hat with a broad, curled brim. My grandfather goes over to greet him. The man in the green pants coughs in the darkness, says something to my grandfather, coughs again; and still coughing he orders the policeman to open the window.

The wooden walls have a slippery look. They seem to be built of cold, compressed ash. When the policeman hits the latch with the butt of his rifle, I have the feeling that the shutters will not open. The house will fall down, the walls will crumble, but noiselessly, like a palace of ash collapsing in the wind. I feel that with a second blow we'll be in the street, in the sunlight, sitting down, our heads covered with debris. But with the second blow the shutter opens and light comes into the room; it bursts in violently, as when a gate is opened for a disoriented animal, who runs and smells, mute; who rages and scratches on the walls, slavering, and then goes back to flop down peacefully in the coolest corner of the cage.

With the window open things become visible, but consolidated in their strange unreality. Then Mama takes a deep breath, takes me by the hand, and tells me: "Come, let's take a look at our house through the window." And I see the town again, as if I were returning to it after a trip. I can see our house, faded and run down, but cool under the almond trees; and I feel from here as if I'd never been inside that green and cordial coolness, as if ours were the perfect imaginary house promised by my mother on nights when I had bad dreams. And I see Pepe, who passes by without seeing us, lost in his thoughts. The boy from the house next door, who passes whistling, changed and unknown, as if he'd just had his hair cut off.

Then the mayor gets up, his shirt open, sweaty, his expression completely upset. He comes over to me all choked up by the excitement brought on by his own argument. "We can't be sure that he's dead until he starts to smell," he says, and he finishes buttoning up his shirt and lights a cigarette, his face turned toward the coffin again, thinking perhaps: *Now they can't say that I don't operate inside the law.* I look into his eyes and I feel that I've looked at him with enough firmness to make him understand that I can penetrate his deepest thoughts. I tell him: "You're operating outside the law in order to please the others." And he, as if that had been exactly what he had expected to hear, answers: "You're a respectable man, colonel. You know that I'm within my rights." I tell him: "You, more than anyone else, know that he's dead." And he says: "That's right, but after all, I'm only a public servant. The only legal way would be with a death certificate." And I tell him: "If the law is on your side, take advantage of it and bring a doctor who can make out the death certificate." And he, with his head lifted but without haughtiness, calmly too, but without the slightest show of weakness or confusion, says: "You're a respectable person and you know that it would be an abuse of authority." When I hear him I see that his brains are not addled so much by liquor as by cowardice.

Now I can see that the mayor shares the anger of the town. It's a feeling fed for ten years, ever since that stormy night when they brought the wounded men to the man's door and shouted to him (because he didn't open the door, he spoke from inside); they shouted to him: "Doctor, take care of these wounded men because there aren't enough doctors to go around," and still without opening (because the door stayed closed with the wounded lying in front of it). "You're the only doctor left. You have to do a charitable act"; and he replied (and he didn't open the door then either), imagined by the crowd to be standing in the middle of the living room, the lamp held high lighting up his hard yellow eyes: "I've forgotten everything I knew about all that. Take them somewhere else," and he kept the door closed (because from that time on the door was never opened again) while the anger grew, spread out, turned into a collective disease which gave no respite to Macondo for the rest of his life, and in every ear the sentence shouted that night—the one that condemned the doctor to rot behind these walls—continued echoing.

Ten years would still pass without his ever drinking the town water, haunted by the fear that it would be poisoned; feeding himself on the vegetables that he and his Indian mistress planted in the courtyard. Now the town feels that the time has come when they can deny him the pity that he denied the town ten years ago, and Macondo, which knows that he's dead (because everyone must have awakened with a lighter feeling this morning), is getting ready to enjoy that longed-for pleasure which everyone considers to be deserved. Their only desire is to smell the odor of organic decomposition behind the doors that he didn't open that other time.

Now I can begin to believe that nothing can help my promise in the face of the ferocity of a town and that I'm hemmed in, surrounded by the hatred and impatience of a band of resentful people. Even the church has found a way to go against my determination. Father Ángel told me a moment ago: "I won't let them bury in consecrated ground a man who hanged himself after having lived sixty years without God. Our Lord would look upon you with good eyes too if you didn't carry out what won't be a work of charity but the sin of rebellion." I told him:"To bury the dead, as is written, is a work of charity." And Father Ángel said: "Yes. But in this case it's not up to us to do it, it's up to the sanitary authorities."

I came. I called the four Guajiros who were raised in my house. I made my daughter Isabel go with me. In that way the act becomes more family, more human, less personal and defiant than if I dragged the corpse to the cemetery through the streets of the town myself. I think Macondo is capable of doing anything after what I've seen happen in this century. But if they won't respect me, not even because I'm old, a Colonel of the Republic, and, to top it off, lame in body and sound in conscience, I hope that at least they'll respect my daughter because she's a woman. I'm not doing it for myself. Maybe not for the peace of the dead man either. Just to fulfill a sacred promise. If I brought Isabel along it wasn't out of cowardice but out of charity. She brought the child (and I can see that she did it for the same reason), and here we are now, the three of us, bearing the weight of this harsh emergency.

We got here a moment ago. I thought we'd find the body still hanging from the ceiling, but the men got here first, laid him on the bed, and almost shrouded him with the secret conviction that the affair wouldn't last more than an hour. When I arrive I hope they'll bring the coffin, I see my daughter and the child sitting in the corner and I examine the room, thinking that the doctor may have left something that will explain why he did it. The desk is open, full of a confusion of papers, none written by him. On the desk I see the same bound formulary that he brought to my house twenty-five years ago when he opened that enormous trunk which could have held the clothing of my whole family. But there was nothing else in the trunk except two cheap shirts, a set of false teeth that couldn't have been his for the simple reason that he still had his own, strong and complete, a portrait, and a formulary. I open the drawers and I find printed sheets of paper in all of them; just papers, old, dusty; and underneath, in the last drawer, the same false teeth that he brought twenty-five years ago, dusty, yellow from age and lack of use. On the small table beside the unlighted lamp there are several bundles of unopened newspapers. I examine them. They're written in French, the most recent ones three months old: *July, 1928.* And there are others, also unopened: *January, 1927; November, 1926.* And the oldest ones: *October, 1919.* I think: *It's been nine years, since one year after the sentence had been pronounced, that he hadn't opened the newspapers. Since that time he's given up the last thing that linked him to his land and his people.*

The men bring the coffin and lower the corpse into it. Then I remember the day twenty-five years ago when he arrived at my house and gave me the letter of recommendation, written in Panama and addressed to me by the Intendant General of the Atlantic Coast at the end of the great war, Colonel

Aureliano Buendía. I search through various trifles in the darkness of the bottomless trunk. There's no clue in the other corner, only the same things he brought twenty-five years ago. I remember: *He had two cheap shirts, a set of teeth, a portrait, and that old bound formulary.* I go about gathering up these things before they close the coffin and I put them inside. The portrait is still at the bottom of the trunk, almost in the same place where it had been that time. It's the daguerreotype of a decorated officer. I throw the picture into the box. I throw in the false teeth and finally the formulary. When I finish I signal the men to close the coffin. I think: *Now he's on another trip. The most natural thing for him on his last trip is to take along the things that were with him on the next to the last one. At least that would seem to be the most natural.* And then I seem to see him, for the first time, comfortably dead.

I examine the room and I see that a shoe was forgotten on the bed. I signal my men again with the shoe in my hand and they lift up the lid at the precise moment when the train whistles, disappearing around the last bend in town. *It's two-thirty,* I think. *Two-thirty on September 12, 1928; almost the same hour of that day in 1903 when this man sat down for the first time at our table and asked for some grass to eat.* Adelaida asked him that time: "What kind of grass, doctor?" And he in his parsimonious ruminant voice, still touched by nasality: "Ordinary grass, ma'am. The kind that donkeys eat."

2

THE FACT IS THAT MEME ISN'T IN THE HOUSE AND THAT PROBA-
bly no one could say exactly when she stopped living here.
The last time I saw her was eleven years ago. She still had the
little *botiquín* on this corner that had been imperceptibly mod-
ified by the needs of the neighbors until it had become a va-
riety store. Everything in order, neatly arranged by the scrupulous and hard-working Meme, who spent her day sewing
for the neighbors on one of the four Domestics that there were
in town in those days or behind the counter attending to customers with that pleasant Indian way which she never lost and
which was at the same time both open and reserved; a mixed-
up combination of innocence and mistrust.

I hadn't seen Meme since the time she left our house, but
actually I can't say exactly when she came here to live with the
doctor on the corner or how she could have reached the extreme of degradation of becoming the mistress of a man who
had refused her his services, in spite of everything and the
fact that they shared my father's house, she as a foster child
and he as a permanent guest. I learned from my stepmother
that the doctor wasn't a good man, that he'd had a long argument with Papa, trying to convince him that what Meme
had wasn't anything serious, not even leaving his room. In any

case, even if what the Guajiro girl had was only a passing illness, he should have taken a look at her, if only because of the consideration with which he was treated in our house during the eight years he lived there.

I don't know how things happened. I just know that one morning Meme wasn't in the house anymore and he wasn't either. Then my stepmother had them close up his room and she didn't mention him again until years later when we were working on my wedding dress.

Three or four Sundays after she'd left our house, Meme went to church, to eight o'clock mass, with a gaudy silk print dress and a ridiculous hat that was topped by a cluster of artificial flowers. She'd always been so simple when I saw her in our house, barefoot most of the time, so that the person who came into church that Sunday looked to me like a different Meme from the one we knew. She heard mass up front, among the ladies, stiff and affected under that pile of things she was wearing, which made her new and complicated, a showy newness made up of cheap things. She was kneeling down up front. And even the devotion with which she followed the Mass was something new in her; even in the way she crossed herself there was something of that flowery and gaudy vulgarity with which she'd entered the church, puzzling people who had known her as a servant in our home and surprising those who'd never seen her.

I (I couldn't have been more than thirteen at the time) wondered what had brought on that transformation, why Meme had disappeared from our house and reappeared in church that Sunday dressed more like a Christmas tree than a lady, or with enough there to dress three women completely for Easter Sunday and the Guajiro girl even had enough drippings and beads left over to dress a fourth one. When mass was over the men and women stopped by the door to watch her come out. They stood on the steps in a double row by the main door, and I think that there might even have been something secretly premeditated in that indolent and mockingly solemn way in which they were waiting, not saying a word until Meme came out the door, closed her eyes and opened them again in perfect rhythm to her seven-colored parasol. That was how she went between the double row of men and women, ridiculous in her high-heeled peacock disguise, until one of the men began to close the circle and Meme was in the middle, startled, confused, trying to smile with a smile of distinction that was as gaudy and false on her as her outfit. But when Meme came out, opened her parasol, and began to walk, Papa, who was next to me, pulled me toward the group. So when the men began closing the circle, my father opened a way out for Meme, who was hurriedly trying to get away. Papa took her by the arm without looking at the people there, and he led her through the center of the square with that haughty and challenging expression he puts on when he does something that other people don't agree with.

Some time passed before I found out that Meme had gone to live with the doctor as his mistress. In those days the shop was open and she still went to Mass like the finest of ladies, not bothered by what was thought or said, as if she'd forgotten what had happened that first Sunday. Still, two months later, she wasn't ever seen in church again.

I remember the doctor when he was staying at our house. I remember his black and twisted mustache and his way of looking at women with his lustful, greedy dog eyes. But I remember that I never got close to him, maybe because I thought of him as the strange animal that stayed seated at the table after everyone had gotten up and ate the same kind of grass that donkeys eat. During Papa's illness three years ago, the doctor didn't leave his corner the same as he hadn't left it one single time after the night he refused to attend to the wounded men, just as six years before that he'd denied the woman who two days later would be his concubine. The small house had been shut up before the town passed sentence on the doctor. But I do know that Meme was still living here for several months or several years after the store was closed. It must have been much later when people found out that she'd disappeared, because that was what the anonymous note tacked on this door said. According to that note, the doctor had murdered his mistress and buried her in the garden because he was afraid the town would use her to poison him. But I'd seen Meme before I was married It was eleven years ago, when I was coming back from rosary and the Guajiro woman came to the door of her shop and said to me in her jolly and somewhat ironic way: "Chabela, you're getting married and you didn't even tell me."

"Yes," I tell him, "that's how it must have been." Then I tug on the noose, where on one of the ends the living flesh of the newly cut rope can be seen. I retie the knot my men had cut in order to take the body down and I toss one of the ends over the beam until the noose is hanging, held with enough strength to contribute many deaths just like this man's. While he fans himself with his hat, his face altered by shortness of breath and liquor, looking at the noose, calculating its strength, he says: "A noose as thin as that couldn't possibly have held his body." And I tell him: "That same rope held up his hammock for many years." And he pulls a chair over, hands me his hat, and hangs from the noose by his hands, his face flushed by the effort. Then he stands on the chair again, looking at the end of the hanging rope. He says: "Impossible. That noose doesn't reach down to my neck." And then I can see that he's being illogical deliberately, looking for ways to hold off the burial.

I look at him straight in the face, scrutinizing him. I tell him: "Didn't you ever notice that he was at least a head taller than you?" And he turns to look at the coffin. He says: "All the same, I'm not sure he did it with this noose."

I'm sure it was done that way. And he knows it too, but he has a scheme for wasting time because he's afraid of compromising himself. His cowardice can be seen in the way he moves around in no direction. A double and contradictory cowardice: to hold off the ceremony and to set it up. Then, when he gets to the coffin, he turns on his heels, looks at me, and says: "I'd have to see him hanging to be convinced."

I would have done it. I would have told my men to open the coffin and put the hanged man back up again the way he was until a moment ago. But it would be too much for my daughter. It would be too much for the child, and she shouldn't have brought him. Even though it upsets me to treat a dead man that way, offending defenseless flesh, disturbing a man who's at rest for the first time; even though the act of moving a corpse who's lying peacefully and deservedly in his coffin is against my principles, I'd hang him up again just to see how far this man will go. But it's impossible. And I tell him so: "You can rest assured that I won't tell them to do that. If you want to, hang him up yourself, and you can be responsible for what happens. Remember that we don't know how long he's been dead."

He hasn't moved. He's still beside the coffin, looking at me, then looking at Isabel and then at the child, and then at the coffin again. Suddenly his expression becomes somber and menacing. He says: "You must know what can happen because of this." And I can see what he means by his threat. I tell him: "Of course I do. I'm a responsible person." And he, his arms folded now, sweating, walking toward me with studied and comical movements that pretend to be threatening, says: "May I ask you how you found out that this man had hanged himself last night?"

I wait for him to get in front of me. I remain motionless, looking at him until my face is hit by his hot, harsh breath, until he stops, his arms still folded, moving his hat behind one armpit. Then I say to him: "When you ask me that in an official capacity, I'll be very pleased to give you an answer." He stands facing me in the same position. When I speak to him he doesn't show the least bit of surprise or upset. He says: "Naturally, colonel, I'm asking you officially."

I'll give him all the rope he wants. I'm sure that no matter how much he tries to twist it, he'll have to give in to an iron-clad position, but one that's patient and calm. I tell him: "These men cut the body down because I couldn't let it stay hanging there until you decided to come. I told you to come two hours ago and you took all this time to walk two blocks."

He still doesn't move. I face him, resting on my cane, leaning forward a little. I say: "In the second place, he was my friend." Before I can finish speaking he smiles ironically, but without changing position, throwing his thick and sour breath into my face. He says: "It's the easiest thing in the world, isn't it?" And suddenly he stops smiling. He says: "So you knew this man was going to hang himself."

Tranquil, patient, convinced that he's only going on like that to complicate things, I say to him: "I repeat. The first thing I did when I found out he'd hanged himself was to go to your place and that was two hours ago." And as if I'd asked him a question and not stated something, he says: "I was having lunch." And I say to him: "I know. I even think you took time out for a siesta."

Then he doesn't know what to say. He moves back. He looks at Isabel sitting beside the child. He looks at the men and finally at me. But his expression is changed now. He seems to be looking for something to occupy his thought for a moment. He turns his back on me, goes to where the policeman is, and tells him something. The policeman nods and leaves the room.

Then he comes back and takes my arm. He says: "I'd like to talk to you in the other room, colonel." Now his voice has changed completely. It's tense and disturbed now. And while I walk into the next room, feeling the uncertain pressure of his hand on my arm, I'm taken with the idea that I know what he's going to tell me.

This room, unlike the other one, is big and cool. The light from the courtyard flows into it. In here I can see his disturbed eyes, the smile that doesn't match the expression of his eyes. I can hear his voice saying: "Colonel, maybe we can settle this another way." And without giving him time to finish, I ask him: "How much?" And then he becomes a different man.

Meme had brought out a plate with jelly and two salt rolls, the kind that she'd learned to make from my mother. The clock had struck nine. Meme was sitting opposite me in the back of the store and was eating listlessly, as if the jelly and rolls were only something to hold together the visit. I understood that and let her lose herself in her labyrinths, sink into the past with that nostalgic and sad enthusiasm that in the light of the oil lamp burning on the counter made her look more withered and old than the day she'd come into church wearing the hat and high heels. It was obvious that Meme felt like recalling things that night. And while she was doing it, one had the impression that over the past years she'd held herself back in some unique and timeless static age and that as she recalled things that night she was putting her personal time into motion again and beginning to go through her long-postponed aging process.

Meme was stiff and somber, talking about the picturesque and feudal splendor of our family during the last years of the previous century, before the great war. Meme recalled my mother. She recalled her that night when I was coming back from church and she told me in her somewhat mocking and ironic way: "Chabela, you're getting married and you didn't even tell me." Those were precisely the days when I'd wanted my mother and was trying to bring her back more strongly in my memory. "She was the living picture of you," she said. And I really believed it. I was sitting across from the Indian woman, who spoke with an accent mixed with precision and vagueness, as if there was a lot of incredible legend in what she was recalling but also as if she was recalling it in good faith and even with the conviction that the passage of time had changed legend into reality that was remote but hard to forget. She spoke to me about the journey my parents had made during the war, about the rough pilgrimage that would end with their settling in Macondo. My parents were fleeing the hazards of war and looking for a prosperous and tranquil bend in the road to settle down in, and they heard about the golden calf and came looking for it in what was then a town in formation, founded by several refugee families whose members were as careful about the preservation of their traditions and religious practices as the fattening of their hogs. Macondo was my parents' promised land, peace, and the Parchment. Here they found the appropriate spot to rebuild the house that a few years later would be a country mansion with three stables and two guest rooms. Meme recalled the details without repentance, and spoke about the most extravagant things with an irrepressible desire to live them again or with the pain that came from the fact that she would never live them again. There was no suffering or privation on the journey, she said. Even the horses slept under mosquito netting, not because my father was a spendthrift or a madman, but because my mother had a strange sense of charity, of humanitarian feelings, and thought that the eyes of God would be just as pleased with the act of protecting an animal from the mosquitoes as protecting a man. Their wild and burdensome cargo was everywhere; the trunks full of clothing of people who had died before they'd been on earth, ancestors who couldn't have been found twenty fathoms under the earth; boxes full of kitchen utensils that hadn't been used for a long time and had belonged to my parents' most distant relatives (my father and mother were first cousins), and even a trunk filled with the images of saints, which they used to reconstruct their family altar everywhere they stopped. It was a strange carnival procession with horses and hens and the four Guajiro Indians (Meme's companions) who had grown up in the house and followed my parents all through the region like trained circus animals.

Meme recalled things with sadness. One had the impression that she considered the passage of time a personal loss, as if she noticed in that heart of hers, lacerated by memories, that if time hadn't passed she'd still be on that pilgrimage, which must have been a punishment for my parents, but which was a kind of lark for the children, with strange sights like that of horses under mosquito netting.

Then everything began to go backward, she said. Their arrival in the newborn village of Macondo during the last days of the century was that of a devastated family, still bound to a recent splendid past, disorganized by the war. The Indian woman recalled my mother's arrival in town, sidesaddle on a mule, pregnant, her face green and malarial and her feet disabled by swelling. Perhaps the seeds of resentment were maturing in my father's soul but he came ready to sink roots against wind and tide while he waited for my mother to bear the child that had been growing in her womb during the crossing and was progressively bringing death to her as the time of birth drew near.

The light of the lamp outlined her profile. Meme, with her stiff Indian expression, her hair straight and thick like a horse's mane or tail, looked like a sitting idol, green and spectral in the small hot room behind the store, speaking the way an idol would have if it had set out to recall its ancient earthly existence. I'd never been close to her, but that night, after that sudden and spontaneous show of intimacy, I felt that I was tied to her by bonds tighter than those of blood.

Suddenly, during one of Meme's pauses, I heard coughing in the next room, in this very bedroom where I am now with the child and my father. It was a short, dry cough, followed by a clearing of the throat, and then I heard the unmistakable sound that a man makes when he rolls over in bed. Meme stopped talking at once, and a gloomy, silent cloud darkened her face. I'd forgotten about him. During the time I was there (it was around ten o'clock) I had felt as if the Guajiro woman and I were alone in the house. Then the tension of the atmosphere changed. I felt fatigue in the arm with which I'd been holding the plate with the jelly and rolls, without tasting any. I leaned over and said: "He's awake." She, expressionless now, cold and completely indifferent, said: "He'll be awake until dawn." And suddenly I understood the disillusionment that could be seen in Meme when she recalled the past of our house. Our lives had changed, the times were good and Macondo was a bustling town where there was even enough money to squander on Saturday nights, but Meme was living tied to a past that had been better. While they were shearing the golden calf outside, inside, in the back of the store, her life was sterile, anonymous, all day behind the counter and spending the night with a man who didn't sleep until dawn, who spent his time walking about the house, pacing, looking at her greedily with those lustful dog eyes that I've never been able to forget. It saddened me to think of Meme with that man who refused his services one night and went on being a hardened animal, without bitterness or compassion, all day long in ceaseless roaming through the house, enough to drive the most balanced person out of his mind.

Recovering the tone of my voice, knowing that he was in his room, awake, maybe opening his lustful dog eyes every time our words were heard in the rear of the store, I tried to give a different turn to the conversation.

"How's business been for you?" I asked.

Meme smiled. Her laugh was sad and taciturn, seeming detached from any feeling of the moment, like something she kept in the cupboard and took out only when she had to, using it with no feeling of ownership, as if the infrequency of her smiles had made her forget the normal way to use them. "There it is," she said, moving her head in an ambiguous way, and she was silent, abstract again. Then I understood that it was time for me to leave. I handed Meme the plate without giving any explanation as to why it was untouched, and I watched her get up and put it on the counter. She looked at me from there and repeated: "You're the living picture of her." I must have been sitting against the light before, clouded by it as it came in the opposite direction and Meme couldn't see my face while she'd been talking. Then when she got up to put the plate on the counter she saw me frontward, from behind the lamp, and that was why she said: "You're the living picture of her." And she came back to sit down.

Then she began to recall the days when my mother had arrived in Macondo. She'd gone directly from the mule to a rocking chair and stayed seated for three months, not moving, taking her food listlessly. Sometimes they would bring her lunch and she'd sit halfway through the afternoon with the plate in her hand, rigid, not rocking, her feet resting on a chair, feeling death growing inside of them until someone would come and take the plate from her hands. When the day came, the labor pains drew her out of her abandonment and she stood up by herself, although they had to help her walk the twenty steps between the porch and the bedroom, martyrized by the occupation of a death that had taken her over during nine months of silent suffering. Her crossing from the rocker to the bed had all the pain, bitterness, and penalties that had been absent during the journey taken a few months before, but she arrived where she knew she had to arrive before she fulfilled the last act of her life.

My father seemed desperate over my mother's death, Meme said. But according to what he himself said afterward when he was alone in the house, "No one trusts the morality of a home where the man doesn't have a legitimate wife by his side." And since he'd read somewhere that when a loved one dies we should set out a bed of jasmine to remember her every night, he planted a vine against the courtyard wall, and a year later, in a second marriage, he was wedded to Adelaida, my stepmother.

Sometimes I thought that Meme was going to cry while she was speaking. But she remained firm, satisfied at expiating the loss of having been happy once and having stopped being so by her own free will. Then she smiled. Then she relaxed in her chair and became completely human. It was as if she'd drawn up mental accounts of her grief when she leaned forward and saw that she still had a favorable balance in good memories left, and then she smiled with her old wide and teasing friendliness. She said that the other thing had started five years later, when she came into the dining room where my father was having lunch and told him: "Colonel, colonel, there's a stranger to see you in your office."

3

BEHIND THE CHURCH, ON THE OTHER SIDE OF THE STREET, THERE was once a lot with no trees. That was toward the end of the last century, when we came to Macondo and they hadn't started to build the church yet. It was a dry, bald plot of land where the children played after school. Later on, when construction on the church began, they set up four beams to one side of the lot and it could be seen that the encircled space was just right for building a hut. Which they did. Inside they kept the materials for the construction of the church.

When the work on the church came to an end, someone finished putting adobe on the walls of the small hut and opened a door in the rear wall, which faced the small, bare, stony plot where there was not even a trace of an aloe bush. A year later the small hut was finished, big enough for two people. Inside there was a smell of quicklime. That was the only pleasant odor that had been smelled for a long time inside that enclosure and the only agreeable one that would be smelled ever after. When they had whitewashed the walls, the same hand that had completed the construction ran a bar across the inside door and put a padlock on the street door.

The hut had no owner. No one worried about making his rights effective over either the lot or the construction materials. When the first parish priest arrived he put up with one of the well-to-do families in Macondo. Then he was transferred to a different parish. But during those days (and possibly before the first priest had left) a woman with a child at her breast had occupied the hut, and no one knew when she had come, nor from where, nor how she had managed to open the door. There was an earthen crock in a corner, black and green with moss, and a jar hanging from a nail. But there wasn't any more whitewash left on the walls. In the yard a crust of earth hardened by the rain had formed over the stones. The woman built a network of branches to protect herself from the sun. And since she had no means to put a roof of palm leaves, tile, or zinc on it, she planted a grapevine beside the branches and hung a clump of *sábila* and a loaf of bread by the street door to protect herself against evil thoughts.

When the coming of the new priest was announced in 1903, the woman was still living in the hut with her child. Half of the population went out to the highway to wait for the priest to arrive. The rural band was playing sentimental pieces until a boy came running, panting to the point of bursting, saying that the priest's mule was at the last bend in the road. Then the musicians changed their position and began to play a march. The person assigned to give the welcoming speech climbed up on an improvised platform and waited for the priest to appear so that he could begin his greeting. But a moment later the martial tune was suspended, the orator got down off the table, and the astonished multitude watched a stranger pass by, riding a mule whose haunches carried the largest trunk ever seen in Macondo. The man went by on his way into town without looking at anyone. Even if the priest had been dressed in civilian clothes for the trip, it would never have occurred to anyone that the bronzed traveler in military leggings was a priest dressed in civilian clothes.

And, in fact, he wasn't, because at that very same moment, along the shortcut on the other side of town, people saw a strange priest coming along, fearfully thin, with a dry and stretched-out face, astride a mule, his cassock lifted up to his knees, and protected from the sun by a faded and run-down umbrella. In the neighborhood of the church the priest asked where the parish house was, and he must have asked someone who didn't have the least idea of anything, because the answer he got was: "It's the hut behind the church, father." The woman had gone out, but the child was playing inside behind the half-open door. The priest dismounted, rolled a swollen suitcase over to the hut. It was unlocked, just barely held together by a leather strap that was different from the hide of the suitcase itself, and after he examined the hut, he brought up the mule and tied it in the yard in the shade of the grape leaves. Then he opened up the suitcase, took out a hammock that must have been the same age and had seen the same use as the umbrella, hung it diagonally across the hut, from beam to beam, took off his boots, and tried to sleep, unconcerned about the child, who was looking at him with great frightened eyes.

When the woman returned she must have felt disconcerted by the strange presence of the priest, whose face was so inexpressive that it was in no way different from the skull of a cow. The woman must have tiptoed across the room. She must have dragged her folding cot to the door, made a bundle of her clothes and the child's rags, and left the hut without even bothering about the crock and the jar, because an hour later, when the delegation went back through town in the opposite direction preceded by the band, which was playing its martial air in the midst of a crowd of boys who had skipped school, they found the priest alone in the hut, stretched out in his hammock in a carefree way, his cassock unbuttoned and his shoes off. Someone must have brought the news to the main road, but it occurred to no one to ask what the priest was doing in that hut. They must have thought that he was related to the woman in some way, just as she must have abandoned the hut because she thought that the priest had orders to occupy it, or that it was church property, or simply out of fear that they would ask her why she had lived for more than two years in a hut that didn't belong to her without paying any rent or without anyone's permission. Nor did it occur to the delegation to ask for any explanation, neither then nor any time after, because the priest wouldn't accept any speeches. He laid the presents on the floor and limited himself to greeting the men and women coldly and quickly, because according to what he said, he hadn't shut his eyes all night.

The delegation dissolved in the face of that cold reception by the strangest priest they'd ever seen. They noticed how his face looked like the skull of a cow, with closely cropped gray hair, and he didn't have any lips, but a horizontal opening that seemed not to have been in the place of his mouth since birth but made later on by a quick and unique knife. But that very afternoon they realized that he looked like someone. And before dawn everyone knew who it was. They remembered having seen him with a sling and a stone, naked, but wearing shoes and a hat, during the time when Macondo was a humble refugee village. The veterans remembered his activities in the civil war of '85. They remembered that he had been a colonel at the age of seventeen and that he was intrepid, hardheaded, and against the government. But nothing had been heard of him again in Macondo until that day when he returned home to take over the parish. Very few remembered his given name. On the other hand, most of the veterans remembered the one his mother had put on him (because he was willful and rebellious) and that it was the same one that his comrades in arms would call him by later on. They all called him the Pup. And that was what he was always called in Macondo until the hour of his death:

"Pup, Puppy."

So it was that this man came to our house on the same day and almost at the same hour that the pup reached Macondo. The former along the main road, unexpected and with no one having the slightest notion of his name or profession; the priest by the shortcut, while the whole town was waiting for him on the main road.

I returned home after the reception. We had just sat down to the table—a little later than usual—when Meme came over to tell me: "Colonel, colonel, colonel, there's a stranger to see you in your office." I said: "Tell him to come in." And Meme said: "He's in the office and says that he has to see you at once." Adelaida stopped feeding soup to Isabel (she couldn't have been more than five at the time) and went to take care of the newcomer. A moment later she came back, visibly worried:

"He's pacing back and forth in the office," she said.

I saw her walk behind the candlesticks. Then she began to feed Isabel her soup again. "You should have had him come in," I said, still eating. And she said: "That's what I was going to do. But he was pacing back and forth in the office when I got there and said good afternoon, but he didn't answer me because he was looking at the leather dancing girl on the shelf. And when I was about to say good afternoon again, he wound up the dancing girl, put her on the desk, and watched her dance. I don't know whether it was the music that prevented him from hearing when I said good afternoon again, but I stood there opposite the desk, where he was leaning over watching the dancing girl, who was still wound up a little." Adelaida was feeding Isabel her soup. I said to her: "He must be very interested in the toy." And she, still feeding Isabel her soup: "He was pacing back and forth in the office, but then, when he saw the dancing girl, he took her down as if he knew beforehand what it was for, as if he knew how it worked. He was winding it up when I said good afternoon to him for the first time, before the music began to play. Then he put it on the desk and stood there watching it, but without smiling, as if he weren't interested in the dance but in the mechanism."

They never announced anyone to me. Visitors came almost every day: travelers we knew, who left their animals in the stable and came in with complete confidence, with the familiarity of one who always expects to find an empty place at our table. I told Adelaida: "He must have a message or something." And she said: "In any case, he's acting very strangely. He's watching the dancing girl until it runs down and in the meantime I'm standing across the desk without knowing what to say to him, because I knew that he wouldn't answer me as long as the music was playing. Then, when the dancing girl gave the little leap she always gives when she runs down, he was still standing there looking at her with curiosity, leaning over the desk but not sitting down. Then he looked at me and I realized that he knew I was in the office but that he hadn't worried about me because he wanted to know how long the dancing girl would keep on dancing. I didn't say good afternoon to him again, but I smiled when he looked at me because I saw that he had huge eyes, with yellow pupils, and they look at a person's whole body all at the same time. When I smiled at him he remained serious, but he nodded his head very formally and said: 'The colonel. It's the colonel I have to see.' He has a deep voice, as if he could speak with his mouth closed. As if he were a ventriloquist."

She was feeding Isabel her soup, and she said: "At first he was pacing back and forth in the office." Then I understood that the stranger had made an uncommon impression on her and that she had a special interest in my taking care of him. Nevertheless, I kept on eating lunch while she fed Isabel her soup and spoke. She said: "Then, when he said he wanted to see the colonel, what I told him was 'Please come into the dining room,' and he straightened up where he was, with the dancing girl in his hand. Then he raised his head and became as rigid and firm as a soldier, I think, because he's wearing high boots and a suit of ordinary cloth, with the shirt buttoned up to his neck. I didn't know what to say when he didn't answer anything and was quiet, with the toy in his hand, as if he were waiting for me to leave the office in order to wind it up again. That was when he suddenly reminded me of someone, when I realized that he was a military man."

And I told her: "So you think it's something serious." I looked at her over the candlesticks. She wasn't looking at me. She was feeding Isabel her soup. She said:

"When I got there he was pacing back and forth in the office and so I couldn't see his face. But then when he stood in the back he had his head held so high and his eyes were so fixed that I think he's a military man, and I said to him: 'You want to see the colonel in private, is that it?' And he nodded. Then I came to tell you that he looks like someone, or rather, that he's the same person that he looks like, although I can't explain how he got here."

I kept on eating, but I was looking at her over the candlesticks. She stopped feeding Isabel her soup. She said:

"I'm sure it's not a message. I'm sure it's not that he looks like someone but that he's the same person he looks like. I'm sure, rather, that he's a military man. He's got a black pointed mustache and a face like copper. He's wearing high boots and I'm sure that it's not that he looks like someone but that he's the same person he looks like."

She was speaking in a level tone, monotonous and persistent. It was hot and maybe for that reason I began to feel irritated. I said to her: "So, who does he look like?" And she said: "When he was pacing back and forth in the office I couldn't see his face, but later on." And I, irritated with the monotony and persistence of her words: "All right, all right, I'll go to see him when I finish my lunch." And she, feeding Isabel her soup again: "At first I couldn't see his face because he was pacing back and forth in the office. But then when I said to him: 'Please come in,' he stood there silent beside the wall with the dancing girl in his hand. That was when I remembered who he looks like and I came to tell you. He has huge, indiscreet eyes, and when I turned to leave I felt that he was looking right at my legs."

She suddenly fell silent. In the dining room the metallic tinkle of the spoon kept vibrating. I finished my lunch and folded the napkin under my plate.

At that moment from the office I heard the festive music of the windup toy.

4

IN THE KITCHEN OF THE HOUSE THERE'S AN OLD CARVED WOODEN chair without crosspieces and my grandfather puts his shoes to dry next to the stove on its broken seat.

Tobías, Abraham, Gilberto, and I left school at this time yesterday and we went to the plantations with a sling, a big hat to hold the birds, and a new knife. On the way I was remembering the useless chair placed in the kitchen corner, which at one time was used for visitors and which now is used by the dead man who sits down every night with his hat on to look at the ashes in the cold stove.

Tobías and Gilberto were walking toward the end of the dark nave. Since it had rained during the morning, their shoes slipped on the muddy grass. One of them was whistling, and his hard, firm whistle echoed in the vegetable cavern the way it does when someone starts to sing inside a barrel. Abraham was bringing up the rear with me. He with his sling and the stone, ready to shoot. I with my open knife.

Suddenly the sun broke the roof of tight, hard leaves and a body of light fell winging down onto the grass like a live bird. "Did you see it?" Abraham asked. I looked ahead and saw Gilberto and Tobías at the end of the nave. "It's not a bird," I said. "It's the sun that's just come out strong."

When they got to the bank they began to get undressed and gave strong kicks in that twilight water, which didn't seem to wet their skin. "There hasn't been a single bird all afternoon," Abraham said. "There aren't any birds after it rains," I said. And I believed it myself then. Abraham began to laugh. His laugh is foolish and simple and it makes a sound like that of a thread of water from a spigot. He got undressed. "I'll take the knife into the water and fill the hat with fish," he said.

Abraham was naked in front of me with his hand open, waiting for the knife. I didn't answer right away. I held the knife tight and I felt its clean and tempered steel in my hand. *I'm not going to give him the knife,* I thought. And I told him: "I'm not going to give you the knife. I only got it yesterday and I'm going to keep it all afternoon." Abraham kept his hand out. Then I told him:

"Incomploruto."

Abraham understood me. He's the only one who can understand my words. "All right," he said and walked toward the water through the hardened, sour air. He said: "Start getting undressed and we'll wait for you on the rock." And he said it as he dove in and reappeared shining like an enormous silver-plated fish, as if the water had turned to liquid as it came in contact with him.

I stayed on the bank, lying on the warm mud. When I opened the knife again I stopped looking at Abraham and lifted my eyes up straight toward the other side, up toward the trees, toward the furious dusk where the sky had the monstrous awfulness of a burning stable.

"Hurry up," Abraham said from the other side. Tobías was whistling on the edge of the rock. Then I thought: *I'm not going swimming today. Tomorrow.*

On the way back Abraham hid behind the hawthorns. I was going to follow him, but he told me: "Don't come back here. I'm doing something." I stayed outside, sitting on the dead leaves in the road, watching a single swallow that was tracing a curve in the sky. I said:

"There's only one swallow this afternoon."

Abraham didn't answer right away. He was silent behind the hawthorns, as if he couldn't hear me, as if he were reading. His silence was deep and concentrated, full of a hidden strength. After a long silence he sighed. Then he said:

"Swallows."

I told him again: "There's only one swallow this afternoon." Abraham was still behind the hawthorns but I couldn't tell anything about him. He was silent and drawn in, but his silence wasn't static. It was a desperate and impetuous immobility. After a moment he said:

"Only one? Ah, yes. You're right, you're right."

I didn't say anything then. Behind the hawthorns, he was the one who began to move. Sitting on the leaves, I could hear the sound of other dead leaves under his feet from where he was. Then he was silent again, as if he'd gone away. Then he breathed deeply and asked:

"What did you say?"

I told him again: "There's only one swallow this afternoon." And while I was saying it I saw the curved wing tracing circles in the sky of incredible blue. "He's flying high," I said.

Abraham replied at once:

"Ah, yes, of course. That must be why then."

He came out from behind the hawthorns, buttoning up his pants. He looked up toward where the swallow was still tracing circles, and, still not looking at me, he said:

"What were you telling me a while back about the swallows?"

That held us up. When we got back the lights in town were on. I ran into the house and on the veranda I came on the fat, blind women with the twins of Saint Jerome who every Tuesday have come to sing for my grandfather since before I was born, according to what my mother says.

All night I was thinking that today we'd get out of school again and go to the river, but not with Gilberto and Tobías. I want to go alone with Abraham, to see the shine of his stomach when he dives and comes up again like a metal fish. All night long I've wanted to go back with him, alone in the darkness of the green tunnel, to brush his thigh as we walk along. Whenever I do that I feel as if someone is biting me with soft nibbles and my skin creeps.

If this man who's come to talk to my grandfather in the other room comes back in a little while maybe we can be home before four o'clock. Then I'll go to the river with Abraham.

He stayed on to live at our house. He occupied one of the rooms off the veranda, the one that opens onto the street, because I thought it would be convenient, for I knew that a man of his type wouldn't be comfortable in the small hotel in town. He put a sign on the door (it was still there until a few years ago when they whitewashed the house, written in pencil in his own hand), and on the following week we had to bring in new chairs to take care of the demands of his numerous patients.

After he gave me the letter from Colonel Aureliano Buendía, our conversation in the office went on so long that Adelaida had no doubts but that it was a matter of some high military official on an important mission, and she set the table as if for a holiday. We spoke about Colonel Buendía, his premature daughter, and his wild firstborn son. The conversation had not gone on too long when I gathered that the man knew the Intendant General quite well and that he had enough regard for him to warrant his confidence. When Meme came to tell us that dinner was served, I thought that my wife had improvised some things in order to take care of the newcomer. But a far cry from improvisation was that splendid table served on the new cloth, on the chinaware destined exclusively for family dinners on Christmas and New Year's Day.

Adelaida was solemnly sitting up straight at one end of the table in a velvet dress closed up to the neck, the one that she wore before our marriage to attend to family business in the city. Adelaida had more refined customs than we did, a certain social experience which, since our marriage, had begun to influence the ways of my house. She had put on the family medallion, the one that she displayed at moments of exceptional importance, and all of her, just like the table, the furniture, the air that was breathed in the dining room, brought on a severe feeling of composure and cleanliness. When we reached the parlor, the man, who was always so careless in his dress and manners, must have felt ashamed and out of place, for he checked the button on his shirt as if he were wearing a tie, and a slight nervousness could be noticed in his unworried and strong walk. I can remember nothing with such precision as that instant in which we went into the dining room and I myself felt dressed too domestically for a table like the one Adelaida had prepared.

There was beef and game on the plates. Everything the same, however, as at our regular meals at that time, except for the presentation on the new china, between the newly polished candlesticks, which was spectacular and different from the norm. In spite of the fact that my wife knew that we would be having only one visitor, she had set eight places, and the bottle of wine in the center was an exaggerated manifestation of the diligence with which she had prepared the homage for the man whom, from the first moment, she had confused with a distinguished military functionary. Never before had I seen in my house an environment more loaded with unreality.

Adelaida's clothing would have been ridiculous had it not been for her hands (they were beautiful, really, and overly white), which balanced, along with her regal distinction, the falsity and arrangement of her appearance. It was when he checked the button on his shirt and hesitated that I got ahead of myself and said: "My second wife, *doctor*." A cloud darkened Adelaida's face and turned it strange and gloomy. She didn't budge from where she was, her hand held out, smiling, but no longer with the air of ceremonious stiffness that she had had when we came into the dining room.

The newcomer clicked his heels like a military man, touched

his forehead with the tips of his extended fingers, and then walked over to where she was.

"Yes, ma'am," he said. But he didn't pronounce any name.

Only when I saw him clumsily shake Adelaida's hand did I become aware that his manners were vulgar and common.

He sat at the other end of the table, between the new crystal ware, between the candlesticks. His disarrayed presence stood out like a soup stain on the tablecloth.

Adelaida poured the wine. Her emotion from the beginning had been changed into a passive nervousness that seemed to say: *It's all right, everything will be done the way it was laid out, but you owe me an explanation.*

And it was after she served the wine and sat down at the other end of the table, while Meme got ready to serve the plates, that he leaned back in his chair, rested his hands on the tablecloth and said with a smile:

"Look, miss, just start boiling a little grass and bring that to me as if it were soup."

Meme didn't move. She tried to laugh, but she couldn't get it out; instead she turned toward Adelaida. Then she, smiling too, but visibly upset, asked him: "What kind of grass, doctor?" And he, in his parsimonious ruminant voice:

"Ordinary grass, ma'am. The kind that donkeys eat."

5

THERE'S A MOMENT WHEN SIESTA TIME RUNS DRY. EVEN THE SE-
cret, hidden, minute activity of the insects ceases at that precise instant; the course of nature comes to a halt; creation
stumbles on the brink of chaos and women get up, drooling,
with the flower of the embroidered pillowcase on their cheeks,
suffocated by temperature and rancor; and they think: *It's still
Wednesday in Macondo.* And then they go back to huddling in
the corner, splicing sleep to reality, and they come to an
agreement, weaving the whispering as if it were an immense
flat surface of thread stitched in common by all the women in
town.

If inside time had the same rhythm as that outside, we
would be in the bright sunlight now, in the middle of the street
with the coffin. It would be later outside: it would be nighttime. It would be a heavy September night with a moon and
women sitting in their courtyards chatting under the green
light, and in the street, us, the renegades, in the full sunlight
of this thirsty September. No one will interfere with the ceremony. I expected the mayor to be inflexible in his determination to oppose it and that we could have gone home; the child
to school and my father to his clogs, the washbasin under his
head dripping with cool water, and on the left-hand side his

pitcher with iced lemonade. But now it's different. My father has once more been sufficiently persuasive to impose his point of view on what I thought at first was the mayor's irrevocable determination. Outside the town is bustling, given over to the work of a long, uniform, and pitiless whispering; and the clean street, without a shadow on the clean dust, virgin since the last wind swept away the tracks of the last ox. And it's a town with no one, with closed houses, where nothing is heard in the rooms except the dull bubbling of words pronounced by evil hearts. And in the room, the sitting child, stiff, looking at his shoes; slowly his eyes go to the lamp, then to the newspapers, again to his shoes, and now quickly to the hanged man, his bitten tongue, his glassy dog eyes that have no lust now; a dog with no appetite, dead. The child looks at him, thinks about the hanged man lying underneath the boards; he has a sad expression and then everything changes: a stool comes out by the door of the barbershop and inside the small altar with the mirror, the powder, and the scented water. The hand becomes freckled and large, it's no longer the hand of my son, it's been changed into a large, deft hand that coldly, with calculated parsimony, begins to strop the razor while the ear hears the metallic buzzing of the tempered blade and the head thinks: *Today they'll be coming earlier because it's Wednesday in Macondo.* And then they come, sit on the chairs in the shade and the coolness of the threshold, grim, squinting, their legs crossed, their hands folded over their knees, biting on the tips of their cigars; looking, talking about the same thing, watching the closed window across from them, the silent house with Señora Rebeca inside. She forgot something too; she forgot to disconnect the fan and she's going through the rooms with screened windows, nervous, stirred up, going through the knickknacks of her sterile and tormented widowhood in order to be convinced by her sense of touch that she won't have died before the hour of burial comes. She's opening and closing the doors of her rooms, waiting for the patriarchal clock to rise up out of its siesta and reward her senses by striking three. All this, while the child's expression ends and he goes back to being hard and stiff, not even delaying half the time a woman needs to give the last stitch on the machine and raise her head full of curlers. Before the child goes back to being upright and pensive, the woman has rolled the machine to the corner of the veranda, and the men have bitten their cigars twice while they watch a complete passage of the razor across the cowhide; and Águeda, the cripple, makes a last effort to awaken her dead knees; and Señora Rebeca turns the lock again and thinks: *Wednesday in Macondo. A good day to bury the devil.* But then the child moves again and there's a new change in time. When something moves you can tell that time has passed. Not till then. Until something moves time is eternal, the sweat, the shirt drooling on the skin, and the unbribable and icy dead man, behind his bitten tongue. That's why time doesn't pass for the hanged man: because even if the child's hand moves, he doesn't know it. And while the dead man doesn't know it (because the child is still moving his hand), Águeda must have gone through another bead on her rosary; Señora Rebeca, lounging in her folding chair, is perplexed, watching the clock remain fixed on the edge of the imminent minute, and Águeda has had time (even though the second hasn't passed on Señora Rebeca's clock) to go through another bead on her rosary and think: *I'd do that if I could get to Father Ángel.* Then the child's hand descends and the razor makes a motion on the strop and one of the men sitting in the coolness of the threshold says: "It must be around three-thirty, right?" Then the hand stops. A dead clock on the brink of the next minute once more, the razor halted once more in the limits of its own steel; and Águeda still waiting for a new movement of the hand to stretch her legs and burst into the sacristy with her arms open, her knees moving again, saying: "Father, Father." And Father Ángel, prostrate in the child's immobility, running his tongue over his lips and the viscous taste of the meatball nightmare, seeing Águeda, would then say: "This is undoubtedly a miracle," and then, rolling about again in the sweaty, drooly drowsiness: "In any case, Águeda, this is no time for saying a mass for the souls in Purgatory." But the new movement is frustrated, my father comes into the room and the two times are reconciled; the two halves become adjusted, consolidate, and Señora Rebecca's clock realizes that it's been caught between the child's parsimony and the widow's impatience, and then it yawns, confused, dives into the prodigious quiet of the moment and comes out afterward dripping with liquid time, with exact and rectified time, and it leans forward and says with ceremonious dignity: "It's exactly two forty-seven." And my father, who, without knowing it, has broken the paralysis of the instant, says: "You're lost in the clouds, daughter." And I say: "Do you think something might happen?" And he, sweating, smiling: "At least I'm sure that the rice will be burned and the milk spilled in lots of houses."

The coffin's closed now, but I can remember the dead man's face. I've got it so clearly that if I look at the wall I can see his open eyes, his tight gray cheeks that are like damp earth, his bitten tongue to one side of his mouth. This gives me a burning, restless feeling. Maybe if my pants weren't so tight on one side of my leg.

My grandfather's sat down beside my mother. When he came back from the next room he brought over the chair and now he's here, sitting next to her, not saying anything, his chin on his cane and his lame leg stretched out in front of him. My grandfather's waiting. My mother, like him, is waiting too. The men have stopped smoking on the bed and they're quiet, all in a row, not looking at the coffin. They're waiting too.

If they blindfolded me, if they took me by the hand and walked me around town twenty times and brought me back to this room I'd recognize it by the smell. I'll never forget how this room smells of trash, piled-up trunks, all the same, even though I've only seen one trunk, where Abraham and I could hide and there'd still be room left over for Tobías. I know rooms by their smell.

Last year Ada sat me on her lap. I had my eyes closed and I saw her through my lashes. I saw her dark, as if she wasn't a woman but just a face that was looking at me and rocking and bleating like a sheep. I was really going to sleep when I got the smell.

There's no smell at home that I can't recognize. When they leave me alone on the veranda I close my eyes, stick out my arms, and walk. I think: *When I get the smell of camphorated rum I'll be by my grandfather's room.* I keep on walking with my eyes closed and my arms stretched out. I think *Now I've gone past my mother's room, because it smells like new playing cards. Then it will smell of pitch and mothballs.* I keep on walking and I get the smell of new playing cards at the exact moment I hear my mother's voice singing in her room. Then I get the smell of pitch and mothballs. I think: *Now I'll keep on smelling mothballs. Then I'll turn to the left of the smell and I'll get the other smell of underwear and closed windows. I'll stop there.* Then, when I take three steps, I get the new smell and I stop, with my eyes closed and my arms outstretched, and I hear Ada's voice shouting: "Child, what are you walking with your eyes closed for?"

That night, when I began to fall asleep, I caught a smell that doesn't exist in any of the rooms in the house. It was a strong and warm smell, as if someone had been shaking a jasmine bush. I opened my eyes, sniffing the thick and heavy air. I said. "Do you smell it?" Ada was looking at me but when I spoke to her she closed her eyes and looked in the other direction. I asked her again: "Do you smell it? It's as if there were some jasmines somewhere." Then she said:

"It's the smell of the jasmines that used to be growing on the wall here nine years ago."

I sat on her lap. "But there aren't any jasmines now," I said. And she said: "Not now. But nine years ago, when you were born, there was a jasmine bush against the courtyard wall. It would be hot at night and it would smell the same as now." I leaned on her shoulder. I looked at her mouth while she spoke. "But that was before I was born," I said. And she said:

"During that time there was a great winter storm and they had to clean out the garden."

The smell was still there, warm, almost touchable, leading the other smells of the night. I told Ada: "I *want* you to tell me that." And she remained silent for an instant, then looked toward the whitewashed wall with moonlight on it and said:

"When you're older you'll learn that the jasmine is a flower that *comes out.*"

I didn't understand, but I felt a strange shudder, as if someone had touched me. I said: "All right," and she said: "The same thing happens with jasmines as with people who come out and wander through the night after they're dead."

I stayed there leaning on her shoulder, not saying anything. I was thinking about other things, about the chair in the kitchen where my grandfather puts his shoes on the seat to dry when it rains. I knew from then on that there's a dead man in the kitchen and every night he sits down, without taking off his hat, looking at the ashes in the cold stove. After a moment I said: "That must be like the dead man who sits in the kitchen." Ada looked at me, opened her eyes, and asked: "What dead man?" And I said to her: "The one who sits every night in the chair where my grandfather puts his shoes to dry." And she said: "There's no dead man there. The chair's next to the stove because it's no good for anything else anymore except to dry shoes on."

That was last year. Now it's different, now I've seen a corpse and all I have to do is close my eyes to keep on seeing him inside, in the darkness of my eyes. I was going to tell my mother, but she's begun to talk to my grandfather. "Do you think something might happen?" she asks. And my grandfather lifts his chin from his cane and shakes his head. "At least I'm sure that the rice will be burned and the milk spilled in lots of houses."

6

AT FIRST HE USED TO SLEEP TILL SEVEN O'CLOCK. HE WOULD AP-
pear in the kitchen with his collarless shirt buttoned up to the
neck, his wrinkled and dirty sleeves rolled up to the elbows,
his filthy pants at chest level with the belt fastened outside,
well below the loops. You had the feeling that his pants were
about to fall down, slide off, because there was no body to
hold them up. He hadn't grown thinner, but you didn't see
the military and haughty look he had the first year on his face
anymore; he had the dreamy and fatigued expression of a man
who doesn't know what his life will be from one minute to the
next and hasn't got the least interest in finding out. He would
drink his black coffee a little after seven and then go back to
his room, passing out his inexpressive "Good morning" along
the way.

He'd been living in our house for four years and in Macondo he was looked upon as a serious professional man in
spite of the fact that his brusque manner and disordered ways
built up an atmosphere about him that was more like fear than
respect.

He was the only doctor in town until the banana company
arrived and work started on the railroad. Then empty seats
began to appear in the small room. The people who visited

him during the first four years of his stay in Macondo began to drift away when the company organized a clinic for its workers. He must have seen the new directions that the leaf storm was leading to, but he didn't say anything. He still opened up the street door, sitting in his leather chair all day long until several days passed without the return of a single patient. Then he threw the bolt on the door, bought a hammock, and shut himself up in the room.

During that time Meme got into the habit of bringing him breakfast, which consisted of bananas and oranges. He would eat the fruit and throw the peels into the corner, where the Indian woman would pick them up on Saturdays, when she cleaned the bedroom. But from the way he acted, anyone would have suspected that it made little difference to him whether or not she would stop cleaning some Saturday and the room would become a dungheap.

He did absolutely nothing now. He spent his time in the hammock, rocking. Through the half-open door he could be seen in the darkness and his thin and inexpressive face, his tangled hair, the sickly vitality of his hard yellow eyes gave him the unmistakable look of a man who has begun to feel defeated by circumstances.

During the first years of his stay in our house, Adelaida appeared to be indifferent or appeared to go along with me or really did agree with my decision that he should stay in the house. But when he closed his office and left his room only at mealtime, sitting at the table with the same silent and painful apathy as always, my wife broke the dikes of her tolerance. She told me: "It's heresy to keep supporting him. It's as if we were feeding the devil." And I, always inclined in his behalf out of a complex feeling of pity, amazement, and sorrow (because even though I may try to change the shape of it now, there was a great deal of sorrow in that feeling), insisted: "We have to take care of him. He's a man who doesn't have anybody in the world and he needs understanding."

Shortly afterward the railroad began to operate. Macondo

was a prosperous town, full of new faces, with a movie theater and several amusement places. At that time there was work for everyone, except for him. He kept shut up, aloof, until that morning when, all of a sudden, he made an appearance in the dining room at breakfast time and spoke spontaneously, even with enthusiaism, about the magnificent prospects for the town. That morning I heard the words for the first time. He said: "All of this will pass when we get used to the *leaf storm.*"

Months later he was frequently seen going out into the street before dusk. He would sit by the barbershop until the last hours of daylight, taking part in the conversation of the groups that gathered by the door, beside the portable dressing table, beside the high stool that the barber brought out into the street so that his customers could enjoy the coolness of dusk.

The company doctors were not satisfied with depriving him of his means of life and in 1907, when there was no longer a single patient in Macondo who remembered him and when he himself had ceased expecting any, one of the banana company doctors suggested to the mayor's office that they require all professionals in town to register their degrees. He must not have felt that he was the one they had in mind when the edict appeared one Monday on the four corners of the square. It was I who spoke to him about the convenience of complying with the requirement. But he, tranquil, indifferent, limited himself to replying: "Not me, colonel. I'm not going to get involved in any of that again." I've never been able to find out whether his papers were really in order or not. I couldn't find out if he was French, as we supposed, or if he had any remembrance of a family, which he must have had but about which he never said a word. A few weeks later, when the mayor and his secretary appeared at my house to demand of him the presentation and registration of his license, he absolutely refused to leave his room. That day—after five years of living in the same house—I suddenly realized that we didn't even know his name.

*   *   *

One probably didn't have to be seventeen years old (as I was then) in order to observe—from the time I saw Meme all decked out in church and afterward, when I spoke to her in the shop— that the small room in our house off the street was closed up. Later on I found out that my stepmother had padlocked it, was opposed to anyone's touching the things that were left inside: the bed that the doctor had used until he bought the hammock; the small table with medicines from which he had removed only the money accumulated during his better years (which must have been quite a bit, because he never had any expenses in the house and it was enough for Meme to open the shop with); and, in addition, in the midst of a pile of trash and old newspapers written in his language, the washstand and some useless personal items. It seemed as if all those things had been contaminated by something my stepmother con- sidered evil, completely diabolical.

I must have noticed that the room was closed in October or November (three years after Meme and he had left the house), because early in the following year I began to dream about Martín staying in that room. I wanted to live in it after my marriage; I prowled about it; in conversation with my stepmother I even suggested that it was already time to open the padlock and lift the unbreakable quarantine imposed on one of the most intimate and friendly parts of the house. But before the time we began sewing my wedding dress, no one spoke to me directly about the doctor and even less about the small room that was still like something of his, a fragment of his personality which could not be detached from our house while anyone who might have remembered him still lived in it.

I was going to be married before the year was up. I don't know if it was the circumstances under which my life had de- veloped during childhood and adolescence that gave me an imprecise notion of happenings and things at that time, but what was certain was that during those months when the preparations for my wedding were going forward, I still didn't know the secret of many things. A year before I married him, I would recall Martín through a vague atmosphere of unreality. Perhaps that was why I wanted him close by, in the small room, so that I could convince myself that it was a question of a concrete man and not a fiancé I had met in a dream. But I didn't feel I had the strength to speak to my stepmother about my project. The natural thing would have been to say: "I'm going to take off the padlock. I'm going to put the table next to the window and the bed against the inside wall. I'm going to put a pot of carnations on the shelf and an aloe branch over the lintel." But my cowardice, my absolute lack of decision, was joined by the foggy image of my betrothed. I remembered him as a vague, ungraspable figure whose only concrete elements seemed to be his shiny mustache, his head tilting slightly to the left, and the ever-present four-button jacket.

He had come to our house toward the end of July. He spent the day with us and chatted with my father in the office, going over some mysterious business that I was never able to find out about. In the afternoon Martín and I would go to the plantations with my stepmother. But when I looked at him on the way back in the mellow light of sunset, when he was closer to me, walking alongside my shoulder, then he became even more abstract and unreal. I knew that I would never be capable of imagining him as human or of finding in him the solidity that was indispensable if his memory was to give me courage, strengthen me at the moment of saying: "I'm going to fix the room up for Martín."

Even the idea that I was going to marry him seemed odd to me a year before the wedding. I had met him in February, during the wake for the Paloquemado child. Several of us girls were singing and clapping, trying to use up every drop of the only fun allowed us. There was a movie theater in Macondo, there was a public phonograph, and other places for amusement existed, but my father and stepmother were opposed to girls my age making use of them. "They're amusements from out of the leaf storm," they said.

Noontime was hot in February. My stepmother and I were sitting on the veranda, backstitching some white cloth while my father took his siesta. We sewed until he went by, dragging along in his clogs, to soak his head in the washbasin. But February was cool and deep at night and in the whole town one could hear the voices of women singing at wakes for children.

The night we went to the Paloquemado child's wake Meme Orozco's voice was probably louder than ever. She was thin, graceless, and stiff, like a broom, but she knew how to make her voice carry better than anyone. And in the first pause Genoveva García said: "There's a stranger sitting outside." I think that all of us stopped singing except Remedios Orozco. "Just think, he's wearing a jacket," Genoveva García said. "He's been talking all night and the others are listening to him without saying a peep. He's wearing a four-button jacket and when he crosses his legs you can see his socks and garters and his shoes have laces." Meme Orozco was still singing when we clapped our hands and said: "Let's marry him."

Afterward, when I thought about it at home, I couldn't find any correspondence between those words and reality. I remembered them as if they had been spoken by a group of imaginary women clapping hands and singing in a house where an unreal child had died. Other women were smoking next to us. They were serious, vigilant, stretching out their long buzzard necks toward us. In the back, against the coolness of the doorstep, another woman, bundled up to her head in a wide black cloth, was waiting for the coffee to boil. Suddenly a male voice joined ours. At first it was disconcerted and directionless, but then it was vibrant and metallic, as if the man were singing in church. Veva García nudged me in the ribs. Then I raised my eyes and saw him for the first time. He was young and neat, with a hard collar and a jacket with all four buttons closed. And he was looking at me.

I heard about his return in December and I thought that no place would be more appropriate for him than the small locked room. But I hadn't thought of it yet. I said to myself: "Martín, Martín, Martín." And the name, examined, savored, broken down into its essential parts, lost all of its meaning for me.

When we came out of the wake he put an empty cup in front of me. He said: "I read your fortune in the coffee." I was going to the door with the other girls and I heard his voice, deep, convincing, gentle: "Count seven stars and you'll dream about me." When we passed by the door we saw the Paloquemado child in his small coffin, his face powdered, a rose in his mouth, and his eyes held open with toothpicks. February was sending us warm gusts of death, and the breath of the jasmines and the violets toasted by the heat floated in the room. But in that silence of a dead person, the other voice was constant and different: "Remember. Only seven stars."

He came to our house in July. He liked to lean back against the flowerpots along the railing. He said: "Remember, I never looked into your eyes. That's the secret of a man who's begun to sense the fear of falling in love." And it was true, I couldn't remember his eyes. In July I probably couldn't have said what color the eyes of the man I was going to marry in December were. Still, six months earlier, February was only a deep silence at noontime, a pair of congorocho worms, male and female, coiled on the bathroom floor, the Tuesday beggar woman asking for a branch of lemon balm, and he, leaning back, smiling, his jacket buttoned all the way up, saying: "I'm going to make you think about me every minute of the day. I put a picture of you behind the door and I stuck two pins in your eyes." And Genoveva García, dying with laughter: "That's the kind of nonsense men pick up from the Guajiro Indians."

Toward the end of March he would be going through the house. He would spend long hours in the office with my father, convincing him of the importance of something I could never decipher. Eleven years have passed now since my marriage; nine since the time I watched him say good-bye from the window of the train, making me promise I would take good care of the child until he came back for us. Those nine years would pass with no one's hearing a word from him, and my father, who had helped him get ready for that endless trip, never said another word about his return. But not even during the two years that our marriage lasted was he more concrete and touchable than he was at the wake for the Paloquemado child or on that Sunday in March when I saw him for the second time as Veva García and I were coming home from church. He was standing in the doorway of the hotel, alone, his hands in the side pockets of his four-button jacket. He said: "Now you're going to think about me for the rest of your life because the pins have fallen out of the picture." He said it in such a soft and tense voice that it sounded like the truth. But even that truth was strange and different. Genoveva insisted: "That's silly Guajiro stuff." Three months later she ran away with the head of a company of puppeteers, but she still seemed scrupulous and serious on that Sunday. Martín said: "It's nice to know that someone will remember me in Macondo." And Genoveva García, looking at him with a face that showed exasperation, said:

"*Airyfay!* That four-button coat's going to rot with you inside of it."

7

EVEN THOUGH HE HOPED IT WOULD BE THE OPPOSITE, HE WAS A strange person in town, apathetic in spite of his obvious efforts to seem sociable and cordial. He lived among the people of Macondo, but at a distance from them because of the memory of a past against which any attempt at rectification seemed useless. He was looked on with curiosity, like a gloomy animal who had spent a long time in the shadows and was reappearing, conducting himself in a way that the town could only consider as superimposed and therefore suspect.

He would come back from the barbershop at nightfall and shut himself up in his room. For some time he had given up his evening meal and at first the impression at home was that he was coming back fatigued and going directly to his hammock to sleep until the following day. But only a short time passed before I began to realize that something extraordinary was happening to him at night. He could be heard moving about in his room with a tormented and maddening insistence, as if on those nights he was receiving the ghost of the man he had been until then, and both of them, the past man and the present one, were locked in a silent struggle in which the past one was defending his wrathful solitude, his invulnerable standoffish way, his intransigent manners; and the pres-

ent one his terrible and unchangeable will to free himself from
his own previous man. I could hear him pacing about the room
until dawn, until the time his own fatigue had exhausted the
strength of his invisible adversary.

I was the only one who noticed the true measure of his
change, from the time he stopped wearing leggings and began
to take a bath every day and perfume his clothing with scented
water. And a few months later his transformation had reached
the level where my feelings toward him stopped being a simple understanding tolerance and changed into compassion. It
was not his new look on the street that moved me. It was
thinking of him shut up in his room at night, scraping the
mud off his boots, wetting a rag in the washstand, spreading
polish on the shoes that had deteriorated through many years
of continuous use. It moved me to think of the brush and box
of shoe polish kept under the mattress, hidden from the eyes
of the world as if they were the elements of a secret and
shameful vice contracted at an age when the majority of men
were becoming serene and methodical. For all practical pur-
poses, he was going through a tardy and sterile adolescence
and, like an adolescent, he took great care in his dress,
smoothing out his clothing every night with the edge of his
hand, coldly, and he was not young enough to have a friend
to whom he could communicate his illusions or his disillusions.

The town must have noticed his change too, for a short
time later it began to be said about that he was in love with
the barber's daughter. I don't know whether there was any
basis for that, but what was certain was that the bit of gossip
made me realize his tremendous sexual loneliness, the biolog-
ical fury that must have tormented him in those years of filth
and abandonment.

Every afternoon he could be seen passing by on his way
to the barbershop, more and more fastidious in his dress. A
shirt with an artificial collar, gold cuff links, and his pants clean
and pressed, except that he still wore his belt outside the loops.
He looked like an afflicted suitor, enveloped in the aura of

cheap lotions; the eternal frustrated suitor, the sunset lover who would always lack the bouquet of flowers on the first visit.

That was how he was during the first months of 1909, with still no basis for the gossip in town except for the fact that he would be seen sitting in the barbershop every afternoon chatting with strangers, but with no one's having been able to be sure that he'd ever seen him a single time with the barber's daughter. I discovered the cruelty of that gossip. Everyone in town knew that the barber's daughter would always be an old maid after going through a year of suffering, as she was pursued by a *spirit,* an invisible lover who spread dirt on her food and muddied the water in the pitcher and fogged the mirrors in the barbershop and beat her until her face was green and disfigured. The efforts of the Pup, with a stroke of his stole, the complex therapy of holy water, sacred relics, and psalms administered with dramatic solicitude, were useless. As an extreme measure, the barber's wife locked her bewitched daughter up in her room, strewed rice about the living room, and turned her over to the invisible lover in a solitary and dead honeymoon, after which even the men of Macondo said that the barber's daughter had conceived.

Not even a year had passed when people stopped waiting for the monstrous event of her giving birth and public curiosity turned to the idea that the doctor was in love with the barber's daughter, in spite of the fact that everyone was convinced that the bewitched girl would lock herself up in her room and crumble to pieces in life long before any possible suitors would be transformed into marriageable men.

That was why I knew that rather than a supposition with some basis, it was a piece of cruel gossip, maliciously premeditated. Toward the end of 1909 he was still going to the barbershop and people were talking, organizing the wedding, with no one able to say that the girl had ever come out when he was present or that they had ever had a chance to speak to each other.

*   *   *

One September that was as broiling and as dead as this one, thirteen years ago, my stepmother began sewing on my wedding dress. Every afternoon while my father took his siesta, we would sit down to sew beside the flowerpots on the railing, next to the burning stove that was the rosemary plant. September has been like this all of my life, since thirteen years ago and much longer. As my wedding was to take place in a private ceremony (because my father had decided on it), we sewed slowly, with the minute care of a person who is in no hurry and has found the best measure of her time in her imperceptible work. We would talk during those times. I was still thinking about the street room, gathering up the courage to tell my stepmother that it was the best place to put up Martín. And that afternoon I told her.

My stepmother was sewing the long train of lace and it seemed in the blinding light of that intolerably clear and sound-filled September that she was submerged up to her shoulders in a cloud of that very September. "No," my stepmother said. And then, going back to her work, feeling eight years of bitter memories passing in front of her: "May God never permit anyone to enter that room again."

Martín had returned in July, but he didn't stay at our house. He liked to lean against the railing and stay there looking in the opposite direction. It pleased him to say: "I'd like to spend the rest of my life in Macondo." In the afternoon we'd go out to the plantations with my stepmother. We'd come back at dinnertime, before the lights in town went on. Then he'd tell me: "Even if it hadn't been for you, I'd like to live in Macondo in any case." And that too, from the way he said it, seemed to be the truth.

Around that time it had been four years since the doctor had left our house. And it was precisely on the afternoon we had begun work on the wedding dress—that suffocating afternoon when I told her about the room for Martín—that my stepmother spoke to me for the first time about his strange ways.

"Five years ago," she said, "he was still there, shut up like an animal. Because he wasn't only that, an animal, but something else: an animal who ate grass, a ruminant like any ox in a yoke. If he'd married the barber's daughter, that little faker who made the whole town believe the great lie that she'd conceived after a murky honeymoon with the spirits, maybe none of this would have happened. But he stopped going to the barbershop all of a sudden and he even showed a last-minute change that was only a new chapter as he methodically went through with his frightful plan. Only your father could have thought that after all that a man of such base habits should still stay in our house, living like an animal, scandalizing the town, giving people cause to talk about us as people who were always defying morals and good habits. His plans would end up with Meme's leaving. But not even then did your father recognize the alarming proportions of his mistake."

"I never heard any of that," I said. The locusts had set up a sawmill in the courtyard. My stepmother was speaking, still sewing without lifting her eyes from the tambour where she was stitching symbols, embroidering white labyrinths. She said: "That night we were sitting at the table (all except him, because ever since the afternoon he came back from the barbershop for the last time he wouldn't take his evening meal) when Meme came to serve us. She was different. 'What's the matter, Meme?' I asked her. 'Nothing, ma'am. Why?' But we could see that she wasn't right because she hesitated next to the lamp and she had a sickly look all over her. 'Good heavens, Meme, you're not well,' I said. But she held herself up as best she could until she turned toward the kitchen with the tray. Then your father, who was watching all the time, said to her: 'If you don't feel well, go to bed.' But she didn't say anything. She went out with the tray, her back to us, until we heard the noise of the dishes as they broke to pieces. Meme was on the veranda, holding herself up against the wall by her fingernails. That was when your father went to get that one in the bedroom to have a look at Meme.

"During the eight years he spent in our house," my step-mother said, "we'd never asked for his services for anything serious. We women went to Meme's room, rubbed her with alcohol, and waited for your father to come back. But they didn't come, Isabel. He didn't come to look at Meme in spite of the fact that the man who had fed him for eight years, had given him lodging and had his clothes washed, had gone to get him in person. Every time I remember him I think that his coming here was God's punishment. I think that all that grass we gave him for eight years, all the care, all the solici-tude was a test of God's, teaching us a lesson in prudence and mistrust of the world. It was as if we'd taken eight years of hospitality, food, clean clothes, and thrown it all to the hogs. Meme was dying (at least we thought she was) and he, right there, was still shut up, refusing to go through with what was no longer a work of charity but one of decency, of thanks, of simple consideration for those who were taking care of him.

"Only at midnight did your father come back. He said weakly: 'Give her some alcohol rubs, but no physics.' And I felt as if I'd been slapped. Meme had responded to our rub-bing. Infuriated, I shouted: 'Yes! Alcohol, that's it! We've al-ready rubbed her and she's better! But in order to do that we didn't have to live eight years sponging off people!' And your father, still condescending, still with that conciliatory non-sense: 'It's nothing serious. You'll realize that someday.' As if that other one were some sort of soothsayer."

That afternoon, because of the vehemence of her voice, the exaltation of her words, it seemed as if my stepmother were seeing again what happened on that remote night when the doctor refused to attend to Meme. The rosemary bush seemed suffocated by the blinding clarity of September, by the drowsiness of the locusts, by the heavy breathing of the men trying to take down a door in the neighborhood.

"But one of those Sundays Meme went to mass all decked out like a lady of quality," she said. "I can remember it as if it were today. She had a parasol with changing colors.

"Meme. Meme. That was God's punishment too. We'd taken her from where her parents were starving her to death, we took care of her, gave her a roof over her head, food, and a name, but the hand of Providence intervened there too. When I saw her at the door the next day, waiting for one of the Indians to carry her trunk out for her, even I didn't know where she was going. She was changed and serious, right over there (I can see her now), standing beside the trunk, talking to your father. Everything had been done without consulting me, Chabela; as if I were a painted puppet on the wall. Before I could ask what was going on, why strange things were happening in my own house without my knowing about them, your father came to tell me: 'You've nothing to ask Meme. She's leaving, but maybe she'll come back after a while.' I asked him where she was going and he didn't answer me. He was dragging along in his clogs as if I weren't his wife but some painted puppet on the wall.

"Only two days later," she said, "did I find out that the other one had left at dawn without the decency of saying goodbye. He'd come here as if the place belonged to him and eight years later he left as if he were leaving his own house, without saying good-bye, without saying anything. Just the way a thief would have done. I thought your father had sent him away for not attending to Meme, but when I asked him that on the same day, he limited himself to answering: 'You and I have to have a long talk about that.' And four years have passed without his ever bringing up the subject with me again.

"Only with your father and in a house as disordered as this one, where everybody does whatever he wants to, could such a thing have happened. In Macondo they weren't talking about anything else and I still didn't know that Meme had appeared in church all decked out, like a nobody raised to the status of a lady, and that your father had had the nerve to lead her across the square by the arm. That was when I found out that she wasn't as far away as I'd thought, but was living in the house on the corner with the doctor. They'd gone to live together like two pigs, not even going through the door of the church even though she'd been baptized. One day I told your father: 'God will punish that bit of heresy too.' And he didn't say anything. He was still the same tranquil man he always was, even after having been the patron of public concubinage and scandal.

"And yet I'm pleased now that things turned out that way, just so that the doctor left our house. If that hadn't happened, he'd still be in the little room. But when I found out that he'd left it and that he was taking his trash to the corner along with that trunk that wouldn't fit through the street door, I felt more peaceful. That was my victory, postponed for eight years.

"Two weeks later Meme opened the store, and she even had a sewing machine. She'd bought a new Domestic with the money she put away in this house. I considered that an affront and that's what I told your father. But even though he didn't answer my protests, you could see that instead of being sorry, he was satisfied with his work, as if he'd saved his soul by going against what was proper and honorable for this house, with his proverbial tolerance, his understanding, his liberality. And even a little empty-headedness. I said to him: 'You've thrown the best part of your beliefs to the swine.' And he, as always:

" 'You'll understand that too someday.' "

8

DECEMBER ARRIVED LIKE AN UNEXPECTED SPRING, AS A BOOK ONCE described it. And Martín arrived along with it. He appeared at the house after lunch, with a collapsible suitcase, still wearing the four-button jacket, clean and freshly pressed now. He said nothing to me but went directly to my father's office to talk to him. The date for the wedding had been set since July. But two days after Martín's arrival in December, my father called my stepmother to the office to tell her that the wedding would take place on Monday. It was Saturday.

My dress was finished. Martín had been to the house every day. He spoke to my father and the latter would give us his impressions at mealtime. I didn't know my fiancé. I hadn't been alone with him at any time. Still, Martín seemed to be linked to my father by a deep and solid friendship, and my father spoke of him as if it were he and not I who was going to marry Martín.

I felt no emotion over the closeness of the wedding date. I was still wrapped up in that gray cloud which Martín came through, stiff and abstract, moving his arms as he spoke, closing and opening his four-button jacket. He had lunch with us on Sunday. My stepmother assigned the places at the table in such a way that Martín was next to my father, separated from me by three places. During lunch my stepmother and I said very little. My father and Martín talked about their business matter; and I, sitting three places away, looked at the man who a year later would be the father of my son and to whom I was not even joined by a superficial friendship.

On Sunday night I tried on the wedding dress in my stepmother's bedroom. I looked pale and clean in the mirror, wrapped in that cloud of powdery froth that reminded me of my mother's ghost. I said to myself in front of the mirror: "That's me. Isabel. I'm dressed as a bride who's going to be married tomorrow morning." And I didn't recognize myself; I felt weighted down with the memory of my dead mother. Meme had spoken to me about her on this same corner a few days before. She told me that after I was born my mother was dressed in her bridal clothes and placed in a coffin. And now, looking at myself in the mirror, I saw my mother's bones covered by the mold of the tomb in a pile of crumpled gauze and compact yellow dust. I was outside the mirror. Inside was my mother, alive again, looking at me, stretching her arms out from her frozen space, trying to touch the death that was held together by the first pins of my bridal veil. And in back, in the center of the bedroom, my father, serious, perplexed: "She looks just like her now in that dress."

That night I received my first, last, and only love letter. A message from Martín written in pencil on the back of a movie program. It said: *Since it will be impossible for me to get there on time tonight, I'll go to confession in the morning. Tell the colonel that the thing we were talking about is almost set and that's why I can't come now. Are you frightened? M.* With the flat, floury taste of that letter in my mouth I went to my bedroom, and my palate was still bitter when I woke up a few hours later as my stepmother shook me.

Actually, many hours passed before I woke up completely. In the wedding dress I felt again as if I were in some cool and damp dawn that smelled of musk. My mouth felt dry, as when a person is starting out on a trip and the saliva refuses to wet the bread. The bridal party had been in the living room since four o'clock. I knew them all but now they looked transformed and new, the men dressed in tweeds and the women with their hats on, talking, filling the house with the dense and enervating vapor of their words.

The church was empty. A few women turned around to look at me as I went down the center aisle like a consecrated youth on his way to the sacrificial stone. The Pup, thin and serious, the only person with a look of reality in that turbulent and silent nightmare, came down the altar steps and gave me to Martín with four movements of his emaciated hands. Martín was beside me, tranquil and smiling, the way I'd seen him at the wake of the Paloquemado child, but wearing a short collar now, as if to show me that even on his wedding day he'd taken pains to be still more abstract than he already was on ordinary days.

That morning, back at the house, after the wedding party had eaten breakfast and contributed the standard phrases, my husband went out and didn't come back until siesta time. My father and stepmother didn't seem to notice my situation. They let the day pass without changing the order of things, so that nothing would make the extraordinary breath of that Monday felt. I took my wedding gown apart, made a bundle of it, and put it in the bottom of the wardrobe, remembering my mother, thinking: *At least these rags can be my shroud.*

The unreal groom returned at two in the afternoon and said that he had had lunch. Then it seemed to me as I watched him come with his short hair that December was no longer a blue month. Martín sat down beside me and we remained there for a moment without speaking. For the first time since I had been born I was afraid for night to begin. I must have shown it in some expression, because all of sudden Martín seemed to come to life; he leaned over my shoulder and asked: "What are you thinking about?" I felt something twisting in my heart: the stranger had begun to address me in the familiar form. I looked up toward where December was a gigantic shining ball, a luminous glass month; I said: "I was thinking that all we need now is for it to start raining."

The last night we spoke on the veranda it was hotter than usual. A few days later he would return for good from the barbershop and shut himself up in his room. But on that last night on the veranda, one of the hottest and heaviest I can remember, he seemed understanding as on few occasions. The only thing that seemed alive in the midst of that immense oven was the dull reverberation of the crickets, aroused by the thirst of nature, and the tiny, insignificant, and yet measureless activity of the rosemary and the nard, burning in the middle of the deserted hour. Both of us remained silent for a moment, exuding that thick and viscous substance that isn't sweat but the loose drivel of decomposing living matter. Sometimes he would look at the stars, in a sky desolate because of the summer splendor; then he would remain silent, as if completely given over to the passage of that night, which was monstrously alive. That was how we were, pensive, face to face, he in his leather chair, I in the rocker. Suddenly, with the passage of a white wing, I saw him tilt his sad and lonely head over his left shoulder. I thought of his life, his solitude, his frightful spiritual disturbances. I thought of the tormented indifference with which he watched the spectacle of life. Previously I had felt drawn to him out of complex feelings, sometimes contradictory and as variable as his personality. But at that moment there wasn't the slightest doubt in me that I'd begun to love him deeply. I thought that inside of myself I'd uncovered the mysterious force that from the first moment had led me to shelter him, and I felt the pain of his dark and stifling room like an open wound. I saw him as somber and defeated, crushed by circumstances. And suddenly, with a new look from his hard and penetrating yellow eyes, I felt the certainty that the secret of his labyrinthine solitude had been revealed to me by the tense pulsation of the night. Before I even had time to think why I was doing it, I asked him:

"Tell me something, doctor. Do you believe in God?"

He looked at me. His hair fell over his forehead and a kind of inner suffocation burned all through him, but his face still showed no shadow of emotion or upset. Having completely recovered his parsimonious ruminant voice, he said:

"It's the first time anyone ever asked me that question."

"What about you, doctor, have you ever asked it?"

He seemed neither indifferent nor concerned. He only seemed interested in my person. Not even in my question and least of all in its intent.

"That's hard to say," he said.

"But doesn't a night like this make you afraid? Don't you get the feeling that there's a man bigger than all of us walking through the plantations while nothing moves and everything seems perplexed at the passage of that man?"

He was silent then. The crickets filled the surrounding space, beyond the warm smell which was alive and almost human as it rose up from the jasmine bush I had planted in memory of my first wife. A man without dimensions was walking alone through the night.

"I really don't think any of that bothers me, colonel." And now he seemed perplexed, he too, like things, like the rosemary and the nard in their burning place. "What bothers me," he said, and he kept on looking into my eyes, directly, sternly, "what bothers me is that there's a person like you capable of saying with such certainty that he's aware of that man walking in the night."

"We try to save our souls, doctor. That's the difference."

And then I went beyond what I had proposed. I said: "You don't hear him because you're an atheist."

And he, serene, unperturbed:

"Believe me, colonel, I'm not an atheist. I get just as upset thinking that God exists as thinking that he doesn't. That's why I'd rather not think about it."

I don't know why, but I had the feeling that that was exactly what he was going to answer. *He's a man disturbed by God,* I thought, listening to what he'd just told me spontaneously, with clarity, precision, as if he'd read it in a book. I was still intoxicated with the drowsiness of the night. I felt that I was in the heart of an immense gallery of prophetic images.

Over there on the other side of the railing was the small garden where Adelaida and my daughter had planted things. That was why the rosemary was burning, because every morning they strengthened it with their attention so that on nights like that its burning vapor would pass through the house and make sleep more restful. The jasmine gave off its insistent breath and we received it because it was the same age as Isabel, because in a certain way that smell was a prolongation of her mother. The crickets were in the courtyard, among the bushes, because we'd neglected to clean out the weeds when it had stopped raining. The only thing incredible, miraculous, was that he was there, with his enormous cheap handkerchief, drying his forehead, which glowed with perspiration.

Then after another pause, he said:

"I'd like to know why you asked me that, colonel."

"It just came to me all of a sudden," I said. "Maybe after seven years I wanted to know what a man like you thinks about."

I was mopping my brow too. I said:

"Or maybe I'm worried about your solitude." I waited for an answer that didn't come. I saw him across from me, still sad and alone. I thought about Macondo, the madness of its people, burning banknotes at parties; about the leaf storm that had no direction and was above everything, wallowing in its slough of instinct and dissipation where it had found the taste it wanted. I thought about his life before the leaf storm had struck. And his life afterward, his cheap perfume, his polished old shoes, the gossip that followed him like a shadow that he himself ignored. I said:

"Doctor, have you ever thought of taking a wife?"

And before I could finish asking the question, he was giving an answer, starting off on one of his usual long meanderings:

"You love your daughter very much, don't you, colonel?"

I answered that it was natural. He went on speaking:

"All right. But you're different. Nobody likes to drive his own nails more than you. I've seen you putting hinges on a door when there are several men working for you who could have done it. You like that. I think that your happiness is to walk about the house with a toolbox looking for something to fix. You're even capable of thanking a person for having broken a hinge, colonel. You thank him because in that way he's giving you a chance to be happy."

"It's a habit," I told him, not knowing what direction he was taking. "They say my mother was the same way."

He'd reacted. His attitude was peaceful but ironclad.

"Fine," he said. "It's a good habit. Besides, it's the cheapest kind of happiness I know. That's why you have a house like this and raised your daughter the way you have. I say that it must be good to have a daughter like yours."

I still didn't know what he was getting at in his long, roundabout way. But even though I didn't know, I asked:

"What about you, doctor, haven't you ever thought about how nice it would be to have a daughter?"

"Not I, colonel," he said. And he smiled, but then he immediately became serious again. "My children wouldn't be like yours."

Then I didn't have the slightest trace of doubt: he was talking seriously and that seriousness, that situation, seemed frightful to me. I was thinking: *He's more to be pitied for that than for anything else.* He needed protection, I thought.

"Have you heard of the Pup?" I asked him.

He said no. I told him: "The Pup is the parish priest, but more than that he's a friend to everybody. You should get to know him."

"Oh, yes, yes," he said. "He had children *too*, right?"

74

"That's not what interests me right now," I said. "People invent bits of gossip about the Pup because they have a lot of love for him. But you have a point there, doctor. The Pup is a long way from being a prayermonger, sanctimonious, as we say. He's a whole man who fulfills his duties as a man."

Now he was listening with attention. He was silent, concentrating, his hard yellow eyes fastened on mine. He said: "That's good, right?"

"I think the Pup will be made a saint," I said. And I was sincere in that too. "We've never seen anything like him in Macondo. At first they didn't trust him because he comes from here, because the older people remembered him from when he used to go out hunting birds like all the boys. He fought in the war, he was a colonel, and that was a problem. You know how people are, no respect for veterans, the same as with priests. Besides, we weren't used to having someone read to us from the Bristol Almanac instead of the Gospels."

He smiled. That must have sounded as odd to him as it had to us during the first days. He said: "That's strange, isn't it?"

"That's the way the Pup is. He'd rather show people by means of atmospheric phenomena. He's got a preoccupation with storms that's almost theological. He talks about them every Sunday. And that's why his sermons aren't based on the Gospels but on the atmospheric predictions in the Bristol Almanac."

He was smiling now and listening with a lively and pleased expression. I felt enthusiastic too. I said: "There's still something else of interest for you, doctor. Do you know how long the Pup has been in Macondo?"

He said no.

"It so happens that he arrived the same day as you," I said. "And what's even stranger still, if you had an older brother, I'm sure that he'd be just like the Pup. Physically, of course."

He didn't seem to be thinking about anything else now. From his seriousnesss, from his concentrated and steady attention, I sensed that I had come to the moment to tell him what I wanted to propose:

"Well, then, doctor," I said. "Pay a call on the Pup and you'll find out that things aren't the way you see them."

And he said yes, he'd visit the Pup.

9

COLDLY, SILENTLY, PROGRESSIVELY, THE PADLOCK GATHERS RUST. Adelaida put it on the room when she found out that the doctor had gone to live with Meme. My wife considered that move as a victory for her, the culmination of a systematic, tenacious piece of work she had started the first moment I decided that he would live with us. Seventeen years later the padlock is still guarding the room.

If there was something in my attitude, unchanged for eight years, that may have seemed unworthy in the eyes of men or ungrateful in those of God, my punishment has come about a long time before my death. Perhaps it was meant for me to expiate in life for what I had considered a human obligation, a Christian duty. Because the rust on the lock had not begun to accumulate when Martín was in my house with a briefcase full of projects, the authenticity of which I've never been able to find out, and the firm desire to marry my daughter. He came to my house in a four-button jacket, exuding youth and dynamism from all his pores, enveloped in a luminous air of pleasantness. He married Isabel in December eleven years ago. Nine has passed since he went off with the briefcase full of notes signed by me and with the promise to return as soon as the deal he was working on and of which he had my financial backing came through. Nine years have gone by but I have no right to think he was a swindler because of that. I have no right to think his marriage was only a pretext to convince me of his good faith.

But eight years of experience have been of some use. Martín could have occupied the small room. Adelaida was against it. Her opposition was adamant, decisive and irrevocable. I knew that my wife wouldn't have been bothered in the least to fix up the stable as a bridal chamber rather than let the newlyweds occupy the small room. I accepted her point of view without hesitation. That was my recognition of her victory, one postponed for eight years. If both of us were mistaken in trusting Martín, it was a mistake that was shared. There was neither victory nor defeat for either one of us. Still, what came later was too much for our efforts, it was like the atmospheric phenomena the almanac foretells, ones that must come no matter what.

When I told Meme to leave our house, to follow the direction she thought best for her life, and afterward, even though Adelaida threw my weaknesses and lack of strength up to me, I was able to rebel, to impose my will on everything (that's what I've always done) and arrange things my way. But something told me that I was powerless before the course that events were taking. It wasn't I who arranged things in my own home, but some other mysterious force, one which decided the course of our existence and of which we were nothing but docile and insignificant instruments. Everything seemed to obey the natural and linked fulfillment of a prophecy.

Since Meme was able to open the shop (underneath it all everybody must have known that a hard-working woman who becomes the mistress of a country doctor overnight will sooner or later end up as a shopkeeper), I realized that in our house he'd accumulated a larger sum of money than one might have imagined, and that he'd kept it in his cabinet, uncounted bills and coins which he tossed into the drawer during the time he saw patients.

When Meme opened the shop it was supposed that he was here, in back of the store, shut up because of God knows what bestial and implacable prophecies. It was known that he wouldn't eat any food from outside, that he'd planted a garden and that during the first months Meme would buy a piece of meat for herself, but that a year later she'd stopped doing that, perhaps because direct contact with the man had made a vegetarian of her. Then the two of them shut themselves up until the time the authorities broke down the door, searched the house, and dug up the garden in an attempt to find Meme's body.

People imagined him there, shut in, rocking in his old and tattered hammock. But I knew, even in those months during which his return to the world of the living was not expected, that his impenitent enclosure, his muted battle against the threat of God, would reach its culmination much sooner than his death. I knew that sooner or later he would come out because there isn't a man alive who can live a half-life, locked up, far away from God, without coming out all of a sudden to render to the first man he meets on the corner the accounts that stocks and pillory, the martyrdom of fire and water, the torture of the rack and the screw, wood and hot iron on his eyes, the eternal salt on his tongue, the torture horse, lashes, the grate, and love could not have made him render to his inquisitors. And that time would come for him a few years before his death.

I knew that truth from before, from the last night we talked on the veranda, and afterward, when I went to get him in the little room to have a look at Meme. Could I have opposed his desire to live with her as man and wife? I might have been able before. Not now, because another chapter of fate had begun to be fulfilled three months before that.

He wasn't in his hammock that night. He'd lain down on his back on the cot and had his head back, his eyes fixed on the spot on the ceiling where the light from the candle must have been most intense. There was an electric light in the room but he never used it. He preferred to lie in the shadows, his eyes fixed on the darkness. He didn't move when I went into the room, but I noticed that the moment I crossed the threshold he felt that he wasn't alone. Then I said: "If it's not too much trouble, doctor, it seems that the Indian girl isn't feeling well." He sat up on the bed. A moment before he'd felt that he wasn't alone in the room. Now he knew that I was the one who was there. Without doubt they were two completely different feelings, because he underwent an immediate change, he smoothed his hair and remained sitting on the edge of the bed waiting.

"It's Adelaida, doctor. She wants you to come look at Meme," I said.

And he, sitting there, gave me the impact of an answer with his parsimonious ruminant voice:

"It won't be necessary. The fact is she's pregnant."

Then he leaned forward, seemed to be examining my face, and said: "Meme's been sleeping with me for years."

I must confess that I was surprised. I didn't feel any upset, perplexity, or anger. I didn't feel anything. Perhaps his confession was too serious to my way of seeing things and was out of the normal course of my comprehension. I remained impassive and I didn't even know why. I was motionless, standing, immutable, as cold as he, like his parsimonious ruminant voice. Then, after a long silence during which he still sat on the cot, not moving, as if waiting for me to take the first step, I understood what he had just told me in all of its intensity. But then it was too late for me to get upset.

"As long as you're aware of the situation, doctor." That was all I could say. He said:

"One takes his precautions, colonel. When a person takes a risk he knows that he's taking it. If something goes wrong it's because there was something unforeseen, out of a person's reach."

I knew that kind of evasion. As always, I didn't know where

he was leading. I brought over a chair and sat down opposite him. Then he left the cot, fastened the buckle of his belt, and pulled up his pants and adjusted them. He kept on talking from the other end of the room. He said:

"Just as sure as the fact that I took my precautions is the fact that this is the second time she's got pregnant. The first time was a year and a half ago and you people didn't notice anything."

He went on talking without emotion, going back to the cot. In the darkness I heard his slow, firm steps against the tiles. He said:

"But she was ready for anything then. Not now. Two months ago she told me she was pregnant again and I told her what I had the first time: 'Come by tonight and be ready for the same thing.' She told me not that day, the next day. When I went to have my coffee in the kitchen I told her that I was waiting for her, but she said that she'd never come back."

He'd come over by the cot, but he didn't sit down. He turned his back on me again and began to walk around the room once more. I heard him speaking. I heard the flow of his voice, back and forth, as if he were rocking in the hammock. He was telling things calmly, but with assurance. I knew that it would have been useless to try to interrupt him. All I could do was listen to him. And he kept on talking:

"Still, she did come two days later. I had everything ready. I told her to sit down there and I went to my table for the glass. Then, when I told her to drink it, I realized that this time she wouldn't. She looked at me without smiling and said with a touch of cruelty: 'I'm not going to get rid of this one, doctor. This one I'm going to have so I can raise it.'"

I felt exasperated by his calmness. I told him: "That doesn't justify anything, doctor. What you've done is something that's twice unworthy: first, because of your relations inside my house, and then because of the abortion."

"But you can see that I did everything I could, colonel. It

was all I could do. Afterward, when I saw there was no way out, I got ready to talk to you. I was going to do it one of these days."

"I imagine you know that there is a way out of this kind of situation if you really want to erase the insult. You know the principles of those of us who live in this house," I said. And he said:

"I don't want to cause you any trouble, colonel. Believe me. What I was going to tell you is this: I'll take the Indian woman and go live in the empty house on the corner."

"Living together openly, doctor?" I asked him. "Do you know what that means for us?"

Then he went back to the cot. He sat down, leaned forward, and spoke with his elbows on his legs. His accent became different. At first it had been cold. Now it began to be cruel and challenging. He said:

"I'm proposing the only solution that won't cause you any distress, colonel. The other thing would be to say that the child isn't mine."

"Meme would say it was," I said. I was beginning to feel indignant. His way of expressing himself was too challenging and aggressive now and I couldn't accept it calmly.

But he, hard, implacable, said:

"You have to believe me absolutely when I say that Meme won't say it is. It's because I'm sure of that that I say I'll take her to the corner, only so I can avoid distress for you. That's the only reason, colonel."

He was so sure that Meme would not attribute the paternity of her child to him that now I did feel upset. Something was making me think that his strength was rooted much deeper than his words. I said:

"We trust Meme as we would our own daughter, doctor. In this case she'd be on our side."

"If you knew what I know, you wouldn't talk that way, colonel. Pardon me for saying it this way, but if you compare that Indian girl to your daughter, you're insulting your daughter."

"You have no reason to say that," I said.

And he answered, still with that bitter hardness in his voice: "I do. And when I tell you that she can't say that I'm the father of her child, I also have reasons for it."

He threw his head back. He sighed deeply and said:

"If you took time to spy on Meme when she goes out at night, you wouldn't even demand that I take her away with me. In this case I'm the one who runs the risk, colonel. I'm taking on a dead man to avoid your having any distress."

Then I understood that he wouldn't even go through the doors of the church with Meme. But what was serious was that after his final words I wouldn't have dared go through with what could have been a tremendous burden on my conscience later on. There were several cards in my favor. But the single one he held would have been enough for him to win a bet against my conscience.

"All right, doctor," I said. "This very night I'll make arrangements to have the house on the corner fixed up. But in any case, I want you to be aware of the fact that I'm throwing you out of my house. You're not leaving of your own free will. Colonel Aureliano Buendía would have made you pay dearly for the way you returned his trust."

And when I thought I'd roused up his instincts and was waiting for him to unleash his dark, primal forces, he threw the whole weight of his dignity on me.

"You're a decent man, colonel," he said. "Everybody knows that, and I've lived in this house long enough for you not to have to remind me of it."

When he stood up he didn't seem victorious. He only seemed satisfied at having been able to repay our attentions of eight years. I was the one who felt upset, the one at fault. That night, seeing the germs of death that were becoming progressively more visible in his hard yellow eyes, I understood that my attitude was selfish and that because of that one single stain on my conscience it would be quite right for me to suffer a tremendous expiation for the rest of my life. He, on the other hand, was at peace with himself. He said:

"As for Meme, have them rub her with alcohol. But they shouldn't give her any physics."

10

MY GRANDFATHER'S COME BACK BESIDE MAMA. SHE'S SITTING
down, completely lost in her thoughts. The dress and the hat
are here, on the chair, but my mother's not in them anymore.
My grandfather comes closer, sees that her mind's somewhere
else, and he moves his cane in front of her eyes, saying: "Wake
up, child." My mother blinks, shakes her head. "What were
you thinking about?" my grandfather asks. And she, smiling
with great effort: "I was thinking about the Pup."

My grandfather sits down beside her again, his chin resting on his cane. He says: "That's a coincidence. I was thinking
about him too."

They understand their words. They talk without looking
at each other, Mama leaning back in her chair and my grandfather sitting next to her, his chin still resting on his cane. But
even like that they understand each other's words, the way
Abraham and I can understand each other when we go to see
Lucrecia.

I tell Abraham: "Now I'm tecky-tacking." Abraham always
walks in front, about three steps ahead of me. Without turning around to look he says: "Not yet, in a minute." And I say
to him: "When I teck somebum hoblows up." Abraham doesn't
turn his head but I can hear him laugh softly with a foolish

and simple laugh that's like the thread of water that trembles down from the snout of an ox when he's finished drinking. He says: "It must be around five o'clock." He runs a little more and says: "If we go now somebum might hoblow." But I insist: "In any case, there's always tecky-tacking." And he turns to me and starts to run, saying: "All right, then, let's go."

In order to see Lucrecia you have to go through five yards full of trees and bushes. You have go to over the low wall that's green with lizards where the midget with a woman's voice used to sing. Abraham goes running along, shining like a sheet of metal in the strong light, his heels harried by the dog's barking. Then he stops. At that point we're by the window. We say: "Lucrecia," making our voices low as if Lucrecia was sleeping. But she's awake, sitting on the bed, her shoes off, wearing a loose nightgown, white and starched, that reaches down to her ankles.

When we speak, Lucrecia lifts her eyes and makes them turn around the room, fastening a round, large eye like that of a curlew on us. Then she laughs and begins to move toward the center of the room. Her mouth is open and she shows her small, broken teeth. She has a round head, with the hair cut like a man's. When she gets to the center of the room she stops laughing, squats down, and looks at the door until her hands reach her ankles, and she slowly begins to lift her gown, with a calculated slowness, cruel and challenging at the same time. Abraham and I are still looking in the window while Lucrecia lifts up her gown, her lips sticking out in a panting and anxious frown, her big curlew eyes staring and shining. Then we can see her white stomach, which turns deep blue farther down, when she covers her face with the nightgown and stays that way, stretched out in the center of the bedroom, her legs together and tight with a trembling force that comes up from her ankles. All of a sudden she quickly uncovers her face, points at us with her forefinger, and the shining eye pops out in the midst of terrible shrieks that echo all through the house. Then the door of the room opens and the woman comes in shouting: "Why don't you go screw the patience of your own mothers?"

We haven't been to see Lucrecia for days. Now we go to the river along the road to the plantations. If we get out of this early, Abraham will be waiting for me. But my grandfather doesn't move. He's sitting next to Mama with his chin on his cane. I keep watching him, watching his eyes behind his glasses, and he must feel that I'm looking at him, because all of a sudden he gives a deep sigh, shakes himself, and says to my mother in a low, sad voice: "The Pup would have made them come if he had to whip them."

The he gets up from his chair and walks over to where the dead man is.

It's the second time that I've been in this room. The first time, ten years ago, things were just the same. It's as if they hadn't been touched since then or as if since that remote dawn when he came here to live with Meme he hadn't worried about his life anymore. The papers were in the same place. The table, the few cheap articles of clothing, everything was in the same place it's in today. As if it were yesterday when the Pup and I came to make peace between the man and the authorities.

By that time the banana company had stopped squeezing us and had left Macondo with the rubbish of the rubbish they'd brought us. And with them went the leaf storm, the last traces of what prosperous Macondo had been like in 1915. A ruined village was left here, with four poor, dark stores; occupied by unemployed and angry people who were tormented by a prosperous past and bitterness of an overwhelming and static present. There was nothing in the future at that time except a gloomy and threatening election Sunday.

Six months before an anonymous note had been found nailed to the door of this house one morning. No one was interested in it and it stayed nailed here for a long time until the final drizzle washed away its dark letters and the paper disappeared, hauled off by the last winds of February. But toward the end of 1918, when the closeness of the elections made the government think about the necessity of keeping the tension of its voters awake and irritated, someone spoke to the new authorities concerning this solitary doctor, about whose existence there would have to be some valid evidence after such a long time. They had to be told that during the first years the Indian woman who lived with him ran a shop that shared in the same prosperity that favored even the most insignificant enterprises in Macondo during those times. One day (no one remembers the date, not even the year) the door of the shop didn't open. It was imagined that Meme and the doctor were still living here, shut up, living on the vegetables they grew themselves in the yard. But in the note that appeared on this corner it said that the physician had murdered his concubine and buried her in the garden, afraid that the town would use her to poison him. The inexplicable thing is that it was said during a time when no one could have had any reason to plot the doctor's death. I think that the authorities had forgotten about his existence until that year when the government reinforced the police and the reserves with men they could trust. Then they dug up the forgotten legend of the anonymous note and the authorities violated these doors, searched the house, dug up the yard, and probed in the privy trying to locate Meme's body. But they couldn't find a trace of her.

On that occasion they would have dragged the doctor out, beaten him, and he most surely would have been one more sacrifice on the public square in the name of official order. But the Pup stepped in; he came to my house and invited me to visit the doctor, certain that I'd be able to get a satisfactory explanation from him.

When we went in the back way we found the ruins of a man abandoned in the hammock. Nothing in this world can be more fearsome than the ruins of a man. And those of this citizen of nowhere who sat up in the hammock when he saw us come in were even worse, and he himself seemed to be covered by the coat of dust that covered everything in the room. His head was steely and his hard yellow eyes still had the powerful inner strength that I had seen in them in my house. I had the impression that if we'd scratched him with our nails his body would have fallen apart, turning into a pile of human sawdust. He'd cut his mustache but he hadn't shaved it off. He'd used shears on his beard so that his chin didn't seem to be sown with hard and vigorous sprouts but with soft, white fuzz. Seeing him in the hammock I thought: *He doesn't look like a man now. Now he looks like a corpse whose eyes still haven't died.*

When he spoke his voice was the same parsimonious ruminant voice that he'd brought to our house. He said that he had nothing to say. He said, as if he thought that we didn't know about it, that the police had violated his doors and had dug in his yard without his consent. But that wasn't a protest. It was only a complaining and melancholy confidence.

As for Meme, he gave us an explanation that might have seemed puerile, but which was said by him with the same accent with which he would have told the truth. He said that Meme had left, that was all. When she closed the shop she began to get restless in the house. She didn't speak to anyone, she had no communication at all with the outside world. He said that one day he saw her packing her bag and he didn't say anything to her. He said that he still didn't say anything when he saw her in her street clothes, high heels, with the suitcase in her hand, standing in the doorway but not speaking, only as if she were showing herself like that so that he would know that she was leaving. "Then," he said, "I got up and gave her the money that was left in the drawer."

I asked him: "How long ago was that, doctor?"

And he said: "You can judge by my hair. She was the one who cut it."

The Pup didn't say much on that visit. From the time he'd entered the room he seemed impressed by the sight of the only man he hadn't met after being in Macondo fifteen years. That time I noticed (and more than ever, maybe because the doctor had cut his mustache) the extraordinary resemblance between those two men. They weren't exact, but they looked like brothers. One was several years older, thinner and more emaciated. But there was the community of features between them that exists between two brothers, even if one looks like the father and the other like the mother. Then I recalled that last night on the veranda. I said:

"This is the Pup, doctor. You promised me you'd visit him once."

He smiled. He looked at the priest and said: "That's right, colonel. I don't know why I didn't." And he continued looking at him, examining him, until the Pup spoke.

"It's never too late for a good beginning," he said. "I'd like to be your friend."

At once I realized that facing the stranger, the Pup had lost his usual strength. He spoke timidly, without the inflexible assurance with which his voice thundered from the pulpit reading the atmospheric predictions of the Bristol Almanac in a transcendental and threatening tone.

That was the first time they'd seen each other. And it was also the last. Still, the doctor's life was prolonged until this morning because the Pup had intervened again in his favor on the night they begged him to take care of the wounded and he wouldn't even open the door, and they shouted that terrible sentence down on him, the fulfillment of which I've now undertaken to prevent.

We were getting ready to leave the house when I remembered something that I'd wanted to ask him for years. I told the Pup I was going to stay awhile with the doctor while he interceded with the authorities. When we were alone I asked him:

"Tell me something, doctor. What was the child?"

He didn't change his expression. "What child, colonel?"

he asked. And I said: "Yours. Meme was pregnant when you left my house." And he, tranquil, imperturbable:

"You're right, colonel. I'd even forgotten about that."

My father was silent. Then he said: "The Pup would have made them come if he had to whip them." My father's eyes show a restrained nervousness. And while this waiting goes on, it's been a half hour already (because it must be around three o'clock), I'm worried about the child's perplexity, his absorbed expression, which doesn't seem to be asking anything, his abstract and cold indifference, which makes him just like his father. My son's going to dissolve in the boiling air of this Wednesday just as it happened to Martín nine years ago, when he waved from the train window and disappeared forever. All my sacrifice for this son will be in vain if he keeps on looking like his father. It won't be of any use for me to beg God to make him a man of flesh and blood, one who has volume, weight, and color like other men. Everything will be in vain as long as he has the seeds of his father in his blood.

Five years ago the child didn't have anything of Martín's. Now he's getting to have it all, ever since Genoveva García came back to Macondo with her six children, with two sets of twins among them. Genoveva was fat and old. Blue veins had come out around her eyes, giving a certain look of dirtiness to her face, which had been clean and firm before. She showed a noisy and disordered happiness in the midst of her flock of small white shoes and organdy frills. I knew that Genoveva had run away with the head of a company of puppeteers and I felt some kind of repugnance at seeing those children of hers, who seemed to have automatic movements, as if run by some single central mechanism; small and upsettingly alike, all six with identical shoes and identical frills on their clothing. Genoveva's disorganized happiness seemed painful and sad to me, as did her presence, loaded with urban accessories, in a ruined town that was annihilated by dust. There was something bitter, something inconsolably ridiculous, in her way of moving, of seeming fortunate and of feeling sorry for our way of life, which was so different, she said, from the one she had known in the company of the puppeteers.

Looking at her I remembered other times. I said to her: "You've gotten very fat." And then she became sad. She said: "It must be that memories make a person fat." And she stood there looking closely at the child. She said: "And what happened to the wizard with four buttons?" And I answered her right out, because I knew that she knew: "He went away." And Genoveva said: "And didn't he leave you anything but that?" And I told her no, he'd only left me the child. Genoveva laughed with a loose and vulgar laugh. "He must have been pretty sloppy to make only one child in five years," she said, and she went on, still moving about and cackling in the midst of her confused flock: "And I was mad about him. I swear I would have taken him away from you if it hadn't been that we'd met him at a child's wake. I was very superstitious in those days."

It was before she said good-bye that Genoveva stood looking at the child and said: "He's really just like him. All he needs is the four-button jacket." And from that moment on the child began to look just like his father to me, as if Genoveva had brought on the curse of his identity. On certain occasions I would catch him with his elbows on the table, his head leaning over his left shoulder, and his foggy look turned nowhere. He was just like Martín when he leaned against the carnation pots on the railing and said: "Even if it hadn't been for you, I'd like to spend the rest of my life in Macondo." Sometimes I get the impression that he's going to say it; how could he say it now that he's sitting next to me silent, touching his nose that's stuffed up with the heat? "Does it hurt you?" I asked him. And he says no, that he was thinking that he couldn't keep glasses on. "You don't have to worry about that," I tell him, and I undo his tie. I say: "When we get home you can rest and have a bath." And then I look toward where my father has just said: "Cataure," calling the oldest of the Guajiros. He's a heavyset and short Indian, who was smoking on the bed, and when he hears his name he lifts his head and looks for my father's face with his small somber eyes. But when my father is about to speak again the steps of the mayor are heard in the back room as he staggers into the bedroom.

11

THIS NOON HAS BEEN TERRIBLE FOR OUR HOUSE. EVEN THOUGH the news of his death was no surprise to me, because I was expecting it for a long time, I couldn't imagine that it would bring on such an upset in my house. Someone had to go to this burial with me and I thought that one would be my wife, especially since my illness three years ago and that afternoon when she found the cane with the silver handle and the wind-up dancer when she was looking through the drawers of my desk. I think that we'd forgotten about the toy by then. But that afternoon we made the mechanism work and the ballerina danced as on other occasions, animated by the music that had been festive before and which then, after the long silence in the drawer, sounded quiet and nostalgic. Adelaida watched it dance and remembered. Then she turned to me, her look moistened by simple sadness:

"Who does it remind you of?" she asked.

And I knew who Adelaida was thinking about, while the toy saddened the room with its worn-out little tune.

"I wonder what's become of him?" my wife asked, remembering, shaken perhaps by the breath of those days when he'd appeared at the door of the room at six in the afternoon and hung the lamp in the doorway.

"He's on the corner," I said. "One of these days he'll die and we'll have to bury him."

Adelaida remained silent, absorbed in the dance of the toy, and I felt infected by her nostalgia. I said to her: "I've always wanted to know who you thought he was the day he came. You set that table because he reminded you of someone."

And Adelaida said with a gray smile:

"You'd laugh at me if I told you who he reminded me of when he stood there in the corner with the ballerina in his hand." And she pointed to the empty space where she'd seen him twenty-two years before, with full boots and a costume that looked like a military uniform.

I thought on that afternoon they'd been reconciled in memory, so today I told my wife to get dressed in black to go with me. But the toy is back in the drawer. The music has lost its effect. Adelaida is wearing herself out now. She's sad, devastated, and she spends hours on end praying in her room. "Only you would have thought of a burial like that," she told me. "After all the misfortunes that befell us, all we needed was that cursed leap year. And then the deluge." I tried to persuade her that my word of honor was involved in this undertaking.

"We can't deny that I owe my life to him," I said.

And she said:

"He's the one who owes his to us. All he did when he saved your life was to repay a debt for eight years of bed, board, and clean clothes."

Then she brought a chair over to the railing. And she must be there still, her eyes foggy with grief and superstition. Her attitude seemed so decided that I tried to calm her down. "All right. In that case I'll go with Isabel," I said. And she didn't answer. She sat there, inviolable, until we got ready to leave and I told her, thinking to please her: "Until we get back, go to the altar and pray for us." Then she turned her head toward the door, saying: "I'm not even going to pray. My prayers will still be useless just as long as that woman comes every Tuesday to ask for a branch of lemon balm." And in her voice there was an obscure and overturned rebellion:

"I'll stay collapsed here until Judgment Day. If the termites haven't eaten up the chair by then."

My father stops, his neck stretched out, listening to the familiar footsteps that are advancing through the back room. Then he forgets what he was going to tell Cataure and tries to turn around, leaning on his cane, but his useless leg fails him in the turn and he's about to fall down, as happened three years ago when he fell into the lemonade bowl, with the noise of the bowl as it rolled along the floor and the clogs and the rocker and the shout of the child, who was the only one who saw him fall.

He's limped ever since then, since then he's dragged the foot that hardened after that week of bitter suffering, from which we thought he'd never recover. Now, seeing him like that, getting his balance back with the help of the mayor, I think that that useless leg holds the secret of the compromise that he's going to fulfill against the will of the town.

Maybe his gratitude goes back to that time. From the time he fell on the veranda, saying that he felt as if he'd been pushed off a tower, and the last two doctors left in Macondo advised him to prepare for a good death. I remember him on the fifth day in bed, shrunken between the sheets; I remember his emaciated body, like the body of the Pup, who'd been carried to the cemetery the year before by all the inhabitants of Macondo in a compressed and moving procession of flowers. Inside the coffin his majesty had the same depth of irremediable and disconsolate abandonment that I saw in the face of my father during those days when the bedroom filled up with his voice and he spoke about that strange soldier who appeared one night in the camp of Colonel Aureliano Buendía during the war of '85, his hat and boots decorated with the skin, teeth, and claws of a tiger, and they asked him: "Who are you?" And the strange soldier didn't answer; and they asked him: "Where do you come from?" And he still didn't answer; and they asked him: "What side are you fighting on?" And they still didn't get any answer from the strange soldier, until an orderly picked up a torch and held it close to his face, examined it for an instant, and exclaimed, scandalized: "Jesus! It's the Duke of Marlborough!"

In the midst of that terrible hallucination, the doctors gave orders to bathe him. It was done. But on the next day you could only see a small change in his stomach. Then the doctors left the house and said that the only thing advisable was to prepare him for a good death.

The bedroom was sunken in a silent atmosphere in which you could hear only the slow and measured flapping of the wings of death, that mysterious flapping that has the smell of a man in the bedrooms of the dying. After Father Ángel administered the last rites, many hours passed before anyone moved, looking at the angular profile of the hopeless man. Then the clock struck and my stepmother got ready to give him his spoonful of medicine. That was when we heard the spaced and affirmative footsteps on the veranda. My stepmother held the spoon in the air, stopped murmuring her prayer, and turned to the door, paralyzed by a sudden blush. "I'd recognize those steps even in purgatory," she managed to say at the precise moment that we looked toward the door and saw the doctor. He was on the threshold, looking at us.

I say to my daughter: "The Pup would have made them come even if he had to whip them," and I go over to where the coffin is, thinking: *Since the time the doctor left our house I've been convinced that our acts were ordained by a higher will against which we couldn't have rebelled, even if we tried with all our strength, or even if we assumed the sterile attitude of Adelaida, who shut herself up to pray.*

And while I cover the distance that separates me from the coffin, looking at my men, impassive, sitting on the bed, I feel that I've breathed in the first breath of air that boils up over the dead man, all that bitter matter of fate that destroyed Macondo. I don't think the mayor will delay with the authorization for the burial. I know that outside, on the streets tormented by the heat, people are waiting. I know that there are women in the windows, anxious for a spectacle, and that they stay there, looking out, forgetting that the milk is boiling on the stove and that the rice is dry. But I think that even this last show of rebellion is beyond the possibilities of this crushed and flayed group of men. Their capacity for fight has been broken ever since that Sunday election day when they moved, drew up their plans, and were defeated, and afterward they still were convinced that they were the ones who determined their own acts. But all of that seemed to have been disposed, ordained, channeling the deeds that would lead us step by step to this fateful Wednesday.

Ten years ago, when ruin came down upon us, the collective strength of those who looked for recovery might have been enough for reconstruction. All that was needed was to go out into the field laid waste by the banana company, clean out the weeds, and start again from scratch. But they'd trained the leaf storm to be impatient, not to believe in either past or future. They'd trained it to believe in the moment and to sate the voracity of its appetite in it. We only needed a short time to realize that the leaf storm had left and that without it reconstruction was impossible. The leaf storm had brought everything and it had taken everything away. After it all that was left was a Sunday in the rubble of a town and the ever-present electoral schemer on Macondo's last night, setting up four demijohns of liquor in the public square at the disposal of the police and the reserves.

If the Pup managed to hold them back that night in spite of the fact that their rebellion was still alive, today he would have been capable of going from house to house armed like a dogcatcher obliging them to bury this man. The Pup held them under an ironclad discipline. Even after the priest died four years ago—one year before my illness—that discipline could be seen in the impassioned way in which they all cut the flowers and shrubs in their gardens and took them to his grave in a final tribute to the Pup.

This man was the only one who didn't go to the burial. The only one, precisely, who owed his life to that unbreakable and contradictory subordination of the town to the priest. Because the night they set out the four demijohns of liquor on the square and Macondo became a town overrun by armed barbarians, a town in terror which buried its dead in a common grave, someone must have remembered that there was a doctor on this corner. That was when they laid the stretchers by the door and shouted to him (because he didn't open up, he spoke from inside); they shouted to him: "Doctor, take care of these wounded people because there aren't enough doctors to go around," and he replied: "Take them somewhere else, I don't know about any of that." And they said to him: "You're the only doctor left. You have to do a charitable act." And he answered (and still hadn't opened the door), imagined by the crowd to be in the middle of the room, the lamp held high, his hard yellow eyes lighted up: "I've forgotten everything I knew about all that. Take them somewhere else," and he stayed there (because the door was never opened) with the door closed, while men and woman of Macondo were dying in front of it. The crowd was capable of anything that night. They were getting ready to set fire to the house and reduce its only occupant to ashes. But then the Pup appeared. They say that it was as if he'd been there invisible, standing guard to stop the destruction of the house and the man. "No one will touch this door," they say the Pup said. And they say that was all he said, his arms open as if on a cross, his inexpressive and cold cowskull face illuminated by the glow of rural fury. And then the impulse was reined in, it changed direction, but it still had sufficient force for them to shout the sentence that would assure the coming of this Wednesday for all the ages.

Walking toward the bed to tell my men to open the door,

I think: *He'll be coming any minute now.* And I think that if he doesn't get here in five minutes we'll take the coffin out without any authorization and put the dead man in the street so he'll have to bury him right in front of the house. "Cataure," I say, calling the oldest of my men, and he barely has time to lift his head when I hear the mayor's footsteps coming through the next room.

I know that he's coming straight toward me and I try to turn quickly on my heels, leaning on my cane, but my bad leg fails me and I go forward, sure that I'm going to fall and hit my face against the coffin, when I stumble across his arm and clutch it firmly, and I hear his voice of peaceful stupidity saying: "Don't worry, colonel, I can assure you that nothing will happen." And I think that's how it is, but I know he's saying it to give himself courage. "I don't think anything will happen," I tell him, thinking just the opposite, and he says something about the ceiba trees in the cemetery and hands me the authorization for the burial. Without reading it I fold it, put it in my vest pocket, and tell him: "In any case, whatever happens, it had to happen. It's as if it had been announced in the almanac."

The mayor goes over to the Indians. He tells them to nail up the coffin and open the door. And I see them moving about, looking for the hammer and nails which will remove the sight of that man forever, that unsheltered gentleman from nowhere whom I saw for the last time three years ago beside my convalescent's bed, his head and face cracked by premature decrepitude. He had just rescued me from death then. The same force that had brought him there, that had given him the news of my illness, seemed to be the one which held him up beside my bed saying:

"You just have to exercise that leg a little. You may have to use a cane from now on."

I would ask him two days later what I owed him and he would answer: "You don't owe me anything, colonel. But if you want to do me a favor, throw a little earth on me when

morning finds me stiff. That's all I need for the buzzards not
to eat me."

In the promise he made me give, in the way he proposed
it, in the rhythm of his footsteps on the tile in the room, it was
evident that this man had begun to die a long time back, even
though three years would pass before that postponed and de-
fective death would be completely realized. That day was today. And I even think that they probably didn't need the noose.
A slight breeze would have been enough to extinguish the last
glow of life that remained in his hard yellow eyes. I'd sensed
all that ever since the night I spoke to him in his little room,
before he came here to live with Meme. So when he made me
promise what I'm about to do now, I didn't feel upset. I told
him simply:

"It's an unnecessary request, doctor. You know me and
you must know that I would have buried you over the heads
of everybody even if I didn't owe my life to you."

And he, smiling, his hard yellow eyes peaceful for the first
time:

"That's all very true, colonel. But don't forget that a dead
man wouldn't have been able to bury me."

Now no one will be able to correct this shame. The mayor has
handed my father the burial order and my father has said:
"In any case, whatever happens, it had to happen. It's as if it
had been announced in the almanac." And he said it with the
same indolence with which he turned himself over to the fate
of Macondo, faithful to the trunks where the clothing of all
those who died before I was born is kept. Since then everything has gone downhill. Even my stepmother's energy, her
ironclad and dominant character have been changed into bitter doubt. She seems more and more distant and silent, and
her disillusionment is such that this afternoon she sat down
beside the railing and said: "I'll stay collapsed here until Judgment Day."

My father hadn't ever imposed his will on anything again.

Only today did he get up to fulfill that shameful promise. He's here, sure that everything will happen with no serious consequences, watching the Guajiros starting to move to open the door and nail up the coffin. I see them coming closer, I stand up, I take the child by the hand and pull the chair toward the window so as not to be seen by the town when they open the door.

The child is puzzled. When I get up he looks me in the face with an indescribable expression, a little upset. But now he's perplexed, beside me, watching the Indians, who are sweating because of the effort to open the bolts. And with a penetrating and sustained lament of rusty metal, the doors open wide. Then I see the street again, the glowing and burning white dust that covers the houses and has given the town the lamentable look of a rundown piece of furniture. It's as if God had declared Macondo unnecessary and had thrown it into the corner where towns that have stopped being of any service to creation are kept.

The child, who at the first moment must have been dazzled by the sudden light (his hand trembled in mine when the door was opened), raises his head suddenly, concentrated, intent, and he asks me: "Did you hear it?" Only then do I realize that in some neighboring courtyard a curlew is telling the time. "Yes," I say. "It must be three o'clock already," and almost at that precise moment the first hammer blow sounds on the nail.

Trying not to listen to the lacerating sound that makes my skin crawl, trying to prevent the child from noticing my confusion, I turn my face to the window and in the next block I see the melancholy and dusty almond trees with our house in the background. Shaken by the invisible breath of destruction, it too is on the eve of a silent and final collapse. All of Macondo has been like that ever since it was squeezed by the banana company. Ivy invades the houses, weeds grow in the alleys, walls crumble, and in the middle of the day a person finds a lizard in her room. Everything has seem destroyed since we stopped cultivating the rosemary and the nard; since the time an invisible hand cracked the Christmas dishes in the cupboard and put moths to fatten on the clothes that nobody wore anymore. When a door becomes loose there isn't a solicitous hand ready to repair it. My father doesn't have the energy to move the way he did before the collapse that left him limping forever. Señora Rebeca, behind her eternal fan, doesn't bother about anything that might repel the hunger of malevolence that's provoked in her by her sterile and tormented widowhood. Águeda is crippled, overwhelmed by a patient religious illness; and Father Ángel doesn't seem to have any other satisfaction except savoring the persevering indigestion of meatballs every day during his siesta. The only thing that seems unchanged is the song of the twins of Saint Jerome and that mysterious beggar woman who doesn't seem to grow old and who for twenty years has come to the house every Tuesday for a branch of lemon balm. Only the whistle of a yellow, dusty train that doesn't take anyone away breaks the silence four times a day. And at night the toom-toom of the electric plant that the banana company left behind when it left Macondo.

I can see the house through the window and I am aware that my stepmother is there, motionless in her chair, thinking perhaps that before we get back that final wind which will wipe out this town will have passed. Everyone will have gone then except us, because we're tied to this soil by a roomful of trunks where the household goods and clothing of grandparents, my grandparents, are kept, and the canopies that my parents' horses used when they came to Macondo, fleeing from the war. We've been sown into this soil by the memory of the remote dead whose bones can no longer be found twenty fathoms under the earth. The trunks have been in the room ever since the last days of the war; and they'll be there this afternoon when we come back from the burial, if that final wind hasn't passed, the one that will sweep away Macondo, its bedrooms full of lizards and its silent people devastated by memories.

*   *   *

Suddenly my grandfather gets up, leans on his cane, and stretches out his bird head where his glasses seem to be fastened on as if they were part of his face. I think it would be hard for me to wear glasses. With the smallest movement they'd slip off my ears. And thinking about that I tap my nose. Mama looks at me and asks: "Does it hurt you?" And I tell her no, that I was just thinking that I wouldn't be able to wear glasses. And she smiles, breathes deeply, and tells me: "You must be soaked." And she's right; my clothes are burning on my skin, the thick, green corduroy, fastened all the way up, is sticking to my body with sweat and gives me an itchy feeling. "Yes," I say. And my mother leans over me, loosens my tie and fans my collar, saying: "When we get home you can rest and have a bath." "Cataure," I hear.

At that point, through the rear door, the man with the revolver comes in again. When he gets in the doorway he takes off his hat and walks carefully, as if he was afraid of waking up the corpse. But he did it to surprise my grandfather, who falls forward, pushed by the man, staggers, and manages to grab the arm of the same man who'd tried to knock him down. The others have stopped smoking and are still sitting on the bed in a row like four crows on a sawhorse. When the man with the revolver comes in the crows lean over and talk secretly and one of them gets up, goes over to the table, and picks up the box of nails and the hammer.

My grandfather is talking to the man beside the coffin. The man says: "Don't worry, colonel. I can assure you that nothing will happen." And my grandfather says: "I don't think anything will happen." And the man says: "They can bury him on the outside, against the left wall of the cemetery where the ceiba trees are the tallest." Then he gives my grandfather a piece of paper, saying: "You'll see that everything will turn out fine." My grandfather leans on his cane with one hand, takes the paper with the other, and puts it into his vest pocket, where he keeps his small, square gold watch with a chain. Then he says: "In any case, whatever happens, it had to happen. It's as if it had been announced in the almanac."

The man says: "There are some people in the windows, but that's just curiosity. The women always look at anything." But I don't think my grandfather heard him, because he's looking through the window at the street. The man moves then, goes over to the bed, and, fanning himself with his hat, he tells the men: "You can nail it up now. In the meantime, open the door so we can get a breath of air."

The men start to move. One of them leans over the box with the hammer and nails and the others go to the door. My mother gets up. She's sweaty and pale. She pulls her chair, takes me by the hand, and tugs me aside so that the men can get by to open the door.

At first they try to turn the bolt, which seems to be soldered to the rusty catches, but they can't move it. It's as if someone were pushing with all his strength from the street side. But when one of the men leans against the door and pounds it, the room is filled with the noise of wood, rusty hinges, locks soldered by time, layer upon layer, and the door opens, enormous, as if a man could go through on another's shoulders; and there's a long creaking of wood and iron that's been awakened. And before we have time to find out what's happened, the light bursts into the room, backward, powerful and perfect, because they've taken away the support that held it for two hundred years with the strength of two hundred oxen, and it falls backward into the room, dragging in the shadow of things in its turbulent fall. The men become brutally visible, like a flash of lightning at noon, and they stumble, and it looks as if they had to hold themselves up so that the light wouldn't knock them down.

When the door opens a curlew begins to sing somewhere in town. Now I can see the street. I can see the bright and burning dust. I can see several men sitting on the opposite sidewalk, their arms folded, looking toward the room. I hear the curlew again and I say to Mama: "Did you hear it?" And she says yes, it must be three o'clock. But Ada told me that curlews sing when they get the smell of a dead man. I'm about to tell my mother just at the moment when I hear the sharp sound of the hammer on the head of the first nail. The hammer pounds, pounds, and fills everything up; it rests a second and pounds again, wounding the wood six times in a row, waking up the long, sad sound of the sleeping boards while my mother, her face turned the other way, looks through the window into the street.

When the hammering is over the song of several curlews can be heard. My grandfather signals his men. They lean over, tip the coffin, while the one who stayed in the corner with his hat says to my grandfather: "Don't worry, colonel." And then my grandfather turns toward the corner, agitated, his neck swollen and purple like that of a fighting cock. But he doesn't say anything. It's the man who speaks again from the corner. He says: "I don't even think there's anyone left in town who remembers this."

At that instant I really feel the quiver in my stomach. *Now I do feel like going out back,* I think; but I see that it's too late now. The men make a last effort; they straighten up, their heels dig into the floor, and the coffin is floating in the light as if they were carrying off a dead ship to be buried.

I think: *Now they'll get the smell. Now all the curlews will start to sing.*

(*1955*)

No One Writes
to the Colonel

translated from the Spanish by J. S. Bernstein

THE COLONEL TOOK THE TOP OFF THE COFFEE CAN AND SAW THAT there was only one little spoonful left. He removed the pot from the fire, poured half the water onto the earthen floor, and scraped the inside of the can with a knife until the last scrapings of the ground coffee, mixed with bits of rust, fell into the pot.

While he was waiting for it to boil, sitting next to the stone fireplace with an attitude of confident and innocent expectation, the colonel experienced the feeling that fungus and poisonous lilies were taking root in his gut. It was October. A difficult morning to get through, even for a man like himself, who had survived so many mornings like this one. For nearly sixty years—since the end of the last civil war—the colonel had done nothing else but wait. October was one of the few things which arrived.

His wife raised the mosquito netting when she saw him come into the bedroom with the coffee. The night before she had suffered an asthma attack, and now she was in a drowsy state. But she sat up to take the cup.

"And you?" she said.

"I've had mine," the colonel lied. "There was still a big spoonful left."

The bells began ringing at that moment. The colonel had

forgotten the funeral. While his wife was drinking her coffee, he unhooked the hammock at one end, and rolled it up on the other, behind the door. The woman thought about the dead man.

' "He was born in 1922," she said. "Exactly a month after our son. April 7th."

She continued sipping her coffee in the pauses of her gravelly breathing. She was scarcely more than a bit of white on an arched, rigid spine. Her disturbed breathing made her put her questions as assertions. When she finished her coffee, she was still thinking about the dead man.

"It must be horrible to be buried in October," she said. But her husband paid no attention. He opened the window. October had moved in on the patio. Contemplating the vegetation, which was bursting out in intense greens, and the tiny mounds the worms made in the mud, the colonel felt the sinister month again in his intestines.

"I'm wet through to the bones," he said.

"It's winter," the woman replied. "Since it began raining I've been telling you to sleep with your socks on."

"I've been sleeping with them for a week."

It rained gently but ceaselessly. The colonel would have preferred to wrap himself in a wool blanket and get back into the hammock. But the insistence of the cracked bells reminded him about the funeral. "It's October," he whispered, and walked toward the center of the room. Only then did he remember the rooster tied to the leg of the bed. It was a fighting cock.

After taking the cup into the kitchen, he wound the pendulum clock in its carved wooden case in the living room. Unlike the bedroom, which was too narrow for an asthmatic's breathing, the living room was large, with four sturdy rockers around a little table with a cover and a plaster cat. On the wall opposite the clock, there was a picture of a woman dressed in tulle, surrounded by cupids in a boat laden with roses.

It was seven-twenty when he finished winding the clock.

Then he took the rooster into the kitchen, tied it to a leg of the stove, changed the water in the can, and put a handful of corn next to it. A group of children came in through a hole in the fence. They sat around the rooster, to watch it in silence.

"Stop looking at that animal," said the colonel. "Roosters wear out if you look at them so much."

The children didn't move. One of them began playing the chords of a popular song on his harmonica. "Don't play that today," the colonel told him. "There's been a death in town." The child put the instrument in his pants pocket, and the colonel went into the bedroom to dress for the funeral.

Because of his wife's asthma, his white suit was not pressed. So he had to wear the old black suit which since his marriage he used only on special occasions. It took some effort to find it in the bottom of the trunk, wrapped in newspapers and protected against moths with little balls of naphthalene. Stretched out in bed, the woman was still thinking about the dead man.

"He must have met Agustín already," she said. "Maybe he won't tell him about the situation we've been left in since his death."

"At this moment they're probably talking roosters," said the colonel.

He found an enormous old umbrella in the trunk. His wife had won it in a raffle held to collect funds for the colonel's party. That same night they had attended an outdoor show which was not interrupted despite the rain. The colonel, his wife, and their son, Agustín—who was then eight—watched the show until the end, seated under the umbrella. Now Agustín was dead, and the bright satin material had been eaten away by the moths.

"Look what's left of our circus clown's umbrella," said the colonel with one of his old phrases. Above his head a mysterious system of little metal rods opened. "The only thing it's good for now is to count the stars."

He smiled. But the woman didn't take the trouble to look

at the umbrella. "Everything's that way," she whispered. "We're rotting alive." And she closed her eyes so she could concentrate on the dead man.

After shaving himself by touch—since he'd lacked a mirror for a long time—the colonel dressed silently. His trousers, almost as tight on his legs as long underwear, closed at the ankles with slip-knotted drawstrings, were held up at the waist by two straps of the same material which passed through two gilt buckles sewn on at kidney height. He didn't use a belt. His shirt, the color of old Manila paper, and as stiff, fastened with a copper stud which served at the same time to hold the detachable collar. But the detachable collar was torn, so the colonel gave up on the idea of a tie.

He did each thing as if it were a transcendent act. The bones in his hands were covered by taut, translucent skin, with light spots like the skin on his neck. Before he put on his patent-leather shoes, he scraped the dried mud from the stitching. His wife saw him at that moment, dressed as he was on their wedding day. Only then did she notice how much her husband had aged.

"You look as if you're dressed for some special event," she said.

"This burial is a special event," the colonel said. "It's the first death from natural causes which we've had in many years."

The weather cleared up after nine. The colonel was getting ready to go out when his wife seized him by the sleeve of his coat.

"Comb your hair," she said.

He tried to subdue his steel-colored, bristly hair with a bone comb. But it was a useless attempt.

"I must look like a parrot," he said.

The woman examined him. She thought he didn't. The colonel didn't look like a parrot. He was a dry man, with solid bones articulated as if with nuts and bolts. Because of the vitality in his eyes, it didn't seem as if he were preserved in formalin.

"You're fine that way," she admitted, and added, when her husband was leaving the room: "Ask the doctor if we poured boiling water on him in this house."

They lived at the edge of town, in a house with a palm-thatched roof and walls whose whitewash was flaking off. The humidity kept up but the rain had stopped. The colonel went down toward the plaza along an alley with houses crowded in on each other. As he came out into the main street, he shivered. As far as the eye could see, the town was carpeted with flowers. Seated in their doorways, the women in black were waiting for the funeral.

In the plaza it began to drizzle again. The proprietor of the pool hall saw the colonel from the door of his place and shouted to him with open arms:

"Colonel, wait, and I'll lend you an umbrella!"

The colonel replied without turning around.

"Thank you. I'm all right this way."

The funeral procession hadn't come out of church yet. The men—dressed in white with black ties—were talking in the low doorway under their umbrellas. One of them saw the colonel jumping between the puddles in the plaza.

"Get under here, friend!" he shouted.

He made room under the umbrella.

"Thanks, friend," said the colonel.

But he didn't accept the invitation. He entered the house directly to give his condolences to the mother of the dead man. The first thing he perceived was the odor of many different flowers. Then the heat rose. The colonel tried to make his way through the crowd which was jammed into the bedroom. But someone put a hand on his back, pushed him toward the back of the room through a gallery of perplexed faces to the spot where—deep and wide open—the nostrils of the dead man were found.

There was the dead man's mother, shooing the flies away from the coffin with a plaited palm fan. Other women, dressed in black, contemplated the body with the same expression with which one watches the current of a river. All at once a voice started up at the back of the room. The colonel put one woman aside, faced the profile of the dead man's mother, and put a hand on her shoulder.

"I'm so sorry," he said.

She didn't turn her head. She opened her mouth and let out a howl. The colonel started. He felt himself being pushed against the corpse by a shapeless crowd which broke out in a quavering outcry. He looked for a firm support for his hands but couldn't find the wall. There were other bodies in its place. Someone said in his ear, slowly, with a very gentle voice, "Careful, Colonel." He spun his head around and was face to face with the dead man. But he didn't recognize him because he was stiff and dynamic and seemed as disconcerted as he, wrapped in white cloths and with his trumpet in his hands. When the colonel raised his head over the shouts, in search of air, he saw the closed box bounding toward the door down a slope of flowers which disintegrated against the walls. He perspired. His joints ached. A moment later he knew he was in the street because the drizzle hurt his eyelids, and someone seized him by the arm and said:

"Hurry up, friend, I was waiting for you."

It was Sabas, the godfather of his dead son, the only leader of his party who had escaped political persecution and had continued to live in town. "Thanks, friend," said the colonel, and walked in silence under the umbrella. The band struck up the funeral march. The colonel noticed the lack of a trumpet, and for the first time was certain that the dead man was dead.

"Poor man," he murmured.

Sabas cleared his throat. He held the umbrella in his left hand, the handle almost at the level of his head, since he was shorter than the colonel. They began to talk when the cortege left the plaza. Sabas turned toward the colonel then, his face disconsolate, and said:

"Friend, what's new with the rooster?"

"He's still there," the colonel replied.

At that moment a shout was heard:

"Where are they going with that dead man?"

The colonel raised his eyes. He saw the Mayor on the balcony of the barracks in an expansive pose. He was dressed in his flannel underwear; his unshaven cheek was swollen. The musicians stopped the march. A moment later the colonel recognized Father Angel's voice shouting at the Mayor. He made out their dialogue through the drumming of the rain on the umbrella.

"Well?" asked Sabas.

"Well nothing," the colonel replied. "The burial may not pass in front of the police barracks."

"I had forgotten," exclaimed Sabas. "I always forget that we are under martial law."

"But this isn't a rebellion," the colonel said. "It's a poor dead musician."

The cortege changed direction. In the poor neighborhoods the women watched it pass, biting their nails in silence. But then they came out into the middle of the street and sent up shouts of praise, gratitude, and farewell, as if they believed the dead man was listening to them inside the coffin. The colonel felt ill at the cemetery. When Sabas pushed him toward the wall to make way for the men who were carrying the dead man, he turned his smiling face toward him, but met a rigid countenance.

"What's the matter, friend?" Sabas asked.

The colonel sighed.

"It's October."

They returned by the same street. It had cleared. The sky was deep, intensely blue. It won't rain any more, thought the colonel, and he felt better, but he was still dejected. Sabas interrupted his thoughts.

"Have a doctor examine you."

"I'm not sick," the colonel said. "The trouble is that in October I feel as if I had animals in my gut."

Sabas went "Ah." He said good-bye at the door to his house, a new building, two stories high, with wrought-iron window gratings. The colonel headed for his home, anxious to take off his dress suit. He went out again a moment later to the store on the corner to buy a can of coffee and half a pound of corn for the rooster.

The colonel attended to the rooster in spite of the fact that on Thursday he would have preferred to stay in his hammock. It didn't clear for several days. During the course of the week, the flora in his belly blossomed. He spent several sleepless nights, tormented by the whistling of the asthmatic woman's lungs. But October granted a truce on Friday afternoon. Agustín's companions—workers from the tailor shop, as he had been, and cockfight fanatics—took advantage of the occasion to examine the rooster. He was in good shape.

The colonel returned to the bedroom when he was left alone in the house with his wife. She had recovered.

"What do they say?" she asked.

"Very enthusiastic," the colonel informed her. "Everyone is saving their money to bet on the rooster."

"I don't know what they see in such an ugly rooster," the woman said. "He looks like a freak to me; his head is too tiny for his feet."

"They say he's the best in the district," the colonel answered. "He's worth about fifty pesos."

He was sure that this argument justified his determination to keep the rooster, a legacy from their son who was shot down nine months before at the cockfights for distributing clandestine literature. "An expensive illusion," the woman said. "When the corn is gone we'll have to feed him on our own livers." The colonel took a good long time to think, while he was looking for his white ducks in the closet.

"It's just for a few months," he said. "We already know that there will be fights in January. Then we can sell him for more."

The pants needed pressing. The woman stretched them out over the stove with two irons heated over the coals.

"What's your hurry to go out?" she asked.

"The mail."

"I had forgotten that today is Friday," she commented, returning to the bedroom. The colonel was dressed but pantless. She observed his shoes.

"Those shoes are ready to throw out," she said. "Keep wearing your patent-leather ones."

The colonel felt desolate.

"They look like the shoes of an orphan," he protested. "Every time I put them on I feel like a fugitive from an asylum."

"We are the orphans of our son," the woman said.

This time, too, she persuaded him. The colonel walked toward the harbor before the whistles of the launches blew. Patent-leather shoes, beltless white ducks, and the shirt without the detachable collar, closed at the neck with the copper stud. He observed the docking of the launches from the shop of Moses the Syrian. The travelers got off, stiff from eight hours of immobility. The same ones as always: traveling salesmen, and people from the town who had left the preceding week and were returning as usual.

The last one was the mail launch. The colonel saw it dock with an anguished uneasiness. On the roof, tied to the boat's smokestacks and protected by an oilcloth, he spied the mailbag. Fifteen years of waiting had sharpened his intuition. The rooster had sharpened his anxiety. From the moment the postmaster went on board the launch, untied the bag, and hoisted it up on his shoulder, the colonel kept him in sight.

He followed him through the street parallel to the harbor, a labyrinth of stores and booths with colored merchandise on display. Every time he did it, the colonel experienced an anxiety very different from, but just as oppressive as, fright. The doctor was waiting for the newspapers in the post office.

"My wife wants me to ask you if we threw boiling water on you at our house," the colonel said.

He was a young physician with his skull covered by sleek black hair. There was something unbelievable in the perfection of his dentition. He asked after the health of the asthmatic. The colonel supplied a detailed report without taking his eyes off the postmaster, who was distributing the letters into cubbyholes. His indolent way of moving exasperated the colonel.

The doctor received his mail with the packet of newspapers. He put the pamphlets of medical advertising to one side. Then he scanned his personal letters. Meanwhile the postmaster was handing out mail to those who were present. The colonel watched the compartment which corresponded to his letter in the alphabet. An air-mail letter with blue borders increased his nervous tension.

The doctor broke the seal on the newspapers. He read the lead items while the colonel—his eyes fixed on the little box—waited for the postmaster to stop in front of it. But he didn't. The doctor interrupted his reading of the newspapers. He looked at the colonel. Then he looked at the postmaster seated in front of the telegraph key, and then again at the colonel.

"We're leaving," he said.

The postmaster didn't raise his head.

"Nothing for the colonel," he said.

The colonel felt ashamed.

"I wasn't expecting anything," he lied. He turned to the doctor with an entirely childish look. "No one writes to me."

They went back in silence. The doctor was concentrating on the newspapers. The colonel with his habitual way of walking which resembled that of a man retracing his steps to look for a lost coin. It was a bright afternoon. The almond trees in the plaza were shedding their last rotted leaves. It had begun to grow dark when they arrived at the door of the doctor's office.

"What's in the news?" the colonel asked.

The doctor gave him a few newspapers.

"No one knows," he said. "It's hard to read between the lines which the censor lets them print."

The colonel read the main headlines. International news. At the top, across four columns, a report on the Suez Canal. The front page was almost completely covered by paid funeral announcements.

"There's no hope of elections," the colonel said.

"Don't be naïve, Colonel," said the doctor. "We're too old now to be waiting for the Messiah."

The colonel tried to give the newspapers back, but the doctor refused them.

"Take them home with you," he said. "You can read them tonight and return them tomorrow."

A little after seven the bells in the tower rang out the censor's movie classifications. Father Angel used this means to announce the moral classification of the film in accordance with the ratings he received every month by mail. The colonel's wife counted twelve bells.

"Unfit for everyone," she said. "It's been almost a year now that the movies are bad for everyone."

She lowered the mosquito netting and murmured, "The world is corrupt." But the colonel made no comment. Before lying down, he tied the rooster to the leg of the bed. He locked the house and sprayed some insecticide in the bedroom. Then he put the lamp on the floor, hung his hammock up, and lay down to read the newspapers.

He read them in chronological order, from the first page to the last, including the advertisements. At eleven the trumpet blew curfew. The colonel finished his reading a half-hour later, opened the patio door on the impenetrable night, and urinated, besieged by mosquitoes, against the wall studs. His wife was awake when he returned to the bedroom.

"Nothing about the veterans?" she asked.

"Nothing," said the colonel. He put out the lamp before

he got into the hammock. "In the beginning at least they published the list of the new pensioners. But it's been about five years since they've said anything."

It rained after midnight. The colonel managed to get to sleep but woke up a moment later, alarmed by his intestines. He discovered a leak in some part of the roof. Wrapped in a wool blanket up to his ears, he tried to find the leak in the darkness. A trickle of cold sweat slipped down his spine. He had a fever. He felt as if he were floating in concentric circles inside a tank of jelly. Someone spoke. The colonel answered from his revolutionist's cot.

"Who are you talking to?" asked his wife.

"The Englishman disguised as a tiger who appeared at Colonel Aureliano Buendía's camp," the colonel answered. He turned over in his hammock, burning with his fever. "It was the Duke of Marlborough."

The sky was clear at dawn. At the second call for Mass, he jumped from the hammock and installed himself in a confused reality which was agitated by the crowing of the rooster. His head was still spinning in concentric circles. He was nauseous. He went out into the patio and headed for the privy through the barely audible whispers and the dark odors of winter. The inside of the little zinc-roofed wooden compartment was rarefied by the ammonia smell from the privy. When the colonel raised the lid, a triangular cloud of flies rushed out of the pit.

It was a false alarm. Squatting on the platform of unsanded boards, he felt the uneasiness of an urge frustrated. The oppressiveness was substituted by a dull ache in his digestive tract. "There's no doubt," he murmured. "It's the same every October." And again he assumed his posture of confident and innocent expectation until the fungus in his innards was pacified. Then he returned to the bedroom for the rooster.

"Last night you were delirious from fever," his wife said. She had begun to straighten up the room, having re-

covered from a week-long attack. The colonel made an effort
to remember.

"It wasn't fever," he lied. "It was the dream about the spider webs again."

As always happened, the woman emerged from her attack
full of nervous energy. In the course of the morning she turned
the house upside down. She changed the position of everything, except the clock and the picture of the young girl. She
was so thin and sinewy that when she walked about in her
cloth slippers and her black dress all buttoned up she seemed
as if she had the power of walking through the walls. But before twelve she had regained her bulk, her human weight. In
bed she was an empty space. Now, moving among the flowerpots of ferns and begonias, her presence overflowed the house.
"If Agustín's year were up, I would start singing," she said
while she stirred the pot where all the things to eat that the
tropical land is capable of producing, cut into pieces, were
boiling.

"If you feel like singing, sing," said the colonel. "It's good
for your spleen."

The doctor came after lunch. The colonel and his wife
were drinking coffee in the kitchen when he pushed open the
street door and shouted:

"Everybody dead?"

The colonel got up to welcome him.

"So it seems, Doctor," he said, going into the living room.
"I've always said that your clock keeps time with the buzzards."

The woman went into the bedroom to get ready for the
examination. The doctor stayed in the living room with the
colonel. In spite of the heat, his immaculate linen suit gave off
a smell of freshness. When the woman announced that she
was ready, the doctor gave the colonel three sheets of paper
in an envelope. He entered the bedroom, saying, "That's what
the newspapers didn't print yesterday."

The colonel had assumed as much. It was a summary of

the events in the country, mimeographed for clandestine cir-
culation. Revelations about the state of armed resistance in the
interior of the country. He felt defeated. Ten years of clandestine reports had not taught him that no news was more
surprising than next month's news. He had finished reading
when the doctor came back into the living room.

"This patient is healthier than I am," he said. "With asthma
like that, I could live to be a hundred."

The colonel glowered at him. He gave him back the
envelope without saying a word, but the doctor refused to
take it.

"Pass it on," he said in a whisper.

The colonel put the envelope in his pants pocket. The
woman came out of the bedroom, saying, "One of these days
I'll up and die, and carry you with me, off to hell, Doctor."
The doctor responded silently with the stereotyped enamel of
his teeth. He pulled a chair up to the little table and took several jars of free samples out of his bag. The woman went on
into the kitchen.

"Wait and I'll warm up the coffee."

"No, thank you very much," said the doctor. He wrote the
proper dosage on a prescription pad. "I absolutely refuse to
give you the chance to poison me."

She laughed in the kitchen. When he finished writing, the
doctor read the prescription aloud, because he knew that no
one could decipher his handwriting. The colonel tried to concentrate. Returning from the kitchen, the woman discovered
in his face the toll of the previous night.

"This morning he had a fever," she said, pointing at her
husband. "He spent about two hours talking nonsense about
the civil war."

The colonel started.

"It wasn't a fever," he insisted, regaining his composure.
"Furthermore," he said, "the day I feel sick I'll throw myself
into the garbage can on my own."

He went into the bedroom to find the newspapers.

"Thank you for the compliment," the doctor said.

They walked together toward the plaza. The air was dry. The tar on the streets had begun to melt from the heat. When the doctor said good-bye, the colonel asked him in a low voice, his teeth clenched:

"How much do we owe you, Doctor?"

"Nothing, for now," the doctor said, and he gave him a pat on the shoulder. "I'll send you a fat bill when the cock wins."

The colonel went to the tailor shop to take the clandestine letter to Agustín's companions. It was his only refuge ever since his co-partisans had been killed or exiled from town and he had been converted into a man with no other occupation than waiting for the mail every Friday.

The afternoon heat stimulated the woman's energy. Seated among the begonias in the veranda next to a box of worn-out clothing, she was again working the eternal miracle of creating new apparel out of nothing. She made collars from sleeves, and cuffs from the backs and square patches, perfect ones, although with scraps of different colors. A cicada lodged its whistle in the patio. The sun faded. But she didn't see it go down over the begonias. She raised her head only at dusk when the colonel returned home. Then she clasped her neck with both hands, cracked her knuckles, and said:

"My head is as stiff as a board."

"It's always been that way," the colonel said, but then he saw his wife's body covered all over with scraps of color. "You look like a magpie."

"One has to be half a magpie to dress you," she said. She held out a shirt made of three different colors of material except for the collar and cuffs, which were the same color. "At the carnival all you have to do is take off your jacket."

The six-o'clock bells interrupted her. "The Angel of the Lord announced unto Mary," she prayed aloud, heading into the bedroom. The colonel talked to the children who had come to look at the rooster after school. Then he remembered that there was no corn for the next day, and entered the bedroom to ask his wife for money.

"I think there's only fifty cents," she said.

She kept the money under the mattress, knotted into the corner of a handkerchief. It was the proceeds of Agustín's sewing machine. For nine months, they had spent that money penny by penny, parceling it out between their needs and the rooster's. Now there were only two twenty-cent pieces and a ten-cent piece left.

"Buy a pound of corn," the woman said. "With the change, buy tomorrow's coffee and four ounces of cheese."

"And a golden elephant to hang in the doorway," the colonel went on. "The corn alone costs forty-two."

They thought a moment. "The rooster is an animal, and therefore he can wait," said the woman at first. But her husband's expression caused her to reflect. The colonel sat on the bed, his elbows on his knees, jingling the coins in his hands. "It's not for my sake," he said after a moment. "If it depended on me I'd make a rooster stew this very evening. A fifty-peso indigestion would be very good." He paused to squash a mosquito on his neck. Then his eyes followed his wife around the room.

"What bothers me is that those poor boys are saving up."

Then she began to think. She turned completely around with the insecticide bomb. The colonel found something unreal in her attitude, as if she were invoking the spirits of the house for a consultation. At last she put the bomb on the little mantel with the prints on it, and fixed her syrup-colored eyes on the syrup-colored eyes of the colonel.

"Buy the corn," she said. "God knows how we'll manage."

"This is the miracle of the multiplying loaves," the colonel repeated every time they sat down to the table during the following week. With her astonishing capacity for darning, sewing, and mending, she seemed to have discovered the key to sustaining the household economy with no money. October prolonged its truce. The humidity was replaced by sleepiness. Comforted by the copper sun, the woman devoted three afternoons to her complicated hairdo. "High Mass has begun," the colonel said one afternoon when she was getting the knots out of her long blue tresses with a comb which had some teeth missing. The second afternoon, seated in the patio with a white sheet in her lap, she used a finer comb to take out the lice which had proliferated during her attack. Lastly, she washed her hair with lavender water, waited for it to dry, and rolled it up on the nape of her neck in two turns held with a barrette. The colonel waited. At night, sleepless in his hammock, he worried for many hours over the rooster's fate. But on Wednesday they weighed him, and he was in good shape.

That same afternoon, when Agustín's companions left the house counting the imaginary proceeds from the rooster's victory, the colonel also felt in good shape. His wife cut his hair. "You've taken twenty years off me," he said, examining his head with his hands. His wife thought her husband was right.

"When I'm well, I can bring back the dead," she said.

But her conviction lasted for a very few hours. There was no longer anything in the house to sell, except the clock and the picture. Thursday night, at the limit of their resources, the woman showed her anxiety over the situation.

"Don't worry," the colonel consoled her. "The mail comes tomorrow."

The following day he waited for the launches in front of the doctor's office.

"The airplane is a marvelous thing," the colonel said, his eyes resting on the mailbag. "They say you can get to Europe in one night."

"That's right," the doctor said, fanning himself with an illustrated magazine. The colonel spied the postmaster among a group waiting for the docking to end so they could jump onto the launch. The postmaster jumped first. He received from the captain an envelope sealed with wax. Then he climbed up onto the roof. The mailbag was tied between two oil drums.

"But still it has its dangers," said the colonel. He lost the postmaster from sight, but saw him again among the colored bottles on the refreshment cart. "Humanity doesn't progress without paying a price."

"Even at this stage it's safer than a launch," the doctor said. "At twenty thousand feet you fly above the weather."

"Twenty thousand feet," the colonel repeated, perplexed, without being able to imagine what the figure meant.

The doctor became interested. He spread out the magazine with both hands until it was absolutely still.

"There's perfect stability," he said.

But the colonel was hanging on the actions of the postmaster. He saw him consume a frothy pink drink holding the glass in his left hand. In his right he held the mailbag.

"Also, on the ocean there are ships at anchor in continual contact with night flights," the doctor went on. "With so many precautions it's safer than a launch."

The colonel looked at him.

"Naturally," he said. "It must be like a carpet."

The postmaster came straight toward them. The colonel stepped back, impelled by an irresistible anxiety, trying to read the name written on the sealed envelope. The postmaster opened the bag. He gave the doctor his packet of newspapers. Then he tore open the envelope with the personal correspondence, checked the correctness of the receipt, and read the addressee's names off the letters. The doctor opened the newspapers.

"Still the problem with Suez," he said, reading the main headlines. "The West is losing ground."

The colonel didn't read the headlines. He made an effort to control his stomach. "Ever since there's been censorship, the newspapers talk only about Europe," he said. "The best thing would be for the Europeans to come over here and for us to go to Europe. That way everybody would know what's happening in his own country."

"To the Europeans, South America is a man with a mustache, a guitar, and a gun," the doctor said, laughing over his newspaper. "They don't understand the problem."

The postmaster delivered his mail. He put the rest in the bag and closed it again. The doctor got ready to read two personal letters, but before tearing open the envelopes he looked at the colonel. Then he looked at the postmaster.

"Nothing for the colonel?"

The colonel was terrified. The postmaster tossed the bag onto his shoulder, got off the platform, and replied without turning his head:

"No one writes to the colonel."

Contrary to his habit, he didn't go directly home. He had a cup of coffee at the tailor's while Agustín's companions leafed through the newspapers. He felt cheated. He would have preferred to stay there until the next Friday to keep from having to face his wife that night with empty hands. But when the tailor shop closed, he had to face up to reality. His wife was waiting for him.

"Nothing?" she asked.

"Nothing," the colonel answered.

The following Friday he went down to the launches again. And, as on every Friday, he returned home without the longed-for letter. "We've waited long enough," his wife told him that night. "One must have the patience of an ox, as you do, to wait for a letter for fifteen years." The colonel got into his hammock to read the newspapers.

"We have to wait our turn," he said. "Our number is 1823."

"Since we've been writing, that number has come up twice in the lottery," his wife replied.

The colonel read, as usual, from the first page to the last, including the advertisements. But this time he didn't concentrate. During his reading, he thought about his veteran's pension. Nineteen years before, when Congress passed the law, it took him eight years to prove his claim. Then it took him six more years to get himself included on the rolls. That was the last letter the colonel had received.

He finished after curfew sounded. When he went to turn off the lamp, he realized that his wife was awake.

"Do you still have that clipping?"

The woman thought.

"Yes. It must be with the other papers."

She got out of her mosquito netting and took a wooden chest out of the closet, with a packet of letters arranged by date and held together by a rubber band. She located the advertisement of a law firm which promised quick action on war pensions.

"We could have spent the money in the time I've wasted trying to convince you to change lawyers," the woman said, handing her husband the newspaper clipping. "We're not getting anything out of their putting us away on a shelf as they do with the Indians."

The colonel read the clipping dated two years before. He put it in the pocket of his jacket which was hanging behind the door.

"The problem is that to change lawyers you need money."

"Not at all," the woman said decisively. "You write them telling them to discount whatever they want from the pension itself when they collect it. It's the only way they'll take the case."

So Saturday afternoon the colonel went to see his lawyer. He found him stretched out lazily in a hammock. He was a monumental Negro, with nothing but two canines in his upper jaw. The lawyer put his feet into a pair of wooden-soled slippers and opened the office window on a dusty pianola with papers stuffed into the compartments where the rolls used to go: clippings from the *Official Gazette,* pasted into old accounting ledgers, and a jumbled collection of accounting bulletins. The keyless pianola did double duty as a desk. The lawyer sat down in a swivel chair. The colonel expressed his uneasiness before revealing the purpose of his visit.

"I warned you that it would take more than a few days," said the lawyer when the colonel paused. He was sweltering in the heat. He adjusted the chair backward and fanned himself with an advertising brochure.

"My agents write to me frequently, saying not to get impatient."

"It's been that way for fifteen years," the colonel answered. "This is beginning to sound like the story about the capon."

The lawyer gave a very graphic description of the administrative ins and outs. The chair was too narrow for his sagging buttocks. "Fifteen years ago it was easier," he said. "Then there was the city's veterans' organization, with members of both parties." His lungs filled with stifling air and he pronounced the sentence as if he had just invented it:

"There's strength in numbers."

"There wasn't in this case," the colonel said, realizing his aloneness for the first time. "All my comrades died waiting for the mail."

The lawyer didn't change his expression.

"The law was passed too late," he said. "Not everybody was as lucky as you to be a colonel at the age of twenty. Furthermore, no special allocation was included, so the government has had to make adjustments in the budget."

Always the same story. Each time the colonel listened to him, he felt a mute resentment. "This is not charity," he said. "It's not a question of doing us a favor. We broke our backs to save the Republic." The lawyer threw up his hands.

"That's the way it is," he said. "Human ingratitude knows no limits."

The colonel also knew that story. He had begun hearing it the day after the Treaty of Neerlandia, when the government promised travel assistance and indemnities to two hundred revolutionary officers. Camped at the base of the gigantic silk-cotton tree at Neerlandia, a revolutionary battalion, made up in great measure of youths who had left school, waited for three months. Then they went back to their homes by their own means, and they kept on waiting there. Almost sixty years later, the colonel was still waiting.

Excited by these memories, he adopted a transcendental attitude. He rested his right hand on his thigh—mere bone sewed together with nerve tissue—and murmured:

"Well, I've decided to take action."

The lawyer waited.

"Such as?"

"To change lawyers."

A mother duck, followed by several little ducklings, entered the office. The lawyer sat up to chase them out. "As you wish, Colonel," he said, chasing the animals. "It will be just as you wish. If I could work miracles, I wouldn't be living in this barnyard." He put a wooden grille across the patio door and returned to his chair.

"My son worked all his life," said the colonel. "My house is mortgaged. That retirement law has been a lifetime pension for lawyers."

"Not for me," the lawyer protested. "Every last cent has gone for my expenses."

The colonel suffered at the thought that he had been unjust.

"That's what I meant," he corrected himself. He dried his forehead with the sleeve of his shirt. "This heat is enough to rust the screws in your head."

A moment later the lawyer was turning the office upside down looking for the power of attorney. The sun advanced toward the center of the tiny room, which was built of unsanded boards. After looking futilely everywhere, the lawyer got down on all fours, huffing and puffing, and picked up a roll of papers from under the pianola.

"Here it is."

He gave the colonel a sheet of paper with a seal on it. "I have to write my agents so they can cancel the copies," he concluded. The colonel shook the dust off the paper and put it in his shirt pocket.

"Tear it up yourself," the lawyer said.

"No," the colonel answered. "These are twenty years of memories." And he waited for the lawyer to keep on looking. But the lawyer didn't. He went to the hammock to wipe off his sweat. From there he looked at the colonel through the shimmering air.

"I need the documents also," the colonel said.

"Which ones?"

"The proof of claim."

The lawyer threw up his hands.

"Now, that would be impossible, Colonel."

The colonel became alarmed. As Treasurer of the revolution in the district of Macondo, he had undertaken a difficult six day journey with the funds for the civil war in two trunks roped to the back of a mule. He arrived at the camp of Neerlandia dragging the mule, which was dead from hunger, half an hour before the treaty was signed. Colonel Aureliano Buendía—quartermaster general of the revolutionary forces on the Atlantic coast—held out the receipt for the funds, and included the two trunks in his inventory of the surrender.

"Those documents have an incalculable value," the colonel said. "There's a receipt from Colonel Aureliano Buendía, written in his own hand."

"I agree," said the lawyer. "But those documents have passed through thousands and thousands of hands, in thousands and thousands of offices, before they reached God knows which department in the War Ministry."

"No official could fail to notice documents like those," the colonel said.

"But the officials have changed many times in the last fifteen years," the lawyer pointed out. "Just think about it; there have been seven Presidents, and each President changed his Cabinet at least ten times, and each Minister changed his staff at least a hundred times."

"But nobody could take the documents home," said the colonel. "Each new official must have found them in the proper file."

The lawyer lost his patience.

"And moreover if those papers are removed from the Ministry now, they will have to wait for a new place on the rolls."

"It doesn't matter," the colonel said.

"It'll take centuries."

"It doesn't matter. If you wait for the big things, you can wait for the little ones."

He took a pad of lined paper, the pen, the inkwell and a blotter to the little table in the living room, and left the bedroom door open in case he had to ask his wife anything. She was saying her beads.

"What's today's date?"

"October 27th."

He wrote with a studious neatness, the hand that held the pen resting on the blotter, his spine straight to ease his breathing, as he'd been taught in school. The heat became unbearable in the close living room. A drop of perspiration fell on the letter. The colonel picked it up on the blotter. Then he tried to erase the letters which had smeared but he smudged them. He didn't lose his patience. He wrote an asterisk and noted in the margin, "acquired rights." Then he read the whole paragraph.

"When was I put on the rolls?"

The woman didn't interrupt her prayer to think.

"August 12, 1949."

A moment later it began to rain. The colonel filled a page with large doodlings which were a little childish, the same ones he learned in public school at Manaure. Then he wrote on a second sheet down to the middle, and he signed it.

He read the letter to his wife. She approved each sentence with a nod. When he finished reading, the colonel sealed the envelope and turned off the lamp.

"You could ask someone to type it for you."

"No," the colonel answered. "I'm tired of going around asking favors."

For half an hour he heard the rain against the palm roof. The town sank into the deluge. After curfew sounded, a leak began somewhere in the house.

"This should have been done a long time ago," the woman said. "It's always better to handle things oneself."

"It's never too late," the colonel said, paying attention to the leak. "Maybe all this will be settled when the mortgage on the house falls due."

"In two years," the woman said.

He lit the lamp to locate the leak in the living room. He put the rooster's can underneath it and returned to the bedroom, pursued by the metallic noise of the water in the empty can.

"It's possible that to save the interest on the money they'll settle it before January," he said, and he convinced himself. "By then, Agustín's year will be up and we can go to the movies."

She laughed under her breath. "I don't even remember the cartoons any more," she said. The colonel tried to look at her through the mosquito netting.

"When did you go to the movies last?"

"In 1931," she said. "They were showing *The Dead Man's Will*."

"Was there a fight?"

"We never found out. The storm broke just when the ghost tried to rob the girl's necklace."

The sound of the rain put them to sleep. The colonel felt a slight queasiness in his intestines. But he wasn't afraid. He was about to survive another October. He wrapped himself in a wool blanket, and for a moment heard the gravelly breathing of his wife—far away—drifting on another dream. Then he spoke, completely conscious.

The woman woke up.

"Who are you speaking to?"

"No one," the colonel said. "I was thinking that at the Macondo meeting we were right when we told Colonel Aureliano Buendía not to surrender. That's what started to ruin everything."

It rained the whole week. The second of November—against the colonel's wishes—the woman took flowers to Agustín's grave. She returned from the cemetery and had another attack. It was a hard week. Harder than the four weeks of October which the colonel hadn't thought he'd survive. The doctor came to see the sick woman, and came out of the room shouting, "With asthma like that, I'd be able to bury the whole town!" But he spoke to the colonel alone and prescribed a special diet.

The colonel also suffered a relapse. He strained for many hours in the privy, in an icy sweat, feeling as if he were rotting and that the flora in his vitals was falling to pieces. "It's winter," he repeated to himself patiently. "Everything will be different when it stops raining." And he really believed it, certain that he would be alive at the moment the letter arrived.

This time it was he who had to repair their household economy. He had to grit his teeth many times to ask for credit in the neighborhood stores. "It's just until next week," he would say, without being sure himself that it was true. "It's a little money which should have arrived last Friday." When her attack was over, the woman examined him in horror.

"You're nothing but skin and bones," she said.

"I'm taking care of myself so I can sell myself," the colonel said. "I've already been hired by a clarinet factory."

But in reality his hoping for the letter barely sustained him. Exhausted, his bones aching from sleeplessness, he couldn't attend to his needs and the rooster's at the same time. In the second half of November, he thought that the animal would die after two days without corn. Then he remembered a handful of beans which he had hung in the chimney in July. He opened the pods and put down a can of dry seeds for the rooster.

"Come here," she said.

"Just a minute," the colonel answered, watching the rooster's reaction. "Beggars can't be choosers."

He found his wife trying to sit up in bed. Her ravaged body gave off the aroma of medicinal herbs. She spoke her words, one by one, with calculated precision:

"Get rid of that rooster right now."

The colonel had foreseen that moment. He had been waiting for it ever since the afternoon when his son was shot down, and he had decided to keep the rooster. He had had time to think.

"It's not worth it now," he said. "The fight will be in two months and then we'll be able to sell him at a better price."

"It's not a question of the money," the woman said. "When the boys come, you'll tell them to take it away and do whatever they feel like with it."

"It's for Agustín," the colonel said, advancing his prepared argument. "Remember his face when he came to tell us the rooster won."

The woman, in fact, did think of her son.

"Those accursed roosters were his downfall!" she shouted. "If he'd stayed home on January 3rd, his evil hour wouldn't have come." She held out a skinny forefinger toward the door and exclaimed:

"It seems as if I can see him when he left with the rooster under his arm. I warned him not to go looking for trouble at the cockfights, and he smiled and told me, 'Shut up; this afternoon we'll be rolling in money.' "

She fell back exhausted. The colonel pushed her gently toward the pillow. His eyes fell upon other eyes exactly like his own. "Try not to move," he said, feeling her whistling within his own lungs. The woman fell into a momentary torpor. She closed her eyes. When she opened them again, her breathing seemed more even.

"It's because of the situation we're in," she said. "It's a sin to take the food out of our mouths to give it to a rooster."

The colonel wiped her forehead with the sheet.

"Nobody dies in three months."

"And what do we eat in the meantime?" the woman asked.

"I don't know," the colonel said. "But if we were going to die of hunger, we would have died already."

The rooster was very much alive next to the empty can. When he saw the colonel, he emitted an almost human, guttural monologue and tossed his head back. He gave him a smile of complicity:

"Life is tough, pal."

The colonel went into the street. He wandered about the town during the siesta, without thinking about anything, without even trying to convince himself that his problem had no solution. He walked through forgotten streets until he found he was exhausted. Then he returned to the house. The woman heard him come in and called him into the bedroom.

"What?"

She replied without looking at him.

"We can sell the clock."

The colonel had thought of that. "I'm sure Alvaro will give you forty pesos right on the spot," said the woman. "Think how quickly he bought the sewing machine."

She was referring to the tailor whom Agustín had worked for.

"I could speak to him in the morning," admitted the colonel.

"None of that 'speak to him in the morning,'" she insisted. "Take the clock to him this minute. You put it on the counter and you tell him, 'Alvaro, I've brought this clock for you to buy from me.' He'll understand immediately."

The colonel felt ashamed.

"It's like walking around with the Holy Sepulcher," he protested. "If they see me in the street with a showpiece like that, Rafael Escalona will put me into one of his songs."

But this time, too, his wife convinced him. She herself took down the clock, wrapped it in newspaper, and put it into his arms. "Don't come back here without the forty pesos," she said. The colonel went off to the tailor's with the package under his arm. He found Agustín's companions sitting in the doorway.

One of them offered him a seat. "Thanks," he said. "I can't stay." Alvaro came out of the shop. A piece of wet duck hung on a wire stretched between two hooks in the hall. He was a boy with a hard, angular body and wild eyes. He also invited him to sit down. The colonel felt comforted. He leaned the stool against the doorjamb and sat down to wait until Alvaro was alone to propose his deal. Suddenly he realized that he was surrounded by expressionless faces.

"I'm not interrupting?" he said.

They said he wasn't. One of them leaned toward him. He said in a barely audible voice:

"Agustín wrote."

The colonel observed the deserted street.

"What does he say?"

"The same as always."

They gave him the clandestine sheet of paper. The colonel put it in his pants pocket. Then he kept silent, drumming on the package, until he realized that someone had noticed it. He stopped in suspense.

"What have you got there, Colonel?"

The colonel avoided Hernán's penetrating green eyes.

"Nothing," he lied. "I'm taking my clock to the German to have him fix it for me."

"Don't be silly, Colonel," said Hernán, trying to take the package. "Wait and I'll look at it."

The colonel held back. He didn't say anything, but his eyelids turned purple. The others insisted.

"Let him, Colonel. He knows mechanical things."

"I just don't want to bother him."

"Bother, it's no bother," Hernán argued. He seized the clock. "The German will get ten pesos out of you and it'll be the same as it is now."

Hernán went into the tailor shop with the clock. Alvaro was sewing on a machine. At the back, beneath a guitar hanging on a nail, a girl was sewing buttons on. There was a sign tacked up over the guitar: "TALKING POLITICS FORBIDDEN." Outside, the colonel felt as if his body were superfluous. He rested his feet on the rail of the stool.

"Goddamn it, Colonel."

He was startled. "No need to swear," he said.

Alfonso adjusted his eyeglasses on his nose to examine the colonel's shoes.

"It's because of your shoes," he said. "You've got on some goddamn new shoes."

"But you can say that without swearing," the colonel said, and showed the soles of his patent-leather shoes. "These monstrosities are forty years old, and it's the first time they've ever heard anyone swear."

"All done," shouted Hernán, inside, just as the clock's bell rang. In the neighboring house, a woman pounded on the partition; she shouted:

"Let that guitar alone! Agustín's year isn't up yet."

Someone guffawed.

"It's a clock."

Hernán came out with the package.

"It wasn't anything," he said. "If you like I'll go home with you to level it."

The colonel refused his offer.

"How much do I owe you?"

"Don't worry about it, Colonel," replied Hernán, taking his place in the group. "In January, the rooster will pay for it."

The colonel now found the chance he was looking for.

"I'll make you a deal," he said.

"What?"

"I'll give you the rooster." He examined the circle of faces. "I'll give the rooster to all of you."

Hernán looked at him in confusion.

"I'm too old now for that," the colonel continued. He gave his voice a convincing severity. "It's too much responsibility for me. For days now I've had the impression that the animal is dying."

"Don't worry about it, Colonel," Alfonso said. "The trouble is that the rooster is molting now. He's got a fever in his quills."

"He'll be better next month," Hernán said.

"I don't want him anyway," the colonel said.

Hernán's pupils bore into his.

"Realize how things are, Colonel," he insisted. "The main thing is for you to be the one who puts Agustín's rooster into the ring."

The colonel thought about it. "I realize," he said. "That's why I've kept him until now." He clenched his teeth, and felt he could go on:

"The trouble is there are still two months."

Hernán was the one who understood.

"If it's only because of that, there's no problem," he said.

And he proposed his formula. The other accepted. At dusk, when he entered the house with the package under his arm, his wife was chagrined.

"Nothing?" she asked.

"Nothing," the colonel answered. "But now it doesn't matter. The boys will take over feeding the rooster."

"Wait and I'll lend you an umbrella, friend."

Sabas opened a cupboard in the office wall. He uncovered a jumbled interior: riding boots piled up, stirrups and reins, and an aluminum pail full of riding spurs. Hanging from the upper part, half a dozen umbrellas and a lady's parasol. The colonel was thinking of the debris from some catastrophe.

"Thanks, friend," the colonel said, leaning on the window. "I prefer to wait for it to clear." Sabas didn't close the cupboard. He settled down at the desk within range of the electric fan. Then he took a little hypodermic syringe wrapped in cotton out of the drawer. The colonel observed the grayish almond trees through the rain. It was an empty afternoon.

"The rain is different from this window," he said. "It's as if it were raining in another town."

"Rain is rain from whatever point," replied Sabas. He put the syringe on to boil on the glass desk top. "This town stinks."

The colonel shrugged his shoulders. He walked toward the middle of the office: a green-tiled room with furniture upholstered in brightly colored fabrics. At the back, piled up in disarray, were sacks of salt, honeycombs, and riding saddles. Sabas followed him with a completely vacant stare.

"If I were in your shoes I wouldn't think that way," said the colonel.

He sat down and crossed his legs, his calm gaze fixed on the man leaning over his desk. A small man, corpulent, but with flaccid flesh, he had the sadness of a toad in his eyes.

"Have the doctor look at you, friend," said Sabas. "You've been a little sad since the day of the funeral."

The colonel raised his head.

"I'm perfectly well," he said.

Sabas waited for the syringe to boil. "I wish I could say the same," he complained. "You're lucky because you've got a cast-iron stomach." He contemplated the hairy backs of his hands which were dotted with dark blotches. He wore a ring with a black stone next to his wedding band.

"That's right," the colonel admitted.

Sabas called his wife through the door between the office and the rest of the house. Then he began a painful explanation of his diet. He took a little bottle out of his shirt pocket and put a white pill the size of a pea on the desk.

"It's torture to go around with this everyplace," he said. "It's like carrying death in your pocket."

The colonel approached the desk. He examined the pill in the palm of his hand until Sabas invited him to taste it.

"It's to sweeten coffee," he explained. "It's sugar, but without sugar."

"Of course," the colonel said, his saliva impregnated with a sad sweetness. "It's something like a ringing but without bells."

Sabas put his elbows on the desk with his face in his hands after his wife gave him the injection. The colonel didn't know what to do with his body. The woman unplugged the electric fan, put it on top of the safe, and then went to the cupboard.

"Umbrellas have something to do with death," she said.

The colonel paid no attention to her. He had left his house at four to wait for the mail, but the rain made him take refuge in Sabas's office. It was still raining when the launches whistled.

"Everybody says death is a woman," the woman continued. She was fat, taller than her husband, and had a hairy mole on her upper lip. Her way of speaking reminded one of the hum of the electric fan. "But I don't think it's a woman," she said. She closed the cupboard and looked into the colonel's eyes again.

"I think it's an animal with claws."

"That's possible," the colonel admitted. "At times very strange things happen."

He thought of the postmaster jumping onto the launch in an oilskin slicker. A month had passed since he had changed lawyers. He was entitled to expect a reply. Sabas's wife kept speaking about death until she noticed the colonel's absent-minded expression.

"Friend," she said. "You must be worried."

The colonel sat up.

"That's right, friend," he lied. "I'm thinking that it's five already and the rooster hasn't had his injection."

She was confused.

"An injection for a rooster, as if he were a human being!" she shouted. "That's sacrilege."

Sabas couldn't stand any more. He raised his flushed face.

"Close your mouth for a minute," he ordered his wife. And in fact she did raise her hands to her mouth. "You've been bothering my friend for half an hour with your foolishness."

"Not at all," the colonel protested.

The woman slammed the door. Sabas dried his neck with a handkerchief soaked in lavender. The colonel approached the window. It was raining steadily. A long-legged chicken was crossing the deserted plaza.

"Is it true the rooster's getting injections?"

"True," said the colonel. "His training begins next week."

"That's madness," said Sabas. "Those things are not for you."

"I agree," said the colonel. "But that's no reason to wring his neck."

"That's just idiotic stubbornness," said Sabas, turning toward the window. The colonel heard him sigh with the breath of a bellows. His friend's eyes made him feel pity.

"It's never too late for anything," the colonel said.

"Don't be unreasonable," insisted Sabas. "It's a two-edged deal. On one side you get rid of that headache, and on the other you can put nine hundred pesos in your pocket."

"Nine hundred pesos!" the colonel exclaimed.

"Nine hundred pesos."

The colonel visualized the figure.

"You think they'd give a fortune like that for the rooster?"

"I don't think," Sabas answered. "I'm absolutely sure."

It was the largest sum the colonel had had in his head since he had returned the revolution's funds. When he left Sabas's office, he felt a strong wrenching in his gut, but he was aware that this time it wasn't because of the weather. At the post office he headed straight for the postmaster:

"I'm expecting an urgent letter," he said. "It's air mail."

The postmaster looked in the cubbyholes. When he finished reading, he put the letters back in the proper box but he didn't say anything. He dusted off his hand and turned a meaningful look on the colonel.

"It was supposed to come today for sure," the colonel said.

The postmaster shrugged.

"The only thing that comes for sure is death, Colonel."

His wife received him with a dish of corn mush. He ate it in silence with long pauses for thought between each spoonful. Seated opposite him, the woman noticed that something had changed in his face.

"What's the matter?" she asked.

"I'm thinking about the employee that pension depends on," the colonel lied. "In fifty years, we'll be peacefully six feet under, while that poor man will be killing himself every Friday waiting for his retirement pension."

"That's a bad sign," the woman said. "It means that you're beginning to resign yourself already." She went on eating her mush. But a moment later she realized that her husband was still far away.

"Now, what you should do is enjoy the mush."

"It's very good," the colonel said. "Where'd it come from?"

"From the rooster," the woman answered. "The boys brought him so much corn that he decided to share it with us. That's life."

"That's right." The colonel sighed. "Life is the best thing that's ever been invented."

He looked at the rooster tied to the leg of the stove and this time he seemed a different animal. The woman also looked at him.

"This afternoon I had to chase the children out with a stick," she said. "They brought an old hen to breed her with the rooster."

"It's not the first time," the colonel said. "That's the same

143

thing they did in those towns with Colonel Aureliano Buendía. They brought him little girls to breed with."

She got a kick out of the joke. The rooster produced a gutteral noise which sounded in the hall like quiet human conversation. "Sometimes I think that animal is going to talk," the woman said. The colonel looked at him again.

"He's worth his weight in gold," he said. He made some calculations while he sipped a spoonful of mush. "He'll feed us for three years."

"You can't eat hope," the woman said.

"You can't eat it, but it sustains you," the colonel replied. "It's something like my friend Sabas's miraculous pills."

He slept poorly that night trying to erase the figures from his mind. The following day at lunch, the woman served two plates of mush, and ate hers with her head lowered, without saying a word. The colonel felt himself catching her dark mood.

"What's the matter?"

"Nothing," the woman said.

He had the impression that this time it had been her turn to lie. He tried to comfort her. But the woman persisted.

"It's nothing unusual," she said. "I was thinking that the man has been dead for two months, and I still haven't been to see the family."

So she went to see them that night. The colonel accompanied her to the dead man's house, and then headed for the movie theater, drawn by the music coming over the loudspeakers. Seated at the door of his office, Father Angel was watching the entrance to find out who was attending the show despite his twelve warnings. The flood of light, the strident music, and the shouts of the children erected a physical resistance in the area. One of the children threatened the colonel with a wooden rifle.

"What's new with the rooster, Colonel?" he said in an authoritative voice.

The colonel put his hands up.

"He's still around."

A four-color poster covered the entire front of the theater: *Midnight Virgin*. She was a woman in an evening gown, with one leg bared up to the thigh. The colonel continued wandering around the neighborhood until distant thunder and lightning began. Then he went back for his wife.

She wasn't at the dead man's house. Nor at home. The colonel reckoned that there was little time left before curfew, but the clock had stopped. He waited, feeling the storm advance on the town. He was getting ready to go out again when his wife arrived.

He took the rooster into the bedroom. She changed her clothes and went to take a drink of water in the living room just as the colonel finished winding the clock, and was waiting for curfew to blow in order to set it.

"Where were you?" the colonel asked.

"Roundabout," the woman answered. She put the glass on the washstand without looking at her husband and returned to the bedroom. "No one thought it was going to rain so soon." The colonel made no comment. When curfew blew, he set the clock at eleven, closed the case, and put the chair back in its place. He found his wife saying her rosary.

"You haven't answered my question," the colonel said.

"What?"

"Where were you?"

"I stayed around there talking," she said. "It had been so long since I'd been out of the house."

The colonel hung up his hammock. He locked the house and fumigated the room. Then he put the lamp on the floor and lay down.

"I understand," he said sadly. "The worst of a bad situation is that it makes us tell lies."

She let out a long sigh.

"I was with Father Angel," she said. "I went to ask him for a loan on our wedding rings."

"And what did he tell you?"

"That it's a sin to barter with sacred things."

She went on talking under her mosquito netting. "Two days ago I tried to sell the clock," she said. "No one is interested because they're selling modern clocks with luminous numbers on the installment plan. You can see the time in the dark." The colonel acknowledged that forty years of shared living, of shared hunger, of shared suffering, had not been enough for him to come to know his wife. He felt that something had also grown old in their love.

"They don't want the picture, either," she said. "Almost everybody has the same one. I even went to the Turk's."

The colonel felt bitter.

"So now everyone knows we're starving."

"I'm tired," the woman said. "Men don't understand problems of the household. Several times I've had to put stones on to boil so the neighbors wouldn't know that we often go for many days without putting on the pot."

The colonel felt offended.

"That's really a humiliation," he said.

The woman got out from under the mosquito netting and went to the hammock. "I'm ready to give up affectation and pretense in this house," she said. Her voice began to darken with rage. "I'm fed up with resignation and dignity."

The colonel didn't move a muscle.

"Twenty years of waiting for the little colored birds which they promised you after every election, and all we've got out of it is a dead son," she went on. "Nothing but a dead son."

The colonel was used to that sort of recrimination.

"We did our duty."

"And they did theirs by making a thousand pesos a month in the Senate for twenty years," the woman answered. "There's my friend Sabas with a two-story house that isn't big enough to keep all his money in, a man who came to this town selling medicines with a snake curled around his neck."

"But he's dying of diabetes," the colonel said.

"And you're dying of hunger," the woman said. "You should realize that you can't eat dignity."

The lightning interrupted her. The thunder exploded in the street, entered the bedroom, and went rolling under the bed like a heap of stones. The woman jumped toward the mosquito netting for her rosary.

The colonel smiled.

"That's what happens to you for not holding your tongue," he said. "I've always said that God is on my side."

But in reality he felt embittered. A moment later he put out the light and sank into thought in a darkness rent by the lightning. He remembered Macondo. The colonel had waited ten years for the promises of Neerlandia to be fulfilled. In the drowsiness of the siesta he saw a yellow, dusty train pull in, with men and women and animals suffocating from the heat, piled up even on the roofs of the cars. It was the banana fever.

In twenty-four hours they had transformed the town. "I'm leaving," the colonel said then. "The odor of the banana is eating at my insides." And he left Macondo on the return train, Wednesday, June 27, 1906, at 2:18 P.M. It took him nearly half a century to realize that he hadn't had a moment's peace since the surrender at Neerlandia.

He opened his eyes.

"Then there's no need to think about it any more," he said.

"What?"

"The problem of the rooster," the colonel said. "Tomorrow I'll sell it to my friend Sabas for nine hundred pesos."

The howls of the castrated animals, fused with Sabas's shouting, came through the office window. If he doesn't come in ten minutes I'll leave, the colonel promised himself after two hours of waiting. But he waited twenty minutes more. He was getting set to leave when Sabas entered the office followed by a group of workers. He passed back and forth in front of the colonel without looking at him.

"Are you waiting for me, friend?"

"Yes, friend," the colonel said. "But if you're very busy, I can come back later."

Sabas didn't hear him from the other side of the door.

"I'll be right back," he said.

Noon was stifling. The office shone with the shimmering of the street. Dulled by the heat, the colonel involuntarily closed his eyes and at once began to dream of his wife. Sabas's wife came in on tiptoe.

"Don't wake up, friend," she said. "I'm going to draw the blinds because this office is an inferno."

The colonel followed her with a blank look. She spoke in the shadow when she closed the window.

"Do you dream often?"

"Sometimes," replied the colonel, ashamed of having fallen asleep. "Almost always I dream that I'm getting tangled up in spider webs."

"I have nightmares every night," the woman said. "Now I've got it in my head to find out who those unknown people are whom one meets in one's dreams."

She plugged in the fan. "Last week a woman appeared at the head of my bed," she said. "I managed to ask her who she was and she replied, 'I am the woman who died in this room twelve years ago.' "

"But the house was built barely two years ago," the colonel said.

"That's right," the woman said. "That means that even the dead make mistakes."

The hum of the fan solidified the shadow. The colonel felt impatient, tormented by sleepiness and by the rambling woman who went directly from dreams to the mystery of the reincarnation. He was waiting for a pause to say good-bye when Sabas entered the office with his foreman.

"I've warmed up your soup four times," the woman said.

"Warm it up ten times if you like," said Sabas. "But stop nagging me now."

He opened the safe and gave his foreman a roll of bills

together with a list of instructions. The foreman opened the blinds to count the money. Sabas saw the colonel at the back of the office but didn't show any reaction. He kept talking with the foreman. The colonel straightened up at the point when the two men were getting ready to leave the office again. Sabas stopped before opening the door.

"What can I do for you, friend?"

The colonel saw that the foreman was looking at him.

"Nothing, friend," he said. "I just wanted to talk to you."

"Make it fast, whatever it is," said Sabas. "I don't have a minute to spare."

He hesitated with his hand resting on the doorknob. The colonel felt the five longest seconds of his life passing. He clenched his teeth.

"It's about the rooster," he murmured.

Then Sabas finished opening the door. "The question of the rooster," he repeated, smiling, and pushed the foreman toward the hall. "The sky is falling in and my friend is worrying about that rooster." And then, addressing the colonel:

"Very well, friend. I'll be right back."

The colonel stood motionless in the middle of the office until he could no longer hear the footsteps of the two men at the end of the hall. Then he went out to walk around the town which was paralyzed in its Sunday siesta. There was no one at the tailor's. The doctor's office was closed. No one was watching the goods set out at the Syrians' stalls. The river was a sheet of steel. A man at the waterfront was sleeping across four oil drums, his face protected from the sun by a hat. The colonel went home, certain that he was the only thing moving in town.

His wife was waiting for him with a complete lunch.

"I bought it on credit; promised to pay first thing tomorrow," she explained.

During lunch, the colonel told her the events of the last three hours. She listened to him impatiently.

"The trouble is you lack character," she said finally. "You

present yourself as if you were begging alms when you ought to go there with you head high and take our friend aside and say, 'Friend, I've decided to sell you the rooster.' "

"Life is a breeze the way you tell it," the colonel said.

She assumed an energetic attitude. That morning she had put the house in order and was dressed very strangely, in her husband's old shoes, and oilcloth apron, and a rag tied around her head with two knots at the ears. "You haven't the slightest sense for business," she said. "When you go to sell something, you have to put on the same face as when you go to buy."

The colonel found something amusing in her figure.

"Stay just the way you are," he interrupted her, smiling. "You're identical to the little Quaker Oats man."

She took the rag off her head.

"I'm speaking seriously," she said. "I'm going to take the rooster to our friend right now, and I'll bet whatever you want that I come back inside of half an hour with the nine hundred pesos."

"You've got zeros on the brain," the colonel said. "You're already betting with the money from the rooster."

It took a lot of trouble for him to dissuade her. She had spent the morning mentally organizing the budget for the next three years without their Friday agony. She had made a list of the essentials they needed, without forgetting a pair of new shoes for the colonel. She set aside a place in the bedroom for the mirror. The momentary frustration of her plans left her with a confused sensation of shame and resentment.

She took a short siesta. When she got up, the colonel was sitting in the patio.

"Now what are you doing?" she asked.

"I'm thinking," the colonel said.

"Then the problem is solved. We will be able to count on that money fifty years from now."

But in reality the colonel had decided to sell the rooster that very afternoon. He thought of Sabas, alone in his office, preparing himself for his daily injection in front of the electric fan. He had his answer ready.

"Take the rooster," his wife advised him as he went out. "Seeing him in the flesh will work a miracle."

The colonel objected. She followed him to the front door with desperate anxiety.

"It doesn't matter if the whole army is in the office," she said. "You grab him by the arm and don't let him move until he gives you the nine hundred pesos."

"They'll think we're planning a hold-up."

She paid no attention.

"Remember that you are the owner of the rooster," she insisted. "Remember that you are the one who's going to do him the favor."

"All right."

Sabas was in the bedroom with the doctor. "Now's your chance, friend," his wife said to the colonel. "The doctor is getting him ready to travel to the ranch, and he's not coming back until Thursday." The colonel struggled with two opposing forces: in spite of his determination to sell the rooster, he wished he had arrived an hour later and missed Sabas.

"I can wait," he said.

But the woman insisted. She led him to the bedroom where her husband was seated on the throne-like bed, in his underwear, his colorless eyes fixed on the doctor. The colonel waited until the doctor had heated the glass tube with the patient's urine, sniffed the odor, and made an approving gesture to Sabas.

"We'll have to shoot him," the doctor said, turning to the colonel. "Diabetes is too slow for finishing off the wealthy."

"You've already done your best with your damned insulin injections," said Sabas, and he gave a jump on his flaccid buttocks. "But I'm a hard nut to crack." And then, to the colonel:

"Come in, friend. When I went out to look for you this afternoon, I couldn't even see your hat."

"I don't wear one, so I won't have to take if off for any-one."

Sabas began to get dressed. The doctor put a glass tube with a blood sample in his jacket pocket. Then he straightened out the things in his bag. The colonel thought he was getting ready to leave.

"If I were in your shoes, I'd send my friend a bill for a hundred thousand pesos, Doctor," the colonel said. "That way he wouldn't be so worried."

"I've already suggested that to him, but for a million," the doctor said. "Poverty is the best cure for diabetes."

"Thanks for the prescription," said Sabas, trying to stuff his voluminous belly into his riding breeches. "But I won't ac-cept it, to save you from the catastrophe of becoming rich." The doctor saw his own teeth reflected in the little chromed lock of his bag. He looked at the clock without showing im-patience. Sabas, putting on his boots, suddenly turned to the colonel:

"Well, friend, what's happening with the rooster?"

The colonel realized that the doctor was also waiting for his answer. He clenched his teeth.

"Nothing, friend," he murmured. "I've come to sell him to you."

Sabas finished putting on his boots.

"Fine, my friend," he said without emotion. "It's the most sensible thing that could have occurred to you."

"I'm too old now for these complications," the colonel said to justify himself before the doctor's impenetrable expression. "If I were twenty years younger it would be different."

"You'll always be twenty years younger," the doctor re-plied.

The colonel regained his breath. He waited for Sabas to say something more, but he didn't. Sabas put on a leather zip-pered jacket and got ready to leave the bedroom.

"If you like, we'll talk about it next week, friend," the col-onel said.

"That's what I was going to say," said Sabas. "I have a customer who might give you four hundred pesos. But we have to wait till Thursday."

"How much?" the doctor asked.

"Four hundred pesos."

"I had heard someone say that he was worth a lot more," the doctor said.

"You were talking in terms of nine hundred pesos," the colonel said, backed by the doctor's perplexity. "He's the best rooster in the whole province."

Sabas answered the doctor.

"At some other time, anyone would have paid a thousand," he explained. "But now no one dares pit a good rooster. There's always the danger he'll come out of the pit shot to death." He turned to the colonel, feigning disappointment:

"That's what I wanted to tell you friend."

The colonel nodded.

"Fine," he said.

He followed him down the hall. The doctor stayed in the living room, detained by Sabas's wife, who asked him for a remedy "for those things which come over one suddenly and which one doesn't know what they are." The colonel waited for him in the office. Sabas opened the safe, stuffed money into all his pockets, and held out four bills to the colonel.

"There's sixty pesos, friend," he said. "When the rooster is sold we'll settle up."

The colonel walked with the doctor past the stalls at the waterfront, which were beginning to revive in the cool of the afternoon. A barge loaded with sugar cane was moving down the thread of current. The colonel found the doctor strangely impervious.

"And you, how are you, Doctor?"

The doctor shrugged.

"As usual," he said. "I think I need a doctor."

"It's the winter," the colonel said. "It eats away my insides."

The doctor examined him with a look absolutely devoid of any professional interest. In succession he greeted the Syrians seated at the doors of their shops. At the door of the doctor's office, the colonel expressed his opinion of the sale of the rooster.

"I couldn't do anything else," he explained. "That animal feeds on human flesh."

"The only animal who feeds on human flesh is Sabas," the doctor said. "I'm sure he'd resell the rooster for the nine hundred pesos."

"You think so?"

"I'm sure of it," the doctor said. "It's as sweet a deal as his famous patriotic pact with the Mayor."

The colonel refused to believe it. "My friend made that pact to save his skin," he said. "That's how he could stay in town."

"And that's how he could buy the property of his fellow-partisans whom the Mayor kicked out at half their price," the doctor replied. He knocked on the door, since he didn't find his keys in his pockets. Then he faced the colonel's disbelief.

"Don't be so naïve," he said. "Sabas is much more interested in money than in his own skin."

The colonel's wife went shopping that night. He accompanied her to the Syrians' stalls, pondering the doctor's revelations.

"Find the boys immediately and tell them that the rooster is sold," she told him. "We musn't leave them with any hopes."

"The rooster won't be sold until my friend Sabas comes back," the colonel answered.

He found Alvaro playing roulette in the pool hall. The place was sweltering on Sunday night. The heat seemed more intense because of the vibrations of the radio turned up full blast. The colonel amused himself with the brightly colored numbers painted on a large black oilcloth cover and lit by an oil lantern placed on a box in the center of the table. Alvaro insisted on losing on twenty-three. Following the game over his shoulder, the colonel observed that the eleven turned up four times in nine spins.

"Bet on eleven," he whispered into Alvaro's ear. "It's the one coming up most."

Alvaro examined the table. He didn't bet on the next spin. He took some money out of his pants pocket, and with it a sheet of paper. He gave the paper to the colonel under the table.

"It's from Agustín." he said.

The colonel put the clandestine note in his pocket. Alvaro bet heavily on the eleven.

"Start with just a little," the colonel said.

"It may be a good hunch," Alvaro replied. A group of neighboring players took their bets off the other numbers and bet on eleven after the enormous colored wheel had already begun to turn. The colonel felt oppressed. For the first time he felt the fascination, agitation, and bitterness of gambling.

The five won.

"I'm sorry," the colonel said, ashamed, and, with an irresistible feeling of guilt, followed the little wooden rake which pulled in Alvaro's money. "That's what I get for butting into what doesn't concern me."

Alvaro smiled without looking at him.

"Don't worry, Colonel. Trust to love."

The trumpets playing a mambo were suddenly interrupted. The gamblers scattered with their hands in the air. The colonel felt the dry snap, articulate and cold, of a rifle being cocked behind his back. He realized that he had been caught fatally in a police raid with the clandestine paper in his pocket. He turned halfway around without raising his hands. And then he saw, close up, for the first time in his life, the man who had shot his son. The man was directly in front of him, with his rifle barrel aimed at the colonel's belly. He was small, Indian-looking, with weather-beaten skin, and his breath smelled like a child's. The colonel gritted his teeth and gently pushed the rifle barrel away with the tips of his fingers.

"Excuse me," he said.

He confronted two round little bat eyes. In an instant, he felt himself being swallowed up by those eyes, crushed, digested, and expelled immediately.

"You may go, Colonel."

He didn't need to open the window to tell it was December. He knew it in his bones when he was cutting up the fruit for the rooster's breakfast in the kitchen. Then he opened the door and the sight of the patio confirmed his feeling. It was a marvelous patio, with the grass and the trees, and the cubicle with the privy floating in the clear air, one millimeter above the ground.

His wife stayed in bed until nine. When she appeared in the kitchen, the colonel had already straightened up the house and was talking to the children in a circle around the rooster. She had to make a detour to get to the stove.

"Get out of the way!" she shouted. She glowered in the animal's direction. "I don't know when I'll ever get rid of that evil-omened bird."

The colonel regarded his wife's mood over the rooster. Nothing about the rooster deserved resentment. He was ready for training. His neck and his feathered purple thighs, his sawtoothed crest: the animal had taken on a slender figure, a defenseless air.

"Lean out the window and forget the rooster," the colonel said when the children left. "On mornings like this, one feels like having a picture taken."

She leaned out the window but her face betrayed no emotion. "I would like to plant the roses," she said, returning to the stove. The colonel hung the mirror on the hook to shave.

"If you want to plant the roses, go ahead," he said.

He tried to make his movements match those in the mirror.

"The pigs eat them up," she said.

"All the better," the colonel said. "Pigs fattened on roses ought to taste very good."

He looked for his wife in the mirror and noticed that she still had the same expression. By the light of the fire her face seemed to be formed of the same material as the stove. Without noticing, his eyes fixed on her, the colonel continued shaving himself by touch as he had done for many years. The woman thought, in a long silence.

"But I don't want to plant them," she said.

"Fine," said the colonel. "Then don't plant them."

He felt well. December had shriveled the flora in his gut. He suffered a disappointment that morning trying to put on his new shoes. But after trying several times he realized that it was a wasted effort, and put on his patent-leather ones. His wife noticed the change.

"If you don't put on the new ones you'll never break them in," she said.

"They're shoes for a cripple," the colonel protested. "They ought to sell shoes that have already been worn for a month."

He went into the street stimulated by the presentiment that the letter would arrive that afternoon. Since it still was not time for the launches, he waited for Sabas in his office. But they informed him that he wouldn't be back until Monday. He didn't lose his patience despite not having foreseen this setback. "Sooner or later he has to come back," he told himself, and he headed for the harbor; it was a marvelous moment, a moment of still-unblemished clarity.

"The whole year ought to be December," he murmured, seated in the store of Moses the Syrian. "One feels as if he were made of glass."

Moses the Syrian had to make an effort to translate the idea into his almost forgotten Arabic. He was a placid Oriental, encased up to his ears in smooth, stretched skin, and he had the clumsy movements of a drowned man. In fact, he seemed as if he had just been rescued from the water.

"That's the way it was before," he said. "If it were the same now, I would be eight hundred and ninety-seven years old. And you?"

"Seventy-five," said the colonel, his eyes pursuing the postmaster. Only then did he discover the circus. He recognized the patched tent on the roof of the mail boat amid a pile of colored objects. For a second he lost the postmaster while he looked for the wild animals among the crates piled up on the other launches. He didn't find them.

"It's a circus," he said. "It's the first one that's come in ten years."

Moses the Syrian verified his report. He spoke to his wife in a pidgin of Arabic and Spanish. She replied from the back of the store. He made a comment to himself, and then translated his worry for the colonel.

"Hide your cat, Colonel. The boys will steal it to sell it to the circus."

The colonel was getting ready to follow the postmaster.

"It's not a wild-animal show," he said.

"It doesn't matter," the Syrian replied. "The tightrope walkers eat cats so they won't break their bones."

He followed the postmaster through the stalls at the waterfront to the plaza. There the loud clamor from the cock-fight took him by surprise. A passer-by said something to him about his rooster. Only then did he remember that this was the day set for the trials.

He passed the post office. A moment later he had sunk into the turbulent atmosphere of the pit. He saw his rooster in the middle of the pit, alone, defenseless, his spurs wrapped in rags, with something like fear visible in the trembling of his feet. His adversary was a sad ashen rooster.

The colonel felt no emotion. There was a succession of identical attacks. A momentary engagement of feathers and feet and necks in the middle of an enthusiastic ovation. Knocked against the planks of the barrier, the adversary did a somersault and returned to the attack. His rooster didn't attack. He rebuffed every attack, and landed again in exactly the same spot. But now his feet weren't trembling.

"Hernán jumped the barrier, picked him up with both

hands, and showed him to the crowd in the stands. There was a frenetic explosion of applause and shouting. The colonel noticed the disproportion between the enthusiasm of the applause and the intensity of the fight. It seemed to him a farce to which—voluntarily and consciously—the roosters had also lent themselves.

Impelled by a slightly disdainful curiosity, he examined the circular pit. An excited crowd was hurtling down the stands toward the pit. The colonel observed the confusion of hot, anxious, terribly alive faces. They were new people. All the new people in town. He relived—with foreboding—an instant which had been erased on the edge of his memory. Then he leaped the barrier, made his way through the packed crowd in the pit, and confronted Hernán's calm eyes. They looked at each other without blinking.

"Good afternoon, Colonel."

The colonel took the rooster away from him. "Good afternoon," he muttered. And he said nothing more because the warm deep throbbing of the animal made him shudder. He thought that he had never had such an alive thing in his hands before.

"You weren't at home," Hernán said, confused.

A new ovation interrupted him. The colonel felt intimidated. He made his way again, without looking at anybody, stunned by the applause and the shouts, and went into the street with his rooster under his arm.

The whole town—the lower-class people—came out to watch him go by followed by the school children. A gigantic Negro standing on a table with a snake wrapped around his neck was selling medicine without a license at a corner of the plaza. A large group returning from the harbor had stopped to listen to his spiel. But when the colonel passed with the rooster, their attention shifted to him. The way home had never been so long.

He had no regrets. For a long time the town had lain in a sort of stupor, ravaged by ten years of history. That afternoon—another Friday without a letter—the people had awakened. The colonel remembered another era. He saw himself with his wife and his son watching under an umbrella a show which was not interrupted despite the rain. He remembered the party's leaders, scrupulously groomed, fanning themselves to the beat of the music in the patio of his house. He almost relived the painful resonance of the bass drum in his intestines.

He walked along the street parallel to the harbor and there, too, found the tumultuous Election Sunday crowd of long ago. They were watching the circus unloading. From inside a tent, a woman shouted something about the rooster. He continued home, self-absorbed, still hearing scattered voices, as if the remnants of the ovation in the pit were pursuing him.

At the door he addressed the children:

"Everyone go home," he said. "Anyone who comes in will leave with a hiding."

He barred the door and went straight into the kitchen. His wife came out of the bedroom choking.

"They took it by force," she said sobbing. "I told them that the rooster would not leave this house while I was alive." The colonel tied the rooster to the leg of the stove. He changed the water in the can, pursued by his wife's frantic voice.

"They said they would take it over our dead bodies," she said. "They said the rooster didn't belong to us but to the whole town."

Only when he finished with the rooster did the colonel turn to the contorted face of his wife. He discovered, without surprise, that it produced neither remorse nor compassion in him.

"They did the right thing," he said quietly. And then, looking through his pockets, he added with a sort of bottomless sweetness:

"The rooster's not for sale."

She followed him to the bedroom. She felt him to be completely human, but untouchable, as if she were seeing him on a movie screen. The colonel took a roll of bills out of the closet, added what he had in his pockets to it, counted the total, and put it back in the closet.

"There are twenty-nine pesos to return to my friend Sabas," he said. "He'll get the rest when the pension arrives."

"And if it doesn't arrive?" the woman asked.

"It will."

"But if it doesn't?"

"Well, then, he won't get paid."

He found his new shoes under the bed. He went back to the closet for the box, cleaned the soles with a rag, and put the shoes in the box, just as his wife had brought them Sunday night. She didn't move.

"The shoes go back," the colonel said. "That's thirteen pesos more for my friend."

"They won't take them back," she said.

"They have to take them back," the colonel replied. "I've only put them on twice."

"The Turks don't understand such things," the woman said.

"They have to understand."

"And if they don't?"

"Well, then, they don't."

They went to bed without eating. The colonel waited for his wife to finish her rosary to turn out the lamp. But he couldn't sleep. He heard the bells for the movie classifications, and almost at once—three hours later—the curfew. The gravelly breathing of his wife became anguished with the chilly night air. The colonel still had his eyes open when she spoke to him in a calm, conciliatory voice:

"You're awake."

"Yes."

"Try to listen to reason," the woman said. "Talk to my friend Sabas tomorrow."

"He's not coming back until Monday."

"Better," said the woman. "That way you'll have three days to think about what you're going to say."

"There's nothing to think about," the colonel said.

A pleasant coolness had taken the place of the viscous air of October. The colonel recognized December again in the timetable of the plovers. When it struck two, he still hadn't been able to fall asleep. But he knew that his wife was also awake. He tried to change his position in the hammock.

"You can't sleep," the woman said.

"No."

She thought for a moment.

"We're in no condition to do that," she said. "Just think how much four hundred pesos in one lump sum is."

"It won't be long now till the pension comes," the colonel said.

"You've been saying the same thing for fifteen years."

"That's why," the colonel said. "It can't be much longer now."

She was silent. But when she spoke again, it didn't seem to the colonel as if any time had passed at all.

"I have the impression the money will never arrive," the woman said.

"It will."

"And if it doesn't?"

He couldn't find his voice to answer. At the first crowing of the rooster he was struck by reality, but he sank back again into a dense, safe, remorseless sleep. When he awoke, the sun was already high in the sky. His wife was sleeping. The colonel methodically repeated his morning activities, two hours behind schedule, and waited for his wife to eat breakfast.

She was uncommunicative when she awoke. They said good morning, and they sat down to eat in silence. The colonel sipped a cup of black coffee and had a piece of cheese and a sweet roll. He spent the whole morning in the tailor shop. At one o'clock he returned home and found his wife mending clothes among the begonias.

"It's lunchtime," he said.

"There is no lunch."

He shrugged. He tried to block up the holes in the patio wall to prevent the children from coming into the kitchen. When he came back into the hall, lunch was on the table.

During the course of lunch, the colonel realized that his wife was making an effort not to cry. This certainty alarmed him. He knew his wife's character, naturally hard, and hardened even more by forty years of bitterness. The death of her son had not wrung a single tear out of her.

He fixed a reproving look directly on her eyes. She bit her lips, dried her eyelids on her sleeve, and continued eating lunch.

"You have no consideration," she said.

The colonel didn't speak.

"You're willful, stubborn, and inconsiderate," she repeated. She crossed her knife and fork on the plate, but immediately rectified their positions superstitiously. "An entire lifetime eating dirt just so that now it turns out that I deserve less consideration than a rooster."

"That's different," the colonel said.

"It's the same thing," the woman replied. "You ought to realize that I'm dying; this thing I have is not a sickness but a slow death."

The colonel didn't speak until he finished eating his lunch.

"If the doctor guarantees me that by selling the rooster you'll get rid of your asthma, I'll sell him immediately," he said. "But if not, not."

That afternoon he took the rooster to the pit. On his return he found his wife on the verge of an attack. She was walking up and down the hall, her hair down her back, her arms spread wide apart, trying to catch her breath above the whistling in her lungs. She was there until early evening. Then she went to bed without speaking to her husband.

She mouthed prayers until a little after curfew. Then the colonel got ready to put out the lamp. But she objected.

"I don't want to die in the dark," she said.

The colonel left the lamp on the floor. He began to feel exhausted. He wished he could forget everything, sleep forty-four days in one stretch, and wake up on January 20th at three in the afternoon, in the pit, and at the exact moment to let the rooster loose. But he felt himself threatened by the sleeplessness of his wife.

"It's the same story as always," she began a moment later. "We put up with hunger so others can eat. It's been the same story for forty years."

The colonel kept silent until his wife paused to ask him if he was awake. He answered that he was. The woman continued in a smooth, fluent, implacable tone.

"Everybody will win with the rooster except us. We're the only ones who don't have a cent to bet."

"The owner of the rooster is entitled to twenty per cent."

"You were also entitled to get a position when they made you break your back for them in the elections," the woman replied. "You were also entitled to the veteran's pension after risking your neck in the civil war. Now everyone has his future assured and you're dying of hunger, completely alone."

"I'm not alone," the colonel said.

He tried to explain, but sleep overtook him. She kept talking dully until she realized that her husband was sleeping. Then she got out of the mosquito net and walked up and down the living room in the darkness. There she continued talking. The colonel called her at dawn.

She appeared at the door, ghostlike, illuminated from below by the lamp which was almost out. She put it out before getting into the mosquito netting. But she kept talking.

"We're going to do one thing," the colonel interrupted her.

"The only thing we can do is sell the rooster," said the woman.

"We can also sell the clock."

"They won't buy it."

"Tomorrow I'll try to see if Alvaro will give me the forty pesos."

"He won't give them to you."

"Then we'll sell the picture."

When the woman spoke again, she was outside the mosquito net again. The colonel smelled her breath impregnated with medicinal herbs.

"They won't buy it," she said.

"We'll see," the colonel said gently, without a trace of change in his voice. "Now, go to sleep. If we can't sell anything tomorrow, we'll think of something else."

He tried to keep his eyes open but sleep broke his resolve. He fell to the bottom of a substance without time and without space, where the words of his wife had a different significance. But a moment later he felt himself being shaken by the shoulder.

"Answer me."

The colonel didn't know if he had heard those words before or after he had slept. Dawn was breaking. The window stood out in Sunday's green clarity. He thought he had a fever. His eyes burned and he had to make a great effort to clear his head.

"What will we do if we can't sell anything?" the woman repeated.

"By then it will be January 20th," the colonel said, completely awake. "They'll pay the twenty per cent that very afternoon."

"If the rooster wins," the woman said. "But if he loses. It hasn't occurred to you that the rooster might lose."

"He's one rooster that can't lose."

"But suppose he loses."

"There are still forty-four days left to begin to think about that," the colonel said.

The woman lost her patience.

"And meanwhile what do we eat?" she asked, and seized the colonel by the collar of his flannel night shirt. She shook him hard.

It had taken the colonel seventy-five years—the seventy-five years of his life, minute by minute—to reach this moment. He felt pure, explicit, invincible at the moment when he replied:

"Shit."

Chronicle of a
Death Foretold

translated from the Spanish by Gregory Rabassa

1

ON THE DAY THEY WERE GOING TO KILL HIM, SANTIAGO NASAR
got up at five-thirty in the morning to wait for the boat the
bishop was coming on. He'd dreamed he was going through a
grove of timber trees where a gentle drizzle was falling, and
for an instant he was happy in his dream, but when he awoke
he felt completely spattered with bird shit.

"He was always dreaming about trees," Plácida Linero, his
mother, told me twenty-seven years later, recalling the details
of that distressing Monday. "The week before, he'd dreamed
that he was alone in a tinfoil airplane and flying through the
almond trees without bumping into anything," she said to me.
She had a well-earned reputation as an accurate interpreter of
other people's dreams, provided they were told her before
eating, but she hadn't noticed any ominous augury in those
two dreams of her son's, or in the other dreams of trees he'd
described to her on the mornings preceding his death.

Nor did Santiago Nasar recognize the omen. He had slept
little and poorly, without getting undressed, and he woke up
with a headache and a sediment of copper stirrup on his palate, and he interpreted them as the natural havoc of the wedding revels that had gone on until after midnight. Furthermore: all the many people he ran into after leaving his house

at five minutes past six and until he was carved up like a pig an hour later remembered him as being a little sleepy but in a good mood, and he remarked to all of them in a casual way that it was a very beautiful day. No one was certain if he was referring to the state of the weather. Many people coincided in recalling that it was a radiant morning with a sea breeze coming in through the banana groves, as was to be expected in a fine February of that period. But most agreed that the weather was funereal, with a cloudy, low sky and the thick smell of still waters, and that at the moment of the misfortune a thin drizzle was falling like the one Santiago Nasar had seen in his dream grove. I was recovering from the wedding revels in the apostolic lap of María Alejandrina Cervantes, and I only awakened with the clamor of the alarm bells, thinking they had turned them loose in honor of the bishop.

Santiago Nasar put on a shirt and pants of white linen. both items unstarched, just like the ones he'd put on the day before the wedding. It was his attire for special occasions. If it hadn't been for the bishop's arrival, he would have dressed in his khaki outfit and the riding boots he wore on Mondays to go to The Divine Face, the cattle ranch he'd inherited from his father and which he administered with very good judgment but without much luck. In the country he wore a .357 Magnum on his belt, and its armored bullets, according to what he said, could cut a horse in two through the middle. During the partridge season he would also carry his falconry equipment. In the closet he kept a Mannlicher Schoenauer .30-06 rifle, a .300 Holland & Holland Magnum rifle, a .22 Hornet with a double-powered telescopic sight, and a Winchester repeater. He always slept the way his father had slept, with the weapon hidden in the pillowcase, but before leaving the house that day he took out the bullets and put them in the drawer of the night table. "He never left it loaded," his mother told me. I knew that, and I also knew that he kept the guns in one place and hid the ammunition in another far removed so that nobody, not even casually, would yield to the temptation of loading them inside the house. It was a wise custom established by his father ever since one morning when a servant girl had shaken the case to get the pillow out and the pistol went off as it hit the floor and the bullet wrecked the cupboard in the room, went through the living room wall, passed through the dining room of the house next door with the thunder of war, and turned a life-size saint on the main altar of the church on the opposite side of the square to plaster dust. Santiago Nasar, who was a young child at the time, never forgot the lesson of that accident.

The last image his mother had of him was of his fleeting passage through the bedroom. He'd wakened her while he was feeling around trying to find an aspirin in the bathroom medicine chest, and she turned on the light and saw him appear in the doorway with a glass of water in his hand. So she would remember him forever. Santiago Nasar told her then about the dream, but she didn't pay any great attention to the trees.

"Any dream about birds means good health," she said.

She had watched him from the same hammock and in the same position in which I found her prostrated by the last lights of old age when I returned to this forgotten village, trying to put the broken mirror of memory back together from so many scattered shards. She could barely make out shapes in full light and had some medicinal leaves on her temples for the eternal headache that her son had left her the last time he went through the bedroom. She was on her side, clutching the cords at the head of the hammock as she tried to get up, and there in the half shadows was the baptistry smell that had startled me on the morning of the crime.

No sooner had I appeared on the threshold than she confused me with the memory of Santiago Nasar. "There he was," she told me. "He was dressed in white linen that had been washed in plain water because his skin was so delicate that it couldn't stand the noise of starch." She sat in the hammock for a long time, chewing pepper cress seeds, until the illusion that her son had returned left her. Then she sighed: "He was the man in my life."

I saw him in her memory. He had turned twenty-one the last week in January, and he was slim and pale and had his father's Arab eyelids and curly hair. He was the only child of a marriage of convenience without a single moment of happiness, but he seemed happy with his father until the latter died suddenly, three years before, and he continued seeming to be so with his solitary mother until the Monday of his death. From her he had inherited a sixth sense. From his father he learned at a very early age the manipulation of firearms, his love for horses, and the mastery of high-flying birds of prey, but from him he also learned the good arts of valor and prudence. They spoke Arabic between themselves, but not in front of Plácida Linero, so that she wouldn't feel excluded. They were never seen armed in town, and the only time they brought in their trained birds was for a demonstration of falconry at a charity bazaar. The death of his father had forced him to abandon his studies at the end of secondary school in order to take charge of the family ranch. By his nature, Santiago Nasar was merry and peaceful, and openhearted.

On the day they were going to kill him, his mother thought he'd got his days mixed up when she saw him dressed in white. "I reminded him that it was Monday," she told me. But he explained to her that he'd got dressed up pontifical style in case he had a chance to kiss the bishop's ring. She showed no sign of interest. "He won't even get off the boat," she told him. "He'll give an obligatory blessing, as always, and go back the way he came. He hates this town."

Santiago Nasar knew it was true, but church pomp had an irresistible fascination for him. "It's like the movies," he'd told me once. The only thing that interested his mother about the bishop's arrival, on the other hand, was for her son not to get soaked in the rain, since she'd heard him sneeze while he was sleeping. She advised him to take along an umbrella, but he waved good-bye and left the room. It was the last time she saw him.

Victoria Guzmán, the cook, was sure that it hadn't rained that day, or during the whole month of February. "On the contrary," she told me when I came to see her, a short time before her death. "The sun warms things up earlier than in August." She had been quartering three rabbits for lunch, surrounded by panting dogs, when Santiago Nasar entered the kitchen. "He always got up with the face of a bad night," Victoria Guzmán recalled without affection. Divina Flor, her daughter, who was just coming into bloom, served Santiago Nasar a mug of mountain coffee with a shot of cane liquor, as on every Monday, to help him bear the burden of the night before. The enormous kitchen, with the whispers from the fire and the hens sleeping on their perches, was breathing stealthily. Santiago Nasar swallowed another aspirin and sat down to drink the mug of coffee in slow sips, thinking just as slowly, without taking his eyes off the two women who were disemboweling the rabbits on the stove. In spite of her age, Victoria Guzmán was still in good shape. The girl, as yet a bit untamed, seemed overwhelmed by the drive of her glands. Santiago Nasar grabbed her by the wrist when she came to take the empty mug from him.

"The time has come for you to be tamed," he told her.

Victoria Guzmán showed him the bloody knife.

"Let go of her, white man," she ordered him seriously. "You won't have a drink of that water as long as I'm alive."

She'd been seduced by Ibrahim Nasar in the fullness of her adolescence. She'd made love to him in secret for several years in the stables of the ranch, and he brought her to be a house servant when the affection was over. Divina Flor, who was the daughter of a more recent mate, knew that she was destined for Santiago Nasar's furtive bed, and that idea brought out a premature anxiety in her. "Another man like that hasn't ever been born again," she told me, fat and faded and surrounded by the children of other loves. "He was just like his father," Victoria Guzmán answered her. "A shit." But she couldn't avoid a wave of fright as she remembered Santiago Nasar's horror when she pulled out the insides of a rabbit by the roots and threw the steaming guts to the dogs.

"Don't be a savage," he told her. "Make believe it was a human being."

Victoria Guzmán needed almost twenty years to understand that a man accustomed to killing defenseless animals could suddenly express such horror. "Good heavens," she explained with surprise. "All that was such a revelation." Nevertheless, she had so much repressed rage the morning of the crime that she went on feeding the dogs with the insides of the other rabbits, just to embitter Santiago Nasar's breakfast. That's what they were up to when the whole town awoke with the earth-shaking bellow of the bishop's steamboat.

The house was a former warehouse, with two stories, walls of rough planks, and a peaked tin roof where the buzzards kept watch over the garbage on the docks. It had been built in the days when the river was so usable that many seagoing barges and even a few tall ships made their way up there through the marshes of the estuary. By the time Ibrahim Nasar arrived with the last Arabs at the end of the civil wars, seagoing ships no longer came there because of shifts in the river, and the warehouse was in disuse. Ibrahim Nasar bought it at a cheap price in order to set up an import store that he never did establish, and only when he was going to be married did he convert it into a house to live in. On the ground floor he opened up a parlor that served for everything, and in back he built a stable for four animals, the servants' quarters, and a country kitchen with windows opening onto the dock, through which the stench of the water came in at all hours. The only thing he left intact in the parlor was the spiral staircase rescued from some shipwreck. On the upper floor, where the customs office had been before, he built two large bedrooms and five cubbyholes for the many children he intended having, and he constructed a wooden balcony that overlooked the almond trees on the square, where Plácida Linero would sit on March afternoons to console herself for her solitude. In the front he kept the main door and built two full-length windows with lathe-turned bars. He also kept the rear door, except a bit taller so that a horse could enter through it, and he kept a part of the old pier in use. That was always the door most used, not only because it was the natural entry to the mangers and the kitchen, but because it opened onto the street that led to the new docks without going through the square. The front door, except for festive occasions, remained closed and barred. Nevertheless, it was there, and not at the rear door, that the men who were going to kill him waited for Santiago Nasar, and it was through there that he went out to receive the bishop, despite the fact that he would have to walk completely around the house in order to reach the docks.

No one could understand such fatal coincidences. The investigating judge who came from Riohacha must have sensed them without daring to admit it, for his impulse to give them a rational explanation was obvious in his report. The door to the square was cited several times with a dime-novel title: "The Fatal Door." In reality, the only valid explanation seemed to be that of Plácida Linero, who answered the question with her mother wisdom: "My son never went out the back door when he was dressed up." It seemed to be such an easy truth that the investigator wrote it down as a marginal note, but he didn't include it in the report.

Victoria Guzmán, for her part, had been categorical with her answer that neither she nor her daughter knew that the men were waiting for Santiago Nasar to kill him. But in the course of her years she admitted that both knew it when he came into the kitchen to have his coffee. They had been told it by a woman who had passed by after five o'clock to beg a bit of milk, and who in addition had revealed the motives and the place where they were waiting. "I didn't warn him because I thought it was drunkards' talk," she told me. Nevertheless, Divina Flor confessed to me on a later visit, after her mother had died, that the latter hadn't said anything to Santiago Nasar because in the depths of her heart she wanted them to kill him. She, on the other hand, didn't warn him because she was nothing but a frightened child at the time, incapable of a decision of her own, and she'd been all the more frightened when he grabbed her by the wrist with a hand that felt frozen and stony, like the hand of a dead man.

Santiago Nasar went through the shadowy house with long strides, pursued by roars of jubilation from the bishop's boat. Divina Flor went ahead of him to open the door, trying not to have him get ahead of her among the cages of sleeping birds in the dining room, among the wicker furniture and the pots of ferns hanging down in the living room, but when she took the bar down, she couldn't avoid the butcher hawk hand again. "He grabbed my whole pussy," Divina Flor told me. "It was what he always did when he caught me alone in some corner of the house, but that day I didn't feel the usual surprise but an awful urge to cry." She drew away to let him go out, and through the half-open door she saw the almond trees on the square, snowy in the light of dawn, but she didn't have the courage to look at anything else. "Then the boat stopped tooting and the cocks began to crow," she told me. "It was such a great uproar that I couldn't believe there were so many roosters in town, and I thought they were coming on the bishop's boat." The only thing she could do for the man who had never been hers was leave the door unbarred, against Plácida Linero's orders, so that he could get back in, in case of emergency. Someone who was never identified had shoved an envelope under the door with a piece of paper warning Santiago Nasar that they were waiting for him to kill him, and, in addition, the note revealed the place, the motive, and other quite precise details of the plot. The message was on the floor when Santiago Nasar left home, but he didn't see it, nor did Divina Flor or anyone else until long after the crime had been consummated.

It had struck six and the street lights were still on. In the branches of the almond trees and on some balconies the colored wedding decorations were still hanging and one might have thought they'd just been hung in honor of the bishop. But the square, covered with paving stones up to the front steps of the church, where the bandstand was, looked like a trash heap, with empty bottles and all manner of debris from the public festivities. When Santiago Nasar left his house, several people were running toward the docks, hastened along by the bellowing of the boat.

The only place open on the square was a milk shop on one side of the church, where the two men were who were waiting for Santiago Nasar in order to kill him. Clotilde Armenta, the proprietress of the establishment, was the first to see him in the glow of dawn, and she had the impression that he was dressed in aluminum. "He already looked like a ghost," she told me. The men who were going to kill him had slept on the benches, clutching the knives wrapped in newspapers to their chests, and Clotilde Armenta held her breath so as not to awaken them.

They were twins: Pedro and Pablo Vicario. They were twenty-four years old, and they looked so much alike that it was difficult to tell them apart. "They were hard-looking, but of a good sort," the report said. I, who had known them since grammar school, would have written the same thing. That morning they were still wearing their dark wedding suits, too heavy and formal for the Caribbean, and they looked devastated by so many hours of bad living, but they'd done their duty and shaved. Although they hadn't stopped drinking since the eve of the wedding, they weren't drunk at the end of three days, but they looked, rather, like insomniac sleepwalkers. They'd fallen asleep with the first breezes of dawn, after almost three hours of waiting in Clotilde Armenta's store, and it was the first sleep they had had since Friday. They had barely awakened with the first bellow of the boat, but instinct awoke them completely when Santiago Nasar came out of his house. Then they both grabbed the rolled-up newspapers and Pedro Vicario started to get up.

"For the love of God," murmured Clotilde Armenta. "Leave him for later, if only out of respect for his grace the bishop."

"It was a breath of the Holy Spirit," she often repeated. Indeed, it had been a providential happening, but of momentary value only. When they heard her, the Vicario twins reflected, and the one who had stood up sat down again. Both followed Santiago Nasar with their eyes as he began to cross the square. "They looked at him more with pity," Clotilde Armenta said. At that moment the girls from the nuns' school crossed the square, trotting in disorder inside their orphans' uniforms.

Plácida Linero was right: the bishop didn't get off his boat. There were a lot of people at the dock in addition to the authorities and the schoolchildren, and everywhere one could see the crates of well-fattened roosters they were bearing as a gift for the bishop, because cockscomb soup was his favorite dish. At the pier there was so much firewood piled up that it would have taken at least two hours to load. But the boat didn't stop. It appeared at the bend in the river, snorting like a dragon, and then the band of musicians started to play the bishop's anthem, and the cocks began to crow in their baskets and aroused all the other roosters in town.

In those days the legendary paddle-wheelers that burned wood were on the point of disappearing, and the few that remained in service no longer had player pianos or bridal staterooms and were barely able to navigate against the current. But this one was new, and it had two smokestacks instead of one, with the flag painted on them like armbands, and the wheel made of planks at the stern gave it the drive of a seagoing ship. On the upper deck, beside the captain's cabin, was the bishop in his white cassock and with his retinue of Spaniards. "It was Christmas weather," my sister Margot said. What happened, according to her, was that the boat whistle let off a shower of compressed steam as it passed by the docks, and it soaked those who were closest to the edge. It was a fleeting illusion: the bishop began to make the sign of the cross in the air opposite the crowd on the pier, and he kept on doing it mechanically afterwards, without malice or inspiration, until the boat was lost from view and all that remained was the uproar of the roosters.

Santiago Nasar had reason to feel cheated. He had contributed several loads of wood to the public solicitudes of Father Carmen Amador, and in addition, he himself had chosen the capons with the most appetizing combs. But it was a passing annoyance. My sister Margot, who was with him on the pier, found him in a good mood and with an urge to go on with the festivities in spite of the fact that the aspirins had given him no relief. "He didn't seem to be chilly and was only thinking about what the wedding must have cost," she told me. Cristo Bedoya, who was with them, revealed figures that added to his surprise. He'd been carousing with Santiago Nasar and me until a little before four; he hadn't gone to sleep at his parents', but stayed chatting at his grandparents' house. There he obtained the bunch of figures that he needed to calculate what the party had cost. He recounted that they had sacrificed forty turkeys and eleven hogs for the guests, and four calves which the bridegroom had set up to be roasted for the people on the public square. He recounted that 205 cases of contraband alcohol has been consumed and almost two thousand bottles of cane liquor, which had been distributed among the crowd. There wasn't a single person, rich or poor, who hadn't participated in some way in the wildest party the town had ever seen. Santiago Nasar was dreaming aloud.

"That's what my wedding's going to be like," he said. "Life will be too short for people to tell about it."

My sister felt the angel pass by. She thought once more about the good fortune of Flora Miguel, who had so many things in life and was going to have Santiago Nasar as well on Christmas of that year. "I suddenly realized that there couldn't have been a better catch than him," she told me. "Just imagine: handsome, a man of his word, and with a fortune of his own at the age of twenty-one." She used to invite him to have breakfast at our house when there were manioc fritters, and my mother was making some that morning. Santiago Nasar accepted with enthusiasm.

"I'll change my clothes and catch up with you," he said, and he realized that he'd left his watch behind on the night table. "What time is it?"

It was six twenty-five. Santiago Nasar took Cristo Bedoya by the arm and led him toward the square.

"I'll be at your house inside of fifteen minutes," he told my sister.

She insisted that they go together right away because breakfast was already made. "It was a strange insistence," Cristo Bedoya told me. "So much so that sometimes I've thought that Margot already knew that they were going to kill him and wanted to hide him in your house." Santiago Nasar persuaded her to go on ahead while he put on his riding clothes, because he had to be at The Divine Face early in order to geld some calves. He took leave of her with the same wave with which he'd said good-bye to his mother and went off toward the square on the arm of Cristo Bedoya. It was the last time she saw him.

Many of those who were on the docks knew that they were going to kill Santiago Nasar. Don Lázaro Aponte, a colonel from the academy making use of his good retirement, and town mayor for eleven years, waved to him with his fingers. "I had my own very real reasons for believing he wasn't in any danger anymore," he told me. Father Carmen Amador wasn't worried either. "When I saw him safe and sound I thought it had all been a fib," he told me. No one even wondered whether Santiago Nasar had been warned, because it seemed impossible to all that he hadn't.

In reality, my sister Margot was one of the few people who still didn't know that they were going to kill him. "If I'd known, I would have taken him home with me even if I had to hog-tie him," she declared to the investigator. It was strange that she hadn't known, but it was even stranger that my mother didn't know either, because she knew about everything before anyone else in the house, in spite of the fact that she hadn't gone out into the street in years, not even to attend mass. I had become aware of that quality of hers ever since I began to get up early for school. I would find her the way she was in those days, pale and stealthy, sweeping the courtyard with a homemade broom in the ashen glow of dawn, and between sips of coffee she would proceed to tell me what had happened in the world while we'd been asleep. She seemed to have secret threads of communication with the other people in town, especially those her age, and sometimes she would surprise us with news so ahead of its time that she could only have known it through powers of divination. That morning, however, she didn't feel the throb of the tragedy that had been gestating since three o'clock. She'd finished sweeping the courtyard, and when my sister Margot went out to meet the bishop she found her grinding manioc for the fritters. "Cocks could be heard," my mother is accustomed to saying, remembering that day. She never associated the distant uproar with the arrival of the bishop, however, but with the last leftovers from the wedding.

Our house was a good distance from the main square, in a mango grove on the river. My sister Margot had gone to the docks by walking along the shore, and the people were too excited with the bishop's visit to worry about any other news. They'd placed the sick people in the archways to receive God's medicine, and women came running out of their yards with turkeys and suckling pigs and all manner of things to eat, and from the opposite shore came canoes bedecked with flowers. But after the bishop passed without setting foot on land, the other repressed news assumed its scandalous dimensions. Then it was that my sister Margot learned about it in a thorough and brutal way: Angela Vicario, the beautiful girl who'd gotten married the day before, had been returned to the house of her parents, because her husband had discovered that she wasn't a virgin. "I felt that I was the one who was going to die," my sister said. "But no matter how much they tossed the story back and forth, no one could explain to me how poor Santiago Nasar ended up being involved in such a mix-up." The only thing they knew for sure was that Angela Vicario's brothers were waiting for him to kill him.

My sister returned home gnawing at herself inside to keep from crying. She found my mother in the dining room, wearing a Sunday dress with blue flowers that she had put on in case the bishop came by to pay us a call, and she was singing the fado about invisible love as she set the table. My sister noted that there was one more place than usual.

"It's for Santiago Nasar," my mother said. "They told me you'd invited him for breakfast."

"Take it away," my sister said.

Then she told her. "But it was as if she already knew," she said to me. "It was the same as always: you begin telling her something and before the story is half over she already knows how it came out." That bad news represented a knotty problem for my mother. Santiago Nasar had been named for her and she was his godmother when he was christened, but she was also a blood relative of Pura Vicario, the mother of the returned bride. Nevertheless, no sooner had she heard the news than she put on her high-heeled shoes and the church shawl she only wore for visits of condolence. My father, who had heard everything from his bed, appeared in the dining room in his pajamas and asked in alarm where she was going.

"To warn my dear friend Plácida," she answered. "It isn't right that everybody should know that they're going to kill her son and she the only one who doesn't."

"We've got the same ties to the Vicarios that we do with her," my father said.

"You always have to take the side of the dead," she said.

My younger brothers began to come out of the other bedrooms. The smallest, touched by the breath of tragedy, began to weep. My mother paid no attention to them; for once in her life she didn't even pay any attention to her husband.

"Wait a minute and I'll get dressed," he told her.

She was already in the street. My brother Jaime, who wasn't more than seven at the time, was the only one who was dressed for school.

"You go with her," my father ordered.

Jaime ran after her without knowing what was happening or where they were going, and grabbed her hand. "She was going along talking to herself," Jaime told me. "Lowlifes," she was saying under her breath, "shitty animals that can't do anything that isn't something awful." She didn't even realize that she was holding the child by the hand. "They must have thought I'd gone crazy," she told me. "The only thing I can remember is that in the distance you could hear the noise of a lot of people, as if the wedding party had started up again, and everybody was running toward the square." She quickened her step, with the determination she was capable of when there was a life at stake, until somebody who was running in the opposite direction took pity on her madness.

"Don't bother yourself, Luisa Santiaga," he shouted as he went by. "They've already killed him."

2

BAYARDO SAN ROMÁN, THE MAN WHO HAD GIVEN BACK HIS BRIDE, had turned up for the first time in August of the year before: six months before the wedding. He arrived on the weekly boat with some saddlebags decorated with silver that matched the buckle of his belt and the rings on his boots. He was around thirty years old, but they were well-concealed, because he had the waist of a novice bullfighter, golden eyes, and a skin slowly roasted by saltpeter. He arrived wearing a short jacket and very tight trousers, both of natural calfskin, and kid gloves of the same color. Magdalena Oliver had been with him on the boat and couldn't take her eyes off him during the whole trip. "He looked like a fairy," she told me. "And it was a pity, because I could have buttered him and eaten him alive." She wasn't the only one who thought so, nor was she the last to realize that Bayardo San Román was not a man to be known at first sight.

My mother wrote to me at school toward the end of August and said in a casual postscript: "A very strange man has come." In the following letter she told me: "The strange man is called Bayardo San Román, and everybody says he's enchanting, but I haven't seen him." Nobody knew what he'd come for. Someone who couldn't resist the temptation of ask-

184

ing him, a little before the wedding, received the answer: "I've been going from town to town looking for someone to marry." It might have been true, but he would have answered anything else in the same way, because he had a way of speaking that served to conceal rather than to reveal.

The night he arrived he gave them to understand at the movies that he was a track engineer, and spoke of the urgency for building a railroad into the interior so that we could keep ahead of the river's fickle ways. On the following day he had to send a telegram and he transmitted it on the key himself, and in addition, he taught the telegrapher a formula of his so that he could keep on using the worn-out batteries. With the same assurance he talked about frontier illnesses with a military doctor who had come through during those months of conscription. He liked noisy and long-lasting festivities, but he was a good drinker, a mediator of fights, and an enemy of cardsharps. One Sunday after mass he challenged the most skillful swimmers, who were many, and left the best behind by twenty strokes in crossing the river and back. My mother told me about it in a letter, and at the end she made a comment that was very much like her: "It also seems that he's swimming in gold." That was in reply to the premature legend that Bayardo San Román not only was capable of doing everything, and doing it quite well, but also had access to endless resources.

My mother gave him the final blessing in a letter in October: "People like him a lot," she told me, "because he's honest and has a good heart, and last Sunday he received communion on his knees and helped with the mass in Latin." In those days it wasn't permitted to receive communion standing and everything was in Latin, but my mother is accustomed to noting that kind of superfluous detail when she wants to get to the heart of the matter. Nevertheless, after that consecrated verdict she wrote me two letters in which she didn't say anything about Bayardo San Román, not even when it was known very well that he wanted to marry Angela Vicario. Only a long time after the unfortunate wedding did she confess to me that she actually knew him when it was already too late to correct the October letter, and that his golden eyes had caused the shudder of a fear in her.

"He reminded me of the devil," she told me, "but you yourself had told me that things like that shouldn't be put into writing."

I met him a short while after she did, when I came home for Christmas vacation, and I found him just as strange as they had said. He seemed attractive, certainly, but far from Magdalena Oliver's idyllic vision. He seemed more serious to me than his antics would have led one to believe, and with a hidden tension that was barely concealed by his excessive good manners. But above all, he seemed to me like a very sad man. At that time he had already formalized his contract of love with Angela Vicario.

It had never been too well-established how they had met. The landlady of the bachelors' boardinghouse where Bayardo San Román lived told of how he'd been napping in a rocking chair in the parlor toward the end of September, when Angela Vicario and her mother crossed the square carrying two baskets of artificial flowers. Bayardo San Román half-awoke, saw the two women dressed in the unforgiving black worn by the only living creatures in the morass of two o'clock in the afternoon, and asked who the young one was. The landlady answered him that she was the youngest daughter of the woman with her and that her name was Angela Vicario. Bayardo San Román followed them with his look to the other side of the square.

"She's well-named," he said.

Then he rested his head on the back of the rocker and closed his eyes again.

"When I wake up," he said, "remind me that I'm going to marry her."

Angela Vicario told me that the landlady of the boarding-house had spoken to her about that occurrence before Bayardo San Román began courting her. "I was quite startled," she told me. Three people who had been in the boarding-house confirmed that it had taken place, but four others weren't sure. On the other hand, all the versions agreed that Angela Vicario and Bayardo San Román had seen each other for the first time on the national holiday in October during a charity bazaar at which she was in charge of singing out the raffle numbers. Bayardo San Román came to the bazaar and went straight to the booth run by the languid raffler, who was in mourning, and he asked her the price of the music box inlaid with mother-of-pearl that must have been the major attraction of the fair. She answered him that it was not for sale but was to be raffled off.

"So much the better," he said. "That makes it easier and cheaper besides."

She confessed to me that he'd managed to impress her, but for reasons opposite those of love. "I detested conceited men, and I'd never seen one so stuck-up," she told me, recalling that day. "Besides, I thought he was a Jew." Her annoyance was greater when she sang out the raffle number for the music box, to the anxiety of all, and indeed, it had been won by Bayardo San Román. She couldn't imagine that he, just to impress her, had bought all the tickets in the raffle.

That night, when she returned home, Angela Vicario found the music box there, gift-wrapped and tied with an organdy bow. "I never did find out how he knew that it was my birthday," she told me. It was hard for her to convince her parents that she hadn't given Bayardo San Román any reason to send her a gift like that, and even worse, in such a visible way that it hadn't gone unnoticed by anyone. So her older brothers, Pedro and Pablo, took the music box to the hotel to give back to its owner, and they did it with such a rush that there was no one to witness them come and then not leave. Since the only thing the family hadn't counted upon was Bayardo San Román's irresistible charm, the twins didn't reappear until dawn of the next day, foggy with drink, bearing once more the music box, and bringing along, besides, Bayardo San Román to continue the revels at home.

Angela Vicario was the youngest daughter of a family of scant resources. Her father, Poncio Vicario, was a poor man's goldsmith, and he'd lost his sight from doing so much fine work in gold in order to maintain the honor of the house. Purísima del Carmen, her mother, had been a schoolteacher until she married for ever. Her meek and somewhat afflicted look hid the strength of her character quite well. "She looked like a nun," my wife Mercedes recalls. She devoted herself with such spirit of sacrifice to the care of her husband and the rearing of her children that at times one forgot she still existed. The two oldest daughters had married very late. In addition to the twins, there was a middle daughter who had died of nighttime fevers, and two years later they were still observing a mourning that was relaxed inside the house but rigorous on the street. The brothers were brought up to be men. The girls had been reared to get married. They knew how to do screen embroidery, sew by machine, weave bone lace, wash and iron, make artificial flowers and fancy candy, and write engagement announcements. Unlike other girls of the time, who had neglected the cult of death, the four were past mistresses in the ancient science of sitting up with the ill, comforting the dying, and enshrouding the dead. The only thing that my mother reproached them for was the custom of combing their hair before sleeping. "Girls," she would tell them, "don't comb your hair at night; you'll slow down seafarers." Except for that, she thought there were no better-reared daughters. "They're perfect," she was frequently heard to say. "Any man will be happy with them because they've been raised to suffer." Yet it was difficult for the men who married the two eldest to break the circle, because they always went together everywhere, and they organized dances for women only and were predisposed to find hidden intentions in the designs of men.

Angela Vicario was the prettiest of the four, and my mother said that she had been born like the great queens of history, with the umbilical cord wrapped around her neck. But she had a helpless air and a poverty of spirit that augured an uncertain future for her. I would see her again year after year during my Christmas vacations, and every time she seemed more destitute in the window of her house, where she would sit in the afternoon making cloth flowers and singing songs about single women with her neighbors. "She's all set to be hooked," Santiago Nasar would tell me, "your cousin the ninny is." Suddenly, a little before the mourning for her sister, I passed her on the street for the first time dressed as a grown woman and with her hair curled, and I could scarcely believe it was the same person. But it was a momentary vision: her penury of spirit had been aggravated with the years. So much so that when it was discovered that Bayardo San Román wanted to marry her, many people thought it was an outsider's scheming.

The family took it not only seriously but with great excitement. Except Pura Vicario, who laid down the condition that Bayardo San Román should identify himself properly. Up till then nobody knew who he was. His past didn't go beyond that afternoon when he disembarked in his actor's getup, and he was so reserved about his origins that even the most demented invention could have been true. It came to be said that he had wiped out villages and sown terror in Casanare as troop commander, that he had escaped from Devil's Island, that he'd been seen in Pernambuco trying to make a living with a pair of trained bears, and that he'd salvaged the remains of a Spanish galleon loaded with gold in the Windward Passage. Bayardo San Román put an end to all those conjectures by a simple recourse: he produced his entire family.

There were four of them: the father, the mother, and two provocative sisters. They arrived in a Model T Ford with official plates, whose duck-quack horn aroused the streets at eleven o'clock in the morning. His mother, Alberta Simonds, a big mulatto woman from Curaçao, who spoke Spanish with a mixture of Papiamento, in her youth had been proclaimed the most beautiful of the two hundred most beautiful women in the Antilles. The sisters, newly come into bloom, were like two restless fillies. But the main attraction was the father: General Petronio San Román, hero of the civil wars of the past century, and one of the major glories of the Conservative regime for having put Colonel Aureliano Buendía to flight in the disaster of Tucurinca. My mother was the only one who wouldn't go to greet him when she found out who he was. "It seems all right to me that they should get married," she told me. "But that's one thing and it's something altogether different to shake hands with the man who gave the orders for Gerineldo Márquez to be shot in the back." As soon as he appeared in the window of the automobile waving his white hat, everybody recognized him because of the fame of his pictures. He was wearing a wheat-colored linen suit, high-laced cordovan shoes, and gold-rimmed glasses held by a clasp on the bridge of his nose and connected by a chain to a buttonhole in his vest. He wore the Medal of Valor on his lapel and carried a cane with the national shield carved on the pommel. He was the first to get out of the automobile, completely covered with the burning dust of our bad roads, and all he had to do was appear on the running board for everyone to realize that Bayardo San Román was going to marry whomever he chose.

It was Angela Vicario who didn't want to marry him. "He seemed too much of a man for me," she told me. Besides, Bayardo San Román hadn't even tried to court her, but had bewitched the family with his charm. Angela Vicario never forgot the horror of the night on which her parents and her older sisters with their husbands, gathered together in the parlor, imposed on her the obligation to marry a man whom she had barely seen. The twins stayed out of it. "It looked to us like woman problems," Pablo Vicario told me. The parents' decisive argument was that a family dignified by modest means had no right to disdain that prize of destiny. Angela Vicario only dared hint at the inconvenience of a lack of love, but her mother demolished it with a single phrase:

"Love can be learned too."

Unlike the engagements of the time, which were long and supervised, theirs lasted only four months due to Bayardo San Román's urgings. It wasn't any shorter because Pura Vicario demanded that they wait until the family mourning was over. But the time passed without anxiety because of the irresistible way in which Bayardo San Román arranged things. "One night he asked me what house I liked best," Angela Vicario told me. "And I answered, without knowing why, that the prettiest house in town was the farmhouse belonging to the widower Xius." I would have said the same. It was on a windswept hill, and from the terrace you could see the limitless paradise of the marshes covered with purple anemones, and on clear summer days you could make out the neat horizon of the Caribbean and the tourist ships from Cartagena de Indias. That very night Bayardo San Román went to the social club and sat down at the widower Xius's table to play a game of dominoes.

"Widower," he told him, "I'll buy your house."

"It's not for sale," the widower said.

"I'll buy it along with everything inside."

The widower Xius explained to him with the good breeding of olden days that the objects in the house had been bought by his wife over a whole lifetime of sacrifice and that for him they were still a part of her. "He was speaking with his heart in his hand," I was told by Dr. Dionisio Iguarán, who was playing with them. "I was sure he would have died before he'd sell a house where he'd been happy for over thirty years." Bayardo San Román also understood his reasons.

"Agreed," he said. "So sell me the house empty."

But the widower defended himself until the end of the game. Three nights later, better prepared, Bayardo San Román returned to the domino table.

"Widower," he began again, "what's the price of the house?"

"It hasn't got a price."

"Name any one you want."

"I'm sorry, Bayardo," the widower said, "but you young people don't understand the motives of the heart."

Bayardo San Román didn't pause to think.

"Let's say five thousand pesos," he said.

"You don't beat around the bush," the widower answered him, his dignity aroused. "The house isn't worth all that."

"Ten thousand," said Bayardo San Román. "Right now and with one bill on top of another."

The widower looked at him, his eyes full of tears. "He was weaping with rage," I was told by Dr. Dionisio Iguarán, who, in addition to being a physician, was a man of letters. "Just imagine: an amount like that within reach and having to say no from a simple weakness of the spirit." The widower Xius's voice didn't come out, but without hesitation he said no with his head.

"Then do me one last favor," said Bayardo San Román. "Wait for me here for five minutes."

Five minutes later, indeed, he returned to the social club with his silver-trimmed saddlebags, and on the table he laid ten bundles of thousand-peso notes with the printed bands of the State Bank still on them. The widower Xius died two months later. "He died because of that," Dr. Dionisio Iguarán said. "He was healthier than the rest of us, but when you listened with the stethoscope you could hear the tears bubbling inside his heart." But not only had he sold the house with everything in it; he asked Bayardo San Román to pay him little by little because he didn't even have an old trunk where he could keep so much consolation money.

No one would have thought, nor did anyone say, that Angela Vicario wasn't a virgin. She hadn't known any previous fiancé and she'd grown up along with her sisters under the rigor of a mother of iron. Even when it was less than two months before she would be married, Pura Vicario wouldn't let her go out alone with Bayardo San Román to see the house where they were going to live, but she and the blind father accompanied her to watch over her honor. "The only thing I

prayed to God for was to give me the courage to kill myself,"
Angela Vicario told me. "But he didn't give it to me." She was
so distressed that she had resolved to tell her mother the truth
so as to free herself from that martyrdom, when her only two
confidantes, who worked with her making cloth flowers, dis-
suaded her from her good intentions. "I obeyed them blindly,"
she told me, "because they made me believe that they were
experts in men's tricks." They assured her that almost all women
lost their virginity in childhood accidents. They insisted that
even the most difficult of husbands resigned themselves to
anything as long as nobody knew about it. They convinced
her, finally, that most men came to their wedding night so
frightened that they were incapable of doing anything without
the woman's help, and at the moment of truth they couldn't
answer for their own acts. "The only thing they believe is what
they see on the sheet," they told her. And they taught her old
wives' tricks to feign her lost possession, so that on her first
morning as a newlywed she could display open under the sun
in the courtyard of her house the linen sheet with the stain of
honor.

She got married with that illusion. Bayardo San Román,
for his part, must have got married with the illusion of buying
happiness with the huge weight of his power and fortune, for
the more the plans for the festival grew, the more delirious
ideas occurred to him to make it even larger. He tried to hold
off the wedding for a day when the bishop's visit was announced so that he could marry them, but Angela Vicario was
against it. "Actually," she told me, "the fact is I didn't want to
be blessed by a man who cut off only the combs for soup and
threw the rest of the rooster into the garbage." Yet, even without the bishop's blessing, the festival took on a force of its own
so difficult to control that it got out of the hands of Bayardo
San Román and ended up being a public event.

General Petronio San Román and his family arrived that
time on the National Congress's ceremonial boat, which remained moored to the dock until the end of the festivities, and

with them came many illustrious people who, even so, passed unnoticed in the tumult of new faces. So many gifts were brought that it was necessary to restore the forgotten site of the first electrical power plant in order to display the most valuable among them, and the rest were immediately taken to the former home of the widower Xius, which had already been prepared to receive the newlyweds. The groom received a convertible with his name engraved in Gothic letters under the manufacturer's seal. The bride was given a chest with table settings in pure gold for twenty-four guests. They also brought in a ballet company and two waltz orchestras that played out of tune with the local bands and all the groups of brass and accordion players who came, animated by the uproar of the revelry.

The Vicario family lived in a modest house with brick walls and a palm roof, topped by two attics where in January swallows got in to breed. In front it had a terrace almost completely covered with flowerpots, and a large yard with hens running loose and with fruit trees. In the rear of the yard the twins had a pigsty, with its sacrificial stone and its disemboweling table, which had been a good source of domestic income ever since Poncio Vicario had lost his sight. Pedro Vicario had started the business, but when he went into military service, his twin brother also learned the slaughterer's trade.

The inside of the house barely had enough room in which to live, and so the older sisters tried to borrow a house when they realized the size of the festival. "Just imagine," Angela Vicario told me, "they'd thought about Plácida Linero's house, but luckily my parents stubbornly held to the old song that our daughters would be married in our pigpen or they wouldn't be married at all." So they painted the house its original yellow color, fixed up the doors, repaired the floors, and left it as worthy as was possible for such a clamorous wedding. The twins took the pigs off elsewhere and sanitized the pigsty with quicklime, but even so it was obvious that there wasn't enough room. Finally, through the efforts of Bayardo San Román, they knocked down the fences in the yard, borrowed the neighboring house for dancing, and set up carpenters' benches to sit and eat on under the leaves of the tamarind trees.

The only unforeseen surprise was caused by the groom on the morning of the wedding, for he was two hours late in coming for Angela Vicario and she had refused to get dressed as a bride until she saw him in the house. "Just imagine," she told me. "I would have been happy even if he hadn't come, but never if he abandoned me dressed up." Her caution seemed natural, because there was no public misfortune more shameful than for a woman to be jilted in her bridal gown. On the other hand, the fact that Angela Vicario dared put on the veil and the orange blossoms without being a virgin would be interpreted afterwards as a profanation of the symbols of purity. My mother was the only one who appreciated as an act of courage the fact that she had played out her marked cards to the final consequences. "In those days," she explained to me, "God understood such things." But no one yet knew what cards Bayardo San Román was playing. From the moment he finally appeared in frock coat and top hat until he fled the dance with the creature of his torment, he was the perfect image of a happy bridegroom.

Nor was it known what cards Santiago Nasar was playing. I was with him all the time, in the church and at the festival, along with Cristo Bedoya and my brother Luis Enrique, and none of us caught a glimpse of any change in his manner. I've had to repeat this many times, because the four of us had grown up together in school and later on in the same gang at vacation time, and nobody could have believed that one of us could have a secret without its being shared, particularly such a big secret.

Santiago Nasar was a man for parties, and he had his best time on the eve of his death calculating the expense of the wedding. He estimated that they'd set up floral decorations in the church equal in cost to those for fourteen first-class funerals. That precision would haunt me for many years, because Santiago Nasar had often told me that the smell of closed-in flowers had an immediate relation to death for him, and that day he repeated it to me as we went into the church. "I don't want any flowers at my funeral," he told me, hardly thinking that I would see to it that there weren't any the next day. En route from the church to the Vicarios' house he drew up the figures for the colored wreaths that decorated the streets, calculated the cost of the music and the rockets, and even the hail of raw rice with which they received us at the party. In the drowsiness of noon, the newlyweds made their rounds in the yard. Bayardo San Román had become our very good friend, a friend of a few drinks, as they said in those days, and he seemed very much at ease at our table. Angela Vicario, without her veil and bridal bouquet and in her sweat-stained satin dress, had suddenly taken on the face of a married woman. Santiago Nasar calculated, and told Bayardo San Román, that up to then the wedding was costing some nine thousand pesos. It was obvious that Angela took this as an impertinence. "My mother taught me never to talk about money in front of other people," she told me. Bayardo San Román, on the other hand, took it very graciously and even with a certain pride.

"Almost," he said, "but we're only beginning. When it's all over it will be twice that, more or less."

Santiago Nasar proposed proving it down to the last penny, and his life lasted just long enough. In fact, with the final figures that Cristo Bedoya gave him the next day on the docks, forty-five minutes before he died, he ascertained that Bayardo San Román's prediction had been exact.

I had a very confused memory of the festival before I decided to rescue it piece by piece from the memory of others. For years they went on talking in my house about the fact that my father had gone back to playing his boyhood violin in honor of the newlyweds, that my sister the nun had danced a merengue in her doorkeeper's habit, and that Dr. Dionisio Iguarán, who was my mother's cousin, had arranged for them to take him off on the official boat so he wouldn't be here the next day when the bishop arrived. In the course of the investigations for this chronicle I recovered numerous marginal experiences, among them the free recollections of Bayardo San Román's sisters, whose velvet dresses with great butterfly wings pinned to their backs with gold brooches drew more attention than the plumed hat and row of war medals worn by their father. Many knew that in the confusion of the bash I had proposed marriage to Mercedes Barcha as soon as she finished primary school, just as she herself would remind me fourteen years later when we got married. Really, the most intense image that I have always held of that unwelcome Sunday was that of old Poncio Vicario sitting alone on a stool in the center of the yard. They had placed him there thinking perhaps that it was the seat of honor, and the guests stumbled over him, confused him with someone else, moved him so he wouldn't be in the way, and he nodded his snow-white head in all directions with the erratic expression of someone too recently blind, answering questions that weren't directed at him and responding to fleeting waves of the hand that no one was making to him, happy in his circle of oblivion, his shirt cardboard-stiff with starch and holding the lignum vitae cane they had bought him for the party.

The formal activities ended at six in the afternoon, when the guests of honor took their leave. The boat departed with all its lights burning, and with a wake of waltzes from the player piano, and for an instant we were cast adrift over an abyss of uncertainty, until we recognized each other again and plunged into the confusion of the bash. The newlyweds appeared a short time later in the open car, making their way with difficulty through the tumult. Bayardo San Román shot off rockets, drank cane liquor from the bottles the crowd held out to him, and got out of the car with Angela Vicario to join the whirl of the *cumbiamba* dance. Finally, he ordered us to keep on dancing at his expense for as long as our lives would reach, and he carried his terrified wife off to his dream house, where the widower Xius had been happy.

The public spree broke up into fragments at around mid-night, and all that remained was Clotilde Armenta's establish-ment on one side of the square. Santiago Nasar and I, with my brother Luis Enrique and Cristo Bedoya, went to María Alejandrina Cervantes's house of mercies. Among so many others, the Vicario brothers were there and they were drink-ing with us and singing with Santiago Nasar five hours before killing him. A few scattered embers from the original party must still have remained, because from all sides waves of mu-sic and distant fights reached us, sadder and sadder, until a short while before the bishop's boat bellowed.

Pura Vicario told my mother that she had gone to bed at eleven o'clock at night after her older daughters had helped her clean up a bit from the devastation of the wedding. Around ten o'clock, when there were still a few drunkards singing in the square, Angela Vicario had sent for a little suitcase of per-sonal things that were in the dresser in her bedroom, and she asked them also to send a suitcase with everyday clothes; the messenger was in a hurry. Pura Vicario had fallen into a deep sleep, when there was knocking on the door. "They were three very slow knocks," she told my mother, "but they had that strange touch of bad news about them." She told her that she'd opened the door without turning on the light so as not to awaken anybody and saw Bayardo San Román in the glow of the street light, his silk shirt unbuttoned and his fancy pants held up by elastic suspenders. "He had that green color of dreams," Pura Vicario told my mother. Angela Vicario was in the shadows, so she saw only her when Bayardo San Román grabbed her by the arm and brought her into the light. Her satin dress was in shreds and she was wrapped in a towel up to the waist. Pura Vicario thought they'd gone off the road in the car and were lying dead at the bottom of the ravine.

"Holy Mother of God," she said in terror. "Answer me if you're still of this world."

Bayardo San Román didn't enter, but softly pushed his wife into the house without speaking a word. Then he kissed

Pura Vicario on the cheek and spoke to her in a very deep, dejected voice, but with great tenderness. "Thank you for everything, Mother," he told her. "You're a saint."

Only Pura Vicario knew what she did during the next two hours, and she went to her grave with her secret. "The only thing I can remember is that she was holding me by the hair with one hand and beating me with the other with such rage that I thought she was going to kill me," Angela Vicario told me. But even that she did with such stealth that her husband and her older daughters, asleep in the other rooms, didn't find out about anything until dawn, when the disaster had already been consummated.

The twins returned home a short time before three, urgently summoned by their mother. They found Angela Vicario lying face down on the dining room couch, her face all bruised, but she'd stopped crying. "I was no longer frightened," she told me. "On the contrary: I felt as if the drowsiness of death had finally been lifted from me, and the only thing I wanted was for it all to be over quickly so I could flop down and go to sleep." Pedro Vicario, the more forceful of the brothers, picked her up by the waist and sat her on the dining room table.

"All right, girl," he said to her, trembling with rage, "tell us who it was."

She only took the time necessary to say the name. She looked for it in the shadows, she found it at first sight among the many, many easily confused names from this world and the other, and she nailed it to the wall with her well-aimed dart, like a butterfly with no will whose sentence has always been written.

"Santiago Nasar," she said.

3

THE LAWYER STOOD BY THE THESIS OF HOMICIDE IN LEGITIMATE
defense of honor, which was upheld by the court in good faith,
and the twins declared at the end of the trial that they would
have done it again a thousand times over for the same reason.
It was they who gave a hint of the direction the defense would
take as soon as they surrendered to their church a few minutes after the crime.

They burst panting into the parish house, closely pursued
by a group of roused-up Arabs, and they laid the knives, with
clean blades, on Father Amador's desk. Both were exhausted
from the barbarous work of death, and their clothes and arms
were soaked and their faces smeared with sweat and still living
blood, but the priest recalled the surrender as an act of great
dignity.

"We killed him openly," Pedro Vicario said, "but we're
innocent."

"Perhaps before God," said Father Amador.

"Before God and before men," Pablo Vicario said. "It was
a matter of honor."

Furthermore, with the reconstruction of the facts, they had
feigned a much more unforgiving bloodthirstiness than really
was true, to such an extreme that it was necessary to use public

funds to repair the main door of Plácida Linero's house, which was all chipped with knife thrusts. In the panopticon of Riohacha, where they spent three years awaiting trial because they couldn't afford bail, the older prisoners remembered them for their good character and sociability, but they never noticed any indication of remorse in them. Still, in reality it seemed that the Vicario brothers had done nothing right with a view to killing Santiago Nasar immediately and without any public spectacle, but had done much more than could be imagined to have someone to stop them from killing him, and they had failed.

According to what they told me years later, they had begun by looking for him at María Alejandrina Cervantes's place, where they had been with him until two o'clock. That fact, like many others, was not reported in the brief. Actually, Santiago Nasar was no longer there at the time the twins said they went looking for him, because we'd left on a round of serenades, but in any case, it wasn't certain that they'd gone. "They never would have left here," María Alejandrina Cervantes told me, and knowing her so well, I never doubted it. On the other hand, they did go to wait for him at Clotilde Armenta's place, where they knew that almost everybody would turn up except Santiago Nasar. "It was the only place open," they declared to the investigator. "Sooner or later he would have to come out," they told me, after they had been absolved. Still, everybody knew that the main door of Plácida Linero's house was always barred on the inside, even during the daytime, and that Santiago Nasar always carried the keys to the back door with him. That was where he went in when he got home, in fact, while the Vicario twins had been waiting for him for more than an hour on the other side, and if he later left by the door on the square when he went to receive the bishop, it was such an unforeseen reason that the investigator who drew up the brief never did understand it.

There had never been a death more foretold. After their sister revealed the name to them, the Vicario twins went to the bin in the pigsty where they kept their sacrificial tools and picked out the two best knives: one for quartering, ten inches long by two and a half inches wide, and the other for trimming, seven inches long by one and a half inches wide. They wrapped them in a rag and went to sharpen them at the meat market, where only a few stalls had begun to open. There weren't very many customers that early, but twenty-two people declared they had heard everything said, and they all coincided in the impression that the only reason the brothers had said it was so that someone would come over to hear them. Faustino Santos, a butcher friend, saw them enter at three-twenty, when he had just opened up his innards table, and he couldn't understand why they were coming on a Monday and so early, and still in their dark wedding suits. He was accustomed to seeing them on Fridays, but a little later, and wearing the leather aprons they put on for slaughtering. "I thought they were so drunk," Faustino Santos told me, "that not only had they forgotten what time it was, but what day it was too." He reminded them that it was Monday.

"Everybody knows that, you dope," Pablo Vicario answered him good-naturedly. "We just came to sharpen our knives."

They sharpened them on the grindstone, and the way they always did: Pedro holding the knives and turning them over on the stone, and Pablo working the crank. At the same time, they talked with the other butchers about the splendor of the wedding. Some of them complained about not having gotten their share of cake, in spite of their being working companions, and they promised them to have some sent over later. Finally, they made the knives sing on the stone, and Pablo laid his beside the lamp so that the steel sparkled.

"We're going to kill Santiago Nasar," he said.

Their reputation as good people was so well-founded that no one paid any attention to them. "We thought it was drunkards' baloney," several butchers declared, just as Victoria Guzmán and so many others did who saw them later. I was to ask the butchers sometime later whether or not the trade of slaughterer didn't reveal a soul predisposed to killing a human being. They protested: "When you sacrifice a steer you don't dare look into its eyes." One of them told me that he couldn't eat the flesh of an animal he had butchered. Another said that he wouldn't be capable of sacrificing a cow if he'd known it before, much less if he'd drunk its milk. I reminded them that the Vicario brothers sacrificed the same hogs they raised, which were so familiar to them that they called them by their names. "That's true," one of them replied, "but remember that they didn't give them people's names but the names of flowers." Faustino Santos was the only one who perceived a glimmer of truth in Pablo Vicario's threat, and he asked him jokingly why they had to kill Santiago Nasar since there were so many other rich people who deserved dying first.

"Santiago Nasar knows why," Pedro Vicario answered him.

Faustino Santos told me that he'd still been doubtful, and that he reported it to a policeman who came by a little later to buy a pound of liver for the mayor's breakfast. The policeman, according to the brief, was named Leandro Pornoy, and he died the following year, gored in the jugular vein by a bull during the national holidays, so I was never able to talk to him. But Clotilde Armenta confirmed for me that he was the first person in her store when the Vicario twins were sitting and waiting there.

Clotilde Armenta had just replaced her husband behind the counter. It was their usual system. The shop sold milk at dawn and provisions during the day and became a bar after six o'clock in the evening. Clotilde Armenta would open at three-thirty in the morning. Her husband, the good Don Rogelio de la Flor, would take charge of the bar until closing time. But that night there had been so many stray customers from the wedding that he went to bed after three o'clock without closing, and Clotilde Armenta was already up earlier than usual because she wanted to finish before the bishop arrived.

The Vicario brothers came in at four-ten. At that time

only things to eat were sold, but Clotilde Armenta sold them a bottle of cane liquor, not only because of the high regard she had for them but also because she was very grateful for the piece of wedding cake they had sent her. They drank down the whole bottle in two long swigs, but they remained stolid. "They were stunned," Clotilde Armenta told me, "and they couldn't have got their blood pressure up even with lamp oil." Then they took off their cloth jackets, hung them carefully on the chair backs, and asked her for another bottle. Their shirts were dirty with dried sweat and a one-day beard gave them a backwoods look. They drank the second bottle more slowly, sitting down, looking insistently toward Plácida Linero's house on the sidewalk across the way, where the windows were dark. The largest one, on the balcony, belonged to Santiago Nasar's bedroom. Pedro Vicario asked Clotilde Armenta if she had seen any light in that window, and she answered him no, but it seemed like a strange thing to be interested in.

"Did something happen to him?" she asked.

"No," Pedro Vicario replied. "Just that we're looking for him to kill him."

It was such a spontaneous answer that she couldn't believe she'd heard right. But she noticed that the twins were carrying two butcher knives wrapped in kitchen rags.

"And might a person know why you want to kill him so early in the morning?" she asked.

"He knows why," Pedro Vicario answered.

Clotilde Armenta examined them seriously: she knew them so well that she could tell them apart, especially ever since Pedro Vicario had come back from the army. "They looked like two children," she told me. And that thought frightened her, because she'd always felt that only children are capable of everything. So she finished getting the jug of milk ready and went to wake her husband to tell him what was going on in the shop. Don Rogelio de la Flor listened to her half-awake.

"Don't be silly," he said to her. "Those two aren't about to kill anybody, much less someone rich."

When Clotilde Armenta returned to the store, the twins were chatting with Officer Leandro Pornoy, who was coming for the mayor's milk. She didn't hear what they were talking about, but she supposed that they had told him something about their plans from the way he looked at the knives when he left.

Colonel Lázaro Aponte had just got up a little before four. He'd finished shaving when Officer Leandro Pornoy revealed the Vicario brothers' intentions to him. He'd settled so many fights between friends the night before that he was in no hurry for another one. He got dressed calmly, tied his bow tie several times until he had it perfect, and around his neck he hung the scapular of the Congregation of Mary, to receive the bishop. While he breakfasted on fried liver smothered with onion rings, his wife told him with great excitement that Bayardo San Román had brought Angela Vicario back home, but he didn't take it dramatically.

"Good Lord!" he mocked. "What will the bishop think!"

Nevertheless, before finishing breakfast he remembered what the orderly had just told him, put the two bits of news together, and discovered immediately that they fit like pieces of a puzzle. Then he went to the square, going along the street to the new dock, where the houses were beginning to liven up for the bishop's arrival. "I can remember with certainty that it was almost five o'clock and it was beginning to rain," Colonel Lázaro Aponte told me. Along the way three people stopped him to inform him in secret that the Vicario brothers were waiting for Santiago Nasar to kill him, but only one person could tell him where.

He found them in Clotilde Armenta's store. "When I saw them I thought they were nothing but a pair of big bluffers," he told me with his personal logic, "because they weren't as drunk as I thought." Nor did he interrogate them concerning their intentions, but took away their knives and sent them off to sleep. He treated them with the same self-assurance with which he had passed off his wife's alarm.

"Just imagine!" he told them. "What will the bishop say if he finds you in that state!"

They left. Clotilde Armenta suffered another disappointment with the mayor's casual attitude, because she thought he should have detained the twins until the truth came out. Colonel Aponte showed her the knives as a final argument.

"Now they haven't got anything to kill anybody with," he said.

"That's not why," said Clotilde Armenta. "It's to spare those poor boys from the horrible duty that's fallen on them."

Because she'd sensed it. She was certain that the Vicario brothers were not as eager to carry out the sentence as to find someone who would do them the favor of stopping them. But Colonel Aponte was at peace with his soul.

"No one is arrested just on suspicion," he said. "Now it's a matter of warning Santiago Nasar, and happy new year."

Clotilde Armenta would always remember that Colonel Aponte's chubby appearance evoked a certain pity in her, but on the other hand I remembered him as a happy man, although a little bit off due to the solitary spiritualist practices he had learned through the mails. His behavior that Monday was the final proof of his silliness. The truth is that he didn't think of Santiago Nasar again until he saw him on the docks, and then he congratulated himself for having made the right decision.

The Vicario brothers had told their plans to more than a dozen people who had gone to buy milk, and these had spread the news everywhere before six o'clock. It seemed impossible to Clotilde Armenta that they didn't know in the house across the way. She didn't think that Santiago Nasar was there, since she hadn't seen the bedroom light go on, and she asked all the people she could to warn him when they saw him. She even sent word to Father Amador through the novice on duty, who came to buy milk for the nuns. After four o'clock, when she saw the lights in the kitchen of Plácida Linero's house, she sent the last urgent message to Victoria Guzmán by the beggar woman who came every day to ask for a little milk in the name of charity. When the bishop's boat bellowed, almost everybody was up to receive him and there were very few of us who didn't know that the Vicario twins were waiting for Santiago Nasar to kill him, and, in addition, the reasons were understood down to the smallest detail.

Clotilde Armenta hadn't finished dispensing her milk when the Vicario brothers returned with two other knives wrapped up in newspapers. One was for quartering, with a strong, rusty blade twelve inches long and three inches wide, which had been put together by Pedro Vicario with the metal from a marquetry saw at a time when German knives were no longer available because of the war. The other one was shorter, but broad and curved. The investigator had made sketches of them in the brief, perhaps because he had trouble describing them, and all he ventured to say was that this one looked like a miniature scimitar. It was with these knives that the crime was committed, and both were rudimentary and had seen a lot of use.

Faustino Santos couldn't understand what had happened. "They came to sharpen their knives a second time," he told me, "and once more they shouted for people to hear that they were going to cut Santiago Nasar's guts out, so I believed they were kidding around, especially since I didn't pay any attention to the knives and thought they were the same ones." This time, however, Clotilde Armenta noticed from the moment she saw them enter that they didn't have the same determination as before.

Actually, they'd had their first disagreement. Not only were they much more different inside than they looked on the outside, but in difficult emergencies they showed opposite characters. We, their friends, had spotted it ever since grammar school. Pablo Vicario was six minutes older than his brother, and he was the more imaginative and resolute until adolescence. Pedro Vicario always seemed more sentimental to me, and by the same token more authoritarian. They presented themselves together for military service at the age of twenty, and Pablo Vicario was excused in order to stay home and take care of the family. Pedro Vicario served for eleven months on police patrol. The army routine, aggravated by the fear of death, had matured his tendency to command and the habit of deciding for his brother. He also came back with a case of sergeant's blennorrhea that resisted the most brutal methods of military medicine as well as the arsenic injections and permanganate purges of Dr. Dionisio Iguarán. Only in jail did they manage to cure it. We, his friends, agreed that Pablo Vicario had suddenly developed the strange dependence of a younger brother when Pedro Vicario returned with a barrackroom soul and with the novel trick of lifting his shirt for anyone who wanted to see a bullet wound with seton on his left side. He even began to develop a kind of fervor over the great man's blennorrhea that his brother wore like a war medal.

Pedro Vicario, according to his own declaration, was the one who made the decision to kill Santiago Nasar, and at first his brother only followed along. But he was also the one who considered his duty fulfilled when the mayor disarmed them, and then it was Pablo Vicario who assumed command. Neither of the two mentioned that disagreement in their separate statements to the investigator, but Pablo Vicario confirmed several times to me that it hadn't been easy for him to convince his brother of their final resolve. Maybe it was really nothing but a wave of panic, but the fact is that Pablo Vicario went into the pigsty alone to get the other two knives, while his brother agonized, drop by drop, trying to urinate under the tamarind trees. "My brother never knew what it was like," Pedro Vicario told me in our only interview. "It was like pissing ground glass." Pablo Vicario found him hugging the tree when he came back with the knives. "He was in a cold sweat from the pain," he said to me, "and he tried to tell me to go on by myself because he was in no condition to kill anybody." He sat down on one of the carpenters' benches they'd set up under the trees for the wedding lunch, and he dropped his

pants down to his knees. "He spent about half an hour changing the gauze he had his prick wrapped in," Pablo Vicario told
me. Actually, he hadn't delayed more than ten minutes, but
this was something so difficult and so puzzling for Pablo Vicario that he interpreted it as some new trick on his brother's
part to waste time until dawn. So he put the knife in his hand
and dragged him off almost by force in search of their sister's
lost honor.

"There's no way out of this," he told him. "It's as if it had
already happened."

They left by way of the pigpen gate with the knives unwrapped, trailed by the uproar of the dogs in the yards. It was
beginning to get light. "It wasn't raining," Pablo Vicario remembered. "Just the opposite," Pedro recalled. "There was a
sea wind and you could still count the stars with your finger."
The news had been so well spread by then that Hortensia Baute
opened her door precisely as they were passing her house,
and she was the first to weep for Santiago Nasar. "I thought
they'd already killed him," she told me, "because I saw the
knives in the light from the street lamp and it looked to me
like they were dripping blood." One of the few houses open
on that misbegotten street was that of Prudencia Cotes, Pablo
Vicario's fiancée. Whenever the twins passed by there at that
time, and especially on Fridays when they were going to the
market, they would drop in to have their first cup of coffee.
They pushed open the door to the courtyard, surrounded by
the dogs, who recognized them in the half light of dawn, and
they greeted Prudencia Cotes's mother in the kitchen. Coffee
wasn't ready yet.

"We'll leave it for later," Pablo Vicario said. "We're in a
hurry now."

"I can imagine, my sons," she said. "Honor doesn't wait."

But in any case, they waited, and this time it was Pedro
Vicario who thought his brother was wasting time on purpose.
While they were drinking their coffee, Prudencia Cotes came
into the kitchen in all her adolescent bloom, carrying a roll of

old newspapers to revive the fire in the stove. "I knew what they were up to," she told me, "and I didn't only agree, I never would have married him if he hadn't done what a man should do." Before leaving the kitchen, Pablo Vicario took two sections of newspaper from her and gave them to his brother to wrap the knives in. Prudencia Cotes stood waiting in the kitchen until she saw them leave by the courtyard door, and she went on waiting for three years without a moment of discouragement until Pablo Vicario got out of jail and became her husband for life.

"Take good care of yourselves," she told them.

So Clotilde Armenta had good reason when it seemed to her that the twins weren't as resolute as before, and she served them a bottle of rotgut rum with the hope of getting them dead drunk. "That day," she told me, "I realized just how alone we women are in the world!" Pedro Vicario asked to borrow her husband's shaving implements, and she brought him the brush, the soap, the hanging mirror, and the safety razor with a new blade, but he shaved with his butcher knife. Clotilde Armenta thought that was the height of machismo. "He looked like a killer in the movies," she told me. But as he explained to me later, and it was true, in the army he'd learned to shave with a straight razor and couldn't do it any other way ever since. His brother, for his part, shaved in a more humble way, with Don Rogelio de la Flor's borrowed safety razor. Finally, they drank the bottle in silence, very slowly, gazing with the boobish look of early risers at the dark window in the house across the way, while fake customers buying milk they didn't need and asking for food items that didn't exist went in and out with the purpose of seeing whether it was true that they were waiting for Santiago Nasar to kill him.

The Vicario brothers would not see that window light up. Santiago Nasar went into the house at four-twenty, but he didn't have to turn on any light to reach his bedroom because the bulb on the stairway stayed lit through the night. He threw himself onto his bed in the darkness and with his clothes on, since he had only an hour in which to sleep, and that was how Victoria Guzmán found him when she came up to wake him so he could receive the bishop. We'd been together at María Alejandrina Cervantes's until after three, when she herself sent the musicians away and turned out the lights in the dancing courtyard so that her pleasurable mulatto girls could go to bed by themselves and get some rest. They'd been working without cease for three days, first taking care of the guests of honor in secret, and then turned loose, the doors wide open for those of us still unsated by the wedding bash. María Alejandrina Cervantes, about whom we used to say that she would go to sleep only once and that would be to die, was the most elegant and the most tender woman I have ever known, and the most serviceable in bed, but she was also the strictest. She'd been born and reared here, and here she lived, in a house with open doors, with several rooms for rent and an enormous courtyard for dancing lit by lantern gourds bought in the Chinese bazaars of Paramaribo. It was she who did away with my generation's virginity. She taught us much more than we should have learned, but she taught us above all that there's no place in life sadder than an empty bed. Santiago Nasar lost his senses the first time he saw her. I warned him: " '*A falcon who chases a warlike crane can only hope for a life of pain.*' " But he didn't listen to me, dazzled by María Alejandrina Cervantes's illusory calls. She was his mad passion, his mistress of tears at the age of fifteen, until Ibrahim Nasar drove him out of the bed with a whip and shut him up for more than a year on The Divine Face. Ever since then they were still linked by a serious affection, but without the disorder of love, and she had so much respect for him that she never again went to bed with anyone if he was present. During those last vacations she would send us off early with the pretext that she was tired, but she left the door unbarred and with a lamp lighted in the hall so that I could come in secretly.

Santiago Nasar had an almost magical talent for disguises, and his favorite sport was to confuse the identities of the mulatto girls. He would rifle the wardrobe of some to disguise the others, so that they all ended up feeling different from themselves and like the ones they weren't. On a certain occasion, one of them found herself repeated in another with such exactness that she had an attack of tears. "I felt like I'd stepped out of the mirror," she said. But that night María Alejandrina Cervantes wouldn't let Santiago Nasar indulge himself for the last time in his tricks as a transformer, and she prevented it with such flimsy pretexts that the bad taste left by that memory changed his life. So we took the musicians with us for a round of serenades, and we continued the party on our own, while the Vicario twins were waiting for Santiago Nasar to kill him. It was he who got the idea, at almost four o'clock, to go up the widower Xius's hill and sing for the newlyweds.

Not only did we sing under the windows, but we set off rockets and fireworks in the gardens, yet we didn't perceive any sign of life inside the farmhouse. It didn't occur to us that there was no one there, especially because the new car was by the door with its top still folded down and with the satin ribbons and bouquets of wax orange blossoms they had hung on it during the festivities. My brother Luis Enrique, who played the guitar like a professional at that time, improvised a song with matrimonial double meanings in honor of the newlyweds. Until then it hadn't rained; on the contrary, the moon was high in the sky and the air was clear, and at the bottom of the precipice you could see the trickle of light from the Saint Elmo's fire in the cemetery. On the other side you could make out the groves of blue banana trees in the moonlight, the sad swamps, and the phosphorescent line of the Caribbean on the horizon. Santiago Nasar pointed to an intermittent light at sea and told us that it was the soul in torment of a slave ship that had sunk with a cargo of blacks from Senegal across from the main harbor mouth at Cartagena de Indias. It wasn't possible to think that his conscience was bothering him, although at that time he didn't know that the ephemeral married life of

Angela Vicario had come to an end two hours before. Bayardo San Román had taken her to her parents' house on foot so that the noise of the motor wouldn't betray his misfortune in advance, and he was back there alone and with the lights out in the widower Xius's happy farmhouse.

When we went down the hill my brother invited us to have some breakfast of fried fish at one of the lunch stands in the market, but Santiago Nasar was against it because he wanted to get an hour's sleep before the bishop arrived. He went along the riverbank with Cristo Bedoya, passing the poor people's eating places that were beginning to light up by the old harbor, and before turning the corner he waved good-bye. It was the last time we saw him.

Cristo Bedoya, whom he had agreed to meet later on at the docks, took leave of him at the back door of his house. The dogs barked at him as usual when they heard him come in, but he calmed them down in the half light with the tinkling of his keys. Victoria Guzmán was keeping watch over the coffeepot on the stove when he passed by the kitchen on his way into the house.

"White man," she called to him, "coffee will be ready soon."

Santiago Nasar told her that he'd have some later, and he asked her to tell Divina Flor to wake him up at five-thirty and bring him a clean change of clothes, just like the ones he had on. An instant after he'd gone to bed, Victoria Guzmán got the message from Clotilde Armenta sent via the milk beggar. At five-thirty she followed his orders to wake him, but she didn't send Divina Flor and went up to the bedroom herself with the suit of pure linen, because she never missed a chance to keep her daughter away from the claws of the seigneur.

María Alejandrina Cervantes had left the door of her house unbarred. I took leave of my brother, crossed the veranda where the mulatto girls' cats were sleeping curled up among the tulips, and opened the bedroom door without knocking. The lights were out, but as soon as I went in I caught the smell of a warm woman and I saw the eyes of an insomniac leopard in the darkness, and then I didn't know anything else about myself until the bells began to ring.

On his way to our house, my brother went in to buy some cigarettes at Clotilde Armenta's store. He'd drunk so much that his memories of that encounter were always quite confused, but he never forgot the fatal drink that Pedro Vicario offered him. "It was liquid fire," he told me. Pablo Vicario, who had fallen asleep, awoke with a start when he heard him come in, and he showed him the knife.

"We're going to kill Santiago Nasar," he told him.

My brother doesn't remember it. "But even if I did remember, I wouldn't have believed it," he told me many times. "Who the fuck would ever think that the twins would kill anyone, much less with a pig knife!" Then they asked him where Santiago Nasar was, because they'd seen the two of them together, and my brother didn't remember his own answer either. But Clotilde Armenta and the Vicario brothers were so startled when they heard it that it was left established in the brief in separate declarations. According to them, my brother said: "Santiago Nasar is dead." Then he delivered an episcopal blessing, stumbled over the threshold, and staggered out. In the middle of the square he crossed paths with Father Amador, who was going to the dock in his vestments, followed by an acolyte ringing the bell and several helpers carrying the altar for the bishop's field mass. The Vicario brothers crossed themselves when they saw them pass.

Clotilde Armenta told me that they'd lost their last hopes when the priest passed by her place. "I thought he hadn't got my message," she said. Nonetheless, Father Amador confessed to me many years later, retired from the world in the gloomy Calafell Rest Home, that he had in fact received Clotilde Armenta's message and others more peremptory while he was getting ready to go the docks. "The truth is I didn't know what to do," he told me. "My first thought was that it wasn't any business of mine but something for the civil authorities, but then I made up my mind to say something in passing to Plácida Linero." Yet when he crossed the square, he'd forgotten completely. "You have to understand," he told me, "that the bishop was coming on that unfortunate day." At the moment of the crime he felt such despair and was so disgusted with himself that the only thing he could think of was to ring the fire alarm.

My brother Luis Enrique entered the house through the kitchen door, which my mother left unlocked so my father wouldn't hear us come in. He went to the bathroom before going to bed, but he fell asleep sitting on the toilet, and when my brother Jaime got up to go to school he found him stretched out face down on the tile floor and singing in his sleep. My sister the nun, who wasn't going to wait for the bishop because she had an eighty-proof hangover, couldn't get him to wake up. "It was striking five when I went to the bathroom," she told me. Later, when my sister Margot went in to bathe before going to the docks, she managed with great effort to drag him to his bedroom. From the other side of sleep he heard the first bellows of the bishop's boat without awakening. Then he fell into a deep sleep, worn out by his carousing, until my sister the nun rushed into the bedroom, trying to put her habit on as she ran, and woke him up with her mad cry:

"They've killed Santiago Nasar!"

4

THE DAMAGE FROM THE KNIVES WAS ONLY A BEGINNING FOR THE
unforgiving autopsy that Father Carmen Amador found himself obliged to perform in Dr. Dionisio Iguarán's absence. "It
was as if we killed him all over again after he was dead," the
aged priest told me in his retirement at Calafell. "But it was
an order from the mayor, and orders from the barbarian, stu-
pid as they might have been, had to be obeyed." It wasn't entirely proper. In the confusion of that absurd Monday, Colonel Aponte had had an urgent telegraphic conversation with
the governor of the province, and the latter authorized him to
take the preliminary steps while he sent an investigating magistrate. The mayor was a former troop commander with no
experience in matters of law, and he was too conceited to ask
anyone who knew where he should begin. The first thing that
bothered him was the autopsy. Cristo Bedoya, who was a medical student, managed to get out of it because of his intimate
friendship with Santiago Nasar. The mayor thought that the
body could be kept under refrigeration until Dr. Dionisio Iguarán came back, but he couldn't find a human-sized freezer,
and the only one in the market that would serve the purpose
was out of order. The body had been exposed to public view

in the center of the living room, lying on a narrow iron cot while they were building a rich man's coffin for it. They'd brought in fans from the bedrooms and some neighboring houses, but there were so many people anxious to see it that they had to push back the furniture and take down the bird cages and pots of ferns, and even then the heat was unbearable. In addition, the dogs, aroused by the smell of death, increased the uneasiness. They hadn't stopped howling since I went into the house, when Santiago Nasar was still in his death throes in the kitchen and I found Divina Flor weeping in great howls and holding them off with a stick.

"Help me," she shouted to me. "What they want is to eat his guts."

We locked them up in the stable. Plácida Linero later ordered them taken to some place far off until after the funeral. But toward noon, no one knew how, they escaped from where they were and burst madly into the house. Plácida Linero, just once, lost her grip.

"Those shitty dogs!" she shouted. "Kill them!"

The order was carried out immediately and the house was silent again. Until then there hadn't been any concern at all for the state of the body. The face had remained intact, with the same expression it wore when he was singing, and Cristo Bedoya had put the intestines back in place and wrapped the body in linen strips. Nevertheless, in the afternoon a syrup-colored liquid began to flow from the wounds, drawing flies, and a purple blotch appeared on the upper lip and spread out very slowly, like the shadow of a cloud on water, up to the hairline. His face, which had always been easy-going, took on a hostile expression, and his mother covered it with a handkerchief. Colonel Aponte understood then that they couldn't wait any longer and he ordered Father Amador to perform the autopsy. "It would be worse digging him up a week later," he said. The priest had studied medicine and surgery at Salamanca, but had entered the seminary before he was graduated, and even the mayor knew that his autopsy would have no legal standing. Nevertheless, he made him carry out the order.

It was a massacre, performed at the public school with the help of the druggist, who took notes, and a first-year medical student who was here on vacation. They had only a few instruments for minor surgery available and the rest were craftsmen's tools. But despite the havoc wrought on the body, Father Amador's report seemed in order and the investigator incorporated it in the brief as a useful piece of evidence.

Seven of the many wounds were fatal. The liver was almost sliced in pieces by two deep cuts on the anterior side. He had four incisions in the stomach, one of them so deep that it went completely through, and destroyed, the pancreas. He had six other, lesser perforations in the transverse colon and multiple wounds in the small intestine. The only one he had in the back, at the level of the third lumbar vertebra, had perforated the right kidney. The abdominal cavity was filled with large clots of blood, and in the midst of the morass of gastric contents appeared a medal of gold that Santiago Nasar had swallowed at the age of four. The thoracic cavity showed two perforations: one in the second right rib space that affected the lung, and another quite close to the left armpit. He also had six minor wounds on his arms and hands, and two horizontal cuts: one on the right thigh and the other in the abdominal muscles. He had a deep stab in the right hand. The report says: "It looked like a stigma of the crucified Christ." The encephalic mass weighed sixty grams more than that of a normal Englishman, and Father Amador noted in the report that Santiago Nasar had a superior intelligence and a brilliant future. Nevertheless, in the final note he pointed out a hypertrophy of the liver that he attributed to a poorly cured case of hepatitis. "That is to say," he told me, "he had only a few years of life left to him in any case." Dr. Dionisio Iguarán, who in fact had treated Santiago Nasar for hepatitis at the age of twelve, recalled that autopsy with indignation. "Only a priest could be so dumb," he told me. "There was never any way to make him understand that we tropical people have larger livers than greenhorn Galician Spaniards." The report concluded that the cause of death had been a massive hemorrhage brought on by any one of the seven major wounds.

They gave us back a completely different body. Half of the cranium had been destroyed by the trepanation, and the lady-killer face that death had preserved ended up having lost its identity. Furthermore, the priest had pulled out the sliced-up intestines by the roots, but in the end he didn't know what to do with them, and he gave them an angry blessing and threw them into the garbage pail. The last onlookers ranged about the schoolhouse windows lost their curiosity, the helper fainted, and Colonel Lázaro Aponte, who had seen and caused so many repressive massacres, became a vegetarian as well as a spiritualist. The empty shell, stuffed with rags and quicklime and sewed up crudely with coarse twine and baling needles, was on the point of falling apart when we put it into the new coffin with its silk quilt lining. "I thought it would last longer that way," Father Amador told me. Just the opposite happened, and we had to bury him hurriedly at dawn because he was in such bad shape that it was already unbearable in the house.

A cloudy Tuesday was breaking through. I didn't have the courage to sleep at the end of that oppressive time, and I pushed on the door of María Alejandrina Cervantes's house in case she hadn't put up the bar. The gourd lamps were burning where they hung from the trees, and in the courtyard for dancing there were several wood fires with huge steaming pots where the mulatto girls were putting mourning dye onto their party clothes. I found María Alejandrina Cervantes awake as always at dawn, and completely naked as always when there weren't any strangers in the house. She was squatting like a Turkish houri on her queenly bed across from a Babylonic platter of things to eat: veal cutlets, a boiled chicken, a pork loin, and a garnishing of plantains and vegetables that would have served five people. Disproportionate eating was always the only way she could ever mourn and I'd never seen her do it with such grief. I lay down by her side with my clothes on, barely speaking, and mourning too in my way. I was thinking about the ferocity of Santiago Nasar's fate, which had collected twenty years of happiness from him not only with his death but also with the dismemberment of his body and its dispersion and extermination. I dreamed that a woman was coming into the room with a little girl in her arms, and that the child was chewing without stopping to take a breath, and that half-chewed kernels of corn were falling into the woman's brassiere. The woman said to me: "She crunches like a nutty nuthatch, kind of sloppy, kind of slurpy." Suddenly I felt the anxious fingers that were undoing the buttons of my shirt, and I caught the dangerous smell of the beast of love lying by my back, and I felt myself sinking into the delights of the quicksand of her tenderness. But suddenly she stopped, coughed from far off, and slipped out of my life.

"I can't," she said. "You smell of him."

Not just I. Everything continued smelling of Santiago Nasar that day. The Vicario brothers could smell him in the jail cell where the mayor had locked them up until he could think of something to do with them. "No matter how much I scrubbed with soap and rags, I couldn't get rid of the smell," Pedro Vicario told me. They'd gone three nights without sleep, but they couldn't rest because as soon as they began to fall asleep they would commit the crime all over again. Now, almost an old man, trying to explain to me his condition on that endless day, Pablo Vicario told me without any effort: "It was like being awake twice over." That phrase made me think that what must have been most unbearable for them in jail was their lucidity.

The room was ten feet square, and had a very high skylight with iron bars, a portable latrine, a washstand with its pitcher and basin, and two makeshift beds with straw mats. Colonel Aponte, under whose orders it had been built, said that no hotel existed that was more humane. My brother Luis Enrique agreed, because one night they'd locked him up after a fight among musicians, and the mayor allowed him the charity of having one of the mulatto girls stay with him. Perhaps the Vicario brothers could have thought the same thing at eight o'clock in the morning, when they felt themselves safe from the Arabs. At that moment they were comforted by the honor of having done their duty, and the only thing that worried them was the persistence of the smell. They asked for lots of water, laundry soap, and rags, and they washed the blood from their arms and faces, and they also washed their shirts, but they couldn't get any rest. Pedro Vicario asked for his laxatives and diuretics and a roll of sterile gauze so he could change his bandage, and he succeeded in having two urinations during the morning. Nevertheless, life was becoming so difficult for him as the day advanced that the smell took second place. At two in the afternoon, when the heaviness of the heat should have melted them, Pedro Vicario couldn't stay there lying on the bed, but the same weariness prevented him from standing. The pain in his groin had reached his throat, his urine was shut off, and he suffered the frightful certainty that he wouldn't sleep ever again for the rest of his life. "I was awake for eleven months," he told me, and I knew him well enough to know that it was true. He couldn't eat any lunch. Pablo Vicario, for his part, ate a little bit of everything they brought him, and fifteen minutes later unloosed a pestilential diarrhea. At six in the afternoon, while they were performing the autopsy on Santiago Nasar's corpse, the mayor was summoned urgently because Pedro Vicario was convinced that his brother had been poisoned. "He was turning into water right in front of me," Pedro Vicario told me, "and we couldn't get rid of the idea that it was some tricks of the Turks." Up till then he'd overflowed the portable latrine twice and the guard on watch had taken him to the town hall washroom another six times. There Colonel Aponte found him, in the doorless toilet boxed in by the guard, and pouring out water so fluently that it wasn't too absurd to think about poison. But they put the idea aside immediately when it was established that he had only drunk the water and eaten the food sent by Pura Vicario. Nonetheless, the mayor was so impressed that he had the prisoners taken to his house under a special guard until the investigating judge came and transferred them to the panoptic prison in Riohacha.

The twins' fear was in response to the mood in the streets. Revenge by the Arabs wasn't dismissed, but no one, except the Vicario brothers, had thought of poison. It was supposed, rather, that they would wait for nightfall in order to pour gasoline through the skylight and burn up the prisoners in their cell. But even that was too easy a supposition. The Arabs comprised a community of peaceful immigrants who had settled at the beginning of the century in Caribbean towns, even in the poorest and most remote, and there they remained, selling colored cloth and bazaar trinkets. They were clannish, hardworking, and Catholic. They married among themselves, imported their wheat, raised lambs in their yards, and grew oregano and eggplants, and playing cards was their only driving passion. The older ones continued speaking the rustic Arabic they had brought from their homeland, and they maintained it intact in the family down to the second generation, but those of the third, with the exception of Santiago Nasar, listened to their parents in Arabic and answered them in Spanish. So it was inconceivable that they would suddenly abandon their pastoral spirit to avenge a death for which we all could have been to blame. On the other hand, no one thought about reprisals from Plácida Linero's family, who had been powerful and fighting people until their fortune ran out, and had bred more than two barroom killers who had been preserved by the salt of their name.

Colonel Aponte, worried by the rumors, visited the Arabs family by family and that time, at least, drew a correct conclusion. He found them perplexed and sad, with signs of mourning on their altars, and some of them sitting on the ground and wailing, but none harbored ideas of vengeance. The reaction that morning had grown out of the heat of the crime, and even the very leaders admitted that in no case would it have gone beyond a beating. Furthermore, it was Susana Abdala, the centenarian matriarch, who recommended the prodigious infusion of passion flowers and absinthe that dried up Pablo Vicario's diarrhea and unleashed at the same time his brother's florid flow. Pedro Vicario then fell into an insomniac drowsiness and his recovered brother earned his first sleep without remorse. That was how Purísima Vicario found them at three o'clock in the morning on Tuesday when the mayor brought her to say good-bye to them.

The whole family left, even the older sisters with their husbands, on Colonel Aponte's initiative. They left without anyone's noticing, sheltered by public exhaustion, while the only survivors of that irreparable day among us who were awake were burying Santiago Nasar. They were leaving until spirits cooled off, according to the mayor's decision, but they never came back. Pura Vicario wrapped the face of the rejected daughter in a cloth so that no one would see the bruises, and she dressed her in bright red so nobody might think she was mourning her secret lover. Before leaving she asked Father Amador to confess her sons in jail, but Pedro Vicario refused, and convinced his brother that they had nothing to repent. They remained alone, and on the day of their transfer to Riohacha they had so far recovered and were so convinced that they were right that they didn't want to be taken out by night, as had happened with the family, but in broad daylight and with their faces showing. Poncio Vicario, the father, died a short time later. "His moral pain carried him off," Angela Vicario told me. When the twins were absolved, they remained in Riohacha, only a day's trip from Manaure, where the family was living. Prudencia Cotes went there to marry Pablo Vicario, who learned to work with precious metals in his father's shop and came to be an elegant goldsmith. Pedro Vicario, without love or a job, reenlisted in the armed forces three years later, earned his first sergeant's stripes, and one fine morning his patrol went into guerrilla territory singing whorehouse songs and was never heard of again.

For the immense majority of people there was only one victim: Bayardo San Román. They took it for granted that the only actors in the tragedy had been fulfilling with dignity, and even with a certain grandeur, their part of the destiny that life had assigned them. Santiago Nasar had expiated the insult, the brothers Vicario had proved their status as men, and the seduced sister was in possession of her honor once more. The only one who had lost everything was Bayardo San Román: "poor Bayardo," as he was remembered over the years. Still, no one had thought of him until after the eclipse of the moon the following Saturday, when the widower Xius told the mayor that he'd seen a phosphorescent bird fluttering over his former home, and he thought it was the soul of his wife, who was going about demanding what was hers. The mayor slapped his brow, but it had nothing to do with the widower's vision.

"Shit!" he shouted. "I'd completely forgotten about that poor man!"

He went up the hill with a patrol and found the car with its top down in front of the farmhouse, and he saw a solitary light in the bedroom, but no one answered his knocks. So they broke down a side door and searched the rooms, which were lighted by the traces of the eclipse. "Things looked like they were under water," the mayor told me. Bayardo San Román was unconscious on the bed, still the way Pura Vicario had seen him early Tuesday morning, wearing his dress pants and silk shirt, but with his shoes off. There were empty bottles on the floor and many more unopened beside the bed, but not a trace of food. "He was in the last stages of ethylic intoxication," I was told by Dr. Dionisio Iguarán, who had given him emergency treatment. But he recovered in a few hours, and as soon as his mind had cleared, he threw them out of the house with the best manners he was capable of.

"Nobody fucks with me," he said. "Not even my father with his war veteran's balls."

The mayor informed General Petronio San Román of the episode, down to the last literal phrase, in an alarming telegram. General San Román must have followed his son's wishes to the letter, because he didn't come for him, but sent his wife with their daughters and two other older women who seemed to be her sisters. They came on a cargo boat, locked in mourning up to their necks because of Bayardo San Román's misfortunes, and with their hair hanging loose in grief. Before stepping onto land, they took off their shoes and went barefoot through the streets up to the hilltop in the burning dust of noon, pulling out strands of hair by the roots and wailing loudly with such high-pitched shrieks that they seemed to be shouts of joy. I watched them pass from Magdalena Oliver's balcony, and I remember thinking that distress like theirs could only be put on in order to hide other, greater shames.

Colonel Lázaro Aponte accompanied them to the house on the hill, and then Dr. Dionisio Iguarán went up on the mule he kept for emergencies. When the sun let up, two men from the town government brought Bayardo San Román down in a hammock hanging from a pole, wrapped up to his neck in a blanket and with a retinue of wailing women. Magdalena Oliver thought he was dead.

"Collons de déu!" she exclaimed. "What a waste!"

He was laid out by alcohol again, but it was hard to believe they were carrying a living person, because his right arm was dragging on the ground, and as soon as his mother put it back inside the hammock it would fall out again, so that he left a trail on the ground from the edge of the precipice to the deck of the boat. That was all that we had left of him: the memory of a victim.

They left the farmhouse the way it was. My brothers and I would go up to explore it on carousing nights when we were home on vacation, and each time we found fewer things of value in the abandoned rooms. Once we rescued the small valise that Angela Vicario had asked her mother for on her wedding night, but we didn't pay any great attention to it. What we discovered inside seemed to be a woman's natural items for hygiene and beauty, and I only learned their real use when Angela Vicario told me many years later which things were the old wives' artifices she had been instructed in so as to deceive her husband. It was the only trace she'd left in what had been her home as a married woman for five hours.

Years later when I came back to search out the last pieces of testimony for this chronicle, not even the embers of Yolanda Xius's happiness remained. Things had been disappearing little by little, despite Colonel Lázaro Aponte's determined vigilance, even the full-length closet with six mirrors that the master craftsmen of Mompox had had to assemble inside the house because it wouldn't fit through the door. At first the widower Xius was overjoyed, thinking that all those were the posthumous recourses of his wife in carrying off what was hers. Colonel Lázaro Aponte made fun of him. But one night it occurred to him to hold a spiritualist séance in order to clear up the mystery, and the soul of Yolanda Xius confirmed in her own handwriting that it was in fact she who was recovering the knickknacks of her happiness for her house of death. The house began to crumble. The wedding car was falling apart by the door, and finally nothing remained except its weather-rotted carcass. For many years nothing was heard again of its owner. There is a declaration by him in the brief, but it is so short and conventional that it seems to have been put together at the last minute in order to comply with an unavoidable requirement. The only time I tried to talk to him, twenty-three years later, he received me with a certain aggressiveness and refused to supply even the most insignificant fact that might clarify a little his participation in the drama. In any case, not even his family knew much more about him than we did, nor did they have the slightest idea of what he had come to do in a mislaid town, with no other apparent aim than to marry a woman he had never seen.

Of Angela Vicario, on the other hand, I was always receiving periodic news that inspired an idealized image in me. My sister the nun had been going about the upper Guajira for some time trying to convert the last idolaters, and she was in the habit of stopping and chatting with Angela in the village baked by Caribbean salt where her mother had tried to bury her alive. "Regards from your cousin," she would always tell me. My sister Margot, who also visited her during the first years, told me she had bought a solid house with a large courtyard with cross ventilation, the only problem being that on nights of high tide the toilets would back up and fish would appear flopping about in the bedrooms at dawn. Everyone who saw her during that time agreed that she was absorbed and skilled at her embroidery machine, and that by her industry she had managed to forget.

Much later, during an uncertain period when I was trying to understand something of myself by selling encyclopedias and medical books in the towns of Guajira, by chance I got as far as that Indian death village. At the window of a house that faced the sea, embroidering by machine during the hottest hour of the day, was a woman half in mourning, with steel-rimmed glasses and yellowish gray hair, and hanging above her head was a cage with a canary that didn't stop singing. When I saw her like that in the idyllic frame of the window, I refused to believe that the woman there was who I thought it was, because I couldn't bring myself to admit that life might end up resembling bad literature so much. But it was she: Angela Vicario, twenty-three years after the drama.

She treated me the same as always, like a distant cousin, and answered my questions with very good judgment and a sense of humor. She was so mature and witty that it was difficult to believe that she was the same person. What surprised me most was the way in which she'd ended up understanding her own life. After a few minutes she no longer seemed as aged to me as at first sight, but almost as young as in my memory, and she had nothing in common with the person who'd been obliged to marry without love at the age of twenty. Her mother, in her grouchy old age, received me like a difficult ghost. She refused to talk about the past, and for this chronicle I had to be satisfied with a few disconnected phrases from her conversations with my mother, and a few others rescued from my memories. She had gone beyond what was possible to make Angela Vicario die in life, but the daughter herself had brought her plans to naught because she never made any mystery out of her misfortune. On the contrary, she would recount it in all its details to anyone who wanted to hear it, except for one item that would never be cleared up: who was the real cause of her damage, and how and why, because no one believed that it had really been Santiago Nasar. They belonged to two completely different worlds. No one had ever seen them together, much less alone together. Santiago Nasar was too haughty to have noticed her: "Your cousin the booby," he would say to me when he had to mention her. Besides, as we said at that time, he was a sparrow hawk. He went about alone, just like his father, nipping the bud of any wayward virgin who began showing up in those woods, but in town no other relationship ever came to be known except for the conventional one he maintained with Flora Miguel, and the stormy one with María Alejandrina Cervantes, which drove him crazy for fourteen months. The most current version, perhaps because it was the most perverse, was that Angela Vicario was protecting someone who really loved her and she had chosen Santiago Naser's name because she thought her brothers would never dare go up against him. I tried to get that truth out of her myself when I visited her the second time, with all my arguments in order, but she barely lifted her eyes from the embroidery to knock them down. "Don't beat it to death, cousin," she told me. "He was the one."

Everything else she told without reticence, even the disaster of her wedding night. She recounted how her friends had instructed her to get her husband drunk in bed until he passed out, to feign more embarrassment than she really felt so he'd turn out the light, to give herself a drastic douche of alum water to fake virginity, and to stain the sheet with Mercurochrome so she could display it the following day in her bridal courtyard. Her bawds hadn't counted on two things: Bayardo San Román's exceptional resistance as a drinker, and the pure decency that Angela Vicario carried hidden inside the stolidity her mother had imposed. "I didn't do any of what they told me," she said, "because the more I thought about it, the more I realized that it was all something dirty that shouldn't be done to anybody, much less to the poor man who had the bad luck to marry me." So she let herself get undressed openly in the lighted bedroom, safe now from all the acquired fears that had ruined her life. "It was very easy," she told me, "because I'd made up my mind to die."

The truth is that she spoke about her misfortune without any shame in order to cover up the other misfortune, the real one, that was burning in her insides. No one would even have suspected until she decided to tell me that Bayardo San Román had been in her life forever from the moment he'd brought her back home. It was a coup de grâce. "Suddenly, when Mama began to hit me, I began to remember him," she told me. The blows hurt less because she knew they were for him. She went on thinking about him with a certain surprise at herself while she was lying on the dining room couch sobbing. "I wasn't crying because of the blows or anything that had happened," she told me. "I was crying because of him." She kept on thinking about him while her mother put arnica compresses on her face, and even more when she heard the shouting in the street and the fire alarm bells in the belfry, and her mother came in to tell her she could sleep now because the worst was over.

She'd been thinking about him for a long time, without any illusions, when she had to go with her mother to get her eyes examined in the hospital at Riohacha. They stopped off on the way at the Hotel del Puerto, whose owner they knew, and Pura Vicario asked for a glass of water at the bar. She was drinking it with her back to her daughter when the latter saw her own thoughts reflected in the mirrors repeated around the room. Angela Vicario turned her head with a last breath and watched him pass by without seeing her and saw him go out of the hotel. Then she looked at her mother with her heart in shreds. Pura Vicario had finished drinking, dried her lips on her sleeve, and smiled at her from the bar with her new glasses. In that smile, for the first time since her birth, Angela Vicario saw her as she was: a poor woman devoted to the cult of her defects. "Shit," she said to herself. She was so upset that she spent the whole trip back home singing aloud, and she threw herself on her bed to weep for three days.

She was reborn. "I went crazy over him," she told me, "out of my mind." She only had to close her eyes to see him, she heard him breathing in the sea, the blaze of his body in bed would awaken her at midnight. Toward the end of that week, unable to get a moment's rest, she wrote him the first letter. It was a conventional missive, in which she told him that she'd seen him come out of the hotel, and that she would have liked it if he had seen her. She waited in vain for a reply. At the end of two months, tired of waiting, she sent him another letter in the same oblique style as the previous one, whose only aim seemed to be to reproach him for lack of courtesy. Six months later she had written six letters with no reply, but she comforted herself with the certainty that he was getting them.

Mistress of her fate for the first time, Angela Vicario then discovered that hate and love are reciprocal passions. The more letters she sent the more the coals of her fever burned, but the happy rancor she felt for her mother also heated up. "Just seeing her would turn my stomach," she told me, "but I couldn't see her without remembering him." Her life as a rejected wife continued on, simple as that of an old maid, still doing machine embroidery with her friends just as before she had made cloth tulips and paper birds, but when her mother went to bed she would stay in the room until dawn writing letters with no future. She became lucid, overbearing, mistress of her own free will, and she became a virgin again just for him, and she recognized no other authority than her own nor any other service than that of her obsession.

She wrote a weekly letter for over half a lifetime. "Sometimes I couldn't think of what to say," she told me, dying with laughter, "but it was enough for me to know that he was getting them." At first they were a fiancée's notes, then they were little messages from a secret lover, perfumed cards from a furtive sweetheart, business papers, love documents, and lastly they were the indignant letters of an abandoned wife who invented cruel illnesses to make him return. One night, in a good mood, she spilled the inkwell over the finished letter and instead of tearing it up she added a postscript: "As proof of my love I send you my tears." On occasion, tired of weeping, she would make fun of her own madness. Six times the postmistresses were changed and six times she wore their complicity. The only thing that didn't occur to her was to give up. Nevertheless, he seemed insensible to her delirium; it was like writing to nobody.

Early one windy morning in the tenth year, she was awakened by the certainty that he was naked in her bed. Then she wrote him a feverish letter, twenty pages long, in which without shame she let out the bitter truths that she had carried rotting in her heart ever since that ill-fated night. She spoke to him of the eternal scars he had left on her body, the salt of his tongue, the fiery furrow of his African tool. On Friday she gave it to the postmistress who came Friday afternoons to embroider with her and pick up the letters, and she was convinced that that final alleviation would be the end of her agony. But there was no reply. From then on she was no longer conscious of what she wrote nor to whom she was really writing, but she kept on without quarter for seventeen years.

Halfway through one August day, while she was embroidering with her friends, she heard someone coming to the door.

She didn't have to look to see who it was. "He was fat and was beginning to lose his hair, and he already needed glasses to see things close by," she told me. "But it was him, God damn it, it was him!" She was frightened because she knew he was seeing her just as diminished as she saw him, and she didn't think he had as much love inside as she to bear up under it. His shirt was soaked in sweat, as she had seen him the first time at the fair, and he was wearing the same belt, and carrying the same unstitched leather saddlebags with silver decorations. Bayardo San Román took a step forward, unconcerned about the other astonished embroiderers, and laid his saddlebags on the sewing machine.

"Well," he said, "here I am."

He was carrying a suitcase with clothing in order to stay and another just like it with almost two thousand letters that she had written him. They were arranged by date in bundles tied with colored ribbons, and they were all unopened.

5

FOR YEARS WE COULDN'T TALK ABOUT ANYTHING ELSE. OUR DAILY conduct, dominated then by so many linear habits, had suddenly begun to spin around a single common anxiety. The cocks of dawn would catch us trying to give order to the chain of many chance events that had made absurdity possible, and it was obvious that we weren't doing it from an urge to clear up mysteries but because none of us could go on living without an exact knowledge of the place and the mission assigned to us by fate.

Many never got to know. Cristo Bedoya, who went on to become a surgeon of renown, never managed to explain to himself why he gave in to the impulse to spend two hours at his grandparents' house until the bishop came instead of going to rest at his parents', who had been waiting for him since dawn to warn him. But most of those who could have done something to prevent the crime and did not consoled themselves with the pretext that affairs of honor are sacred monopolies, giving access only to those who are part of the drama. "Honor is love," I heard my mother say. Hortensia Baute, whose only participation was having seen two bloody knives that weren't bloody yet, felt so affected by the hallucination that she fell into a penitential crisis, and one day, unable to stand it any longer, she ran out naked into the street. Flora Miguel, Santiago Nasar's fiancée, ran away out of spite with a lieutenant of the border patrol, who prostituted her among the rubber workers on the Vichada. Aura Villeros, the midwife who had helped bring three generations into the world, suffered a spasm of the bladder when she heard the news and to the day of her death had to use a catheter in order to urinate. Don Rogelio de la Flor, Clotilde Armenta's good husband, who was a marvel of vitality at the age of eighty-six, got up for the last time to see how they had hewn Santiago Nasar to bits against the locked door of his own house, and he didn't survive the shock. Plácida Linero had locked that door at the last moment, but with the passage of time she freed herself from blame. "I locked it because Divina Flor had sworn to me that she'd seen my son come in," she told me, "and it wasn't true." On the other hand, she never forgave herself for having mixed up the magnificent augury of trees with the unlucky one of birds, and she succumbed to the pernicious habit of her time of chewing pepper cress seeds.

Twelve days after the crime, the investigating magistrate came upon a town that was an open wound. In the squalid wooden office in the town hall, drinking pot coffee laced with cane liquor against the mirages of the heat, he had to ask for troop reinforcements to control the crowd that was pouring in to testify without having been summoned, everyone eager to show off his own important role in the drama. The magistrate was newly graduated and still wore his black linen law school suit and the gold ring with the emblem of his degree, and he had the airs and the lyricism of a happy new parent. But I never discovered his name. Everything we know about his character has been learned from the brief, which several people helped me look for twenty years later in the Palace of Justice in Riohacha. There was no classification of files whatever, and more then a century of cases were piled up on the floor of the decrepit colonial building that had been Sir Francis Drake's headquarters for two days. The ground floor would be flooded by high tides and the unbound volumes floated about the deserted offices. I searched many times with the water up to my ankles in that lagoon of lost causes, and after five years rummaging around only chance let me rescue some 322 pages filched from the more than 500 that the brief must have contained.

The judge's name didn't appear on any of them, but it was obvious that he was a man burning with the fever of literature. He had doubtless read the Spanish classics and a few Latin ones, and he was quite familiar with Nietzsche, who was the fashionable author among magistrates of his time. The marginal notes, and not just because of the color of the ink, seemed to be written in blood. He was so perplexed by the enigma that fate had touched him with, that he kept falling into lyrical distractions that ran contrary to the rigor of his profession. Most of all, he never thought it legitimate that life should make use of so many coincidences forbidden literature, so that there should be the untrammeled fulfillment of a death so clearly foretold.

Nevertheless, what had alarmed him most at the conclusion of his excessive diligence was not having found a single clue, not even the most improbable, that Santiago Nasar had been the cause of the wrong. The friends of Angela Vicario who had been her accomplices in the deception went on saying for a long time that she had shared her secret with them before the wedding, but that she hadn't revealed any name. In the brief, they declared: "She told us about the miracle but not the saint." Angela Vicario, for her part, wouldn't budge. When the investigating magistrate asked her with his oblique style if she knew who the decedent Santiago Nasar was, she answered him impassively:

"He was my perpetrator."

That's the way she swears in the brief, but with no further precision of either how or where. During the trial, which lasted only three days, the representative of the people put his greatest effort into the weakness of that charge. Such was the perplexity of the investigating magistrate over the lack of proof against Santiago Nasar that his good work at times seemed ruined by disillusionment. On folio 416, in his own handwriting and with the druggist's red ink, he wrote a marginal note: *Give me a prejudice and I will move the world.* Under that paraphrase of discouragement, in a merry sketch with the same blood ink, he drew a heart pierced by an arrow. For him, just as for Santiago Nasar's closest friends, the victim's very behavior during his last hours was overwhelming proof of his innocence.

On the morning of his death, in fact, Santiago Nasar hadn't had a moment of doubt, in spite of the fact that he knew very well what the price of the insult imputed to him was. He was aware of the prudish disposition of his world, and he must have understood that the twins' simple nature was incapable of resisting an insult. No one knew Bayardo San Román very well, but Santiago Nasar knew him well enough to know that underneath his worldly airs he was as subject as anyone else to his native prejudices. So the murdered man's refusal to worry could have been suicide. Besides, when he finally learned at the last moment that the Vicario brothers were waiting for him to kill him, his reaction was not one of panic, as has so often been said, but rather the bewilderment of innocence.

My personal impression is that he died without understanding his death. After he'd promised my sister Margot that he would come and have breakfast at our house, Cristo Bedoya took him by the arm as they strolled along the dock and both seemed so unconcerned that they gave rise to false impressions. "They were both going along so contentedly," Meme Loiza told me, "that I gave thanks to God, because I thought the matter had been cleared up." Not everybody loved Santiago Nasar so much, of course. Polo Carrillo, the owner of the electric plant, thought that his serenity wasn't innocence but cynicism. "He thought that his money made him untouchable," he told me. Fausta López, his wife, commented: "Just like all Turks." Indalecio Pardo had just passed by Clotilde

Armenta's store and the twins had told him that as soon as the bishop left, they were going to kill Santiago Nasar. Like so many others, he thought these were the usual fantasies of very early risers, but Clotilde Armenta made him see that it was true, and she asked him to get to Santiago Nasar and warn him.

"Don't bother," Pedro Vicario told him. "No matter what, he's as good as dead already."

It was too obvious a challenge: the twins knew the bonds between Indalecio Pardo and Santiago Nasar, and they must have thought that he was just the right person to stop the crime without bringing any shame on them. But Indalecio found Santiago Nasar being led by the arm by Cristo Bedoya among the groups that were leaving the docks, and he didn't dare warn him. "I lost my nerve," he told me. He gave each one a pat on the back and let them go their way. They scarcely noticed, because they were still taken up with the costs of the wedding.

The people were breaking up and heading toward the square the same way they were. It was a thick crowd, but Escolástica Cisneros thought she noticed that the two friends were walking in the center of it without any difficulty, inside an empty circle, because everyone knew that Santiago Nasar was about to die and they didn't dare touch him. Cristo Bedoya also remembered a strange attitude toward them. "They were looking at us as if we had our faces painted," he told me. Also, Sara Noriega was opening her shoe store at the moment they passed and she was frightened at Santiago Nasar's paleness. But he calmed her down.

"You can imagine, Missy Sara," he told her without stopping, "with this hangover!"

Celeste Dangond was sitting in his pajamas by the door of his house, mocking those who had gone to greet the bishop, and he invited Santiago Nasar to have some coffee. "It was in order to gain some time to think," he told me. But Santiago Nasar answered that he was in a hurry to change clothes to have breakfast with my sister. "I got all mixed up," Celeste Dangond told me, "because it suddenly seemed to me that they couldn't be killing him if he was so sure of what he was going to do." Yamil Shaium was the only one who did what he had proposed doing. As soon as he heard the rumor, he went out to the door of his dry goods store and waited for Santiago Nasar so he could warn him. He was one of the last Arabs who had come with Ibrahim Nasar, had been his partner in cards until his death, and was still the hereditary counselor of the family. No one had as much authority as he to talk to Santiago Nasar. Nevertheless, he thought that if the rumor was baseless it would alarm him unnecessarily, and he preferred to consult first with Cristo Bedoya in case the latter was better informed. He called to him as he went by. Cristo Bedoya gave a pat on the back to Santiago Nasar, who was already at the corner of the square, and answered Yamil Shaium's call. "See you Saturday," he told him.

Santiago Nasar didn't reply, but said something in Arabic to Yamil Shaium, and the latter answered him, also in Arabic, twisting with laughter. "It was a play on words we always had fun with," Yamil Shaium told me. Without stopping, Santiago Nasar waved good-bye to both of them and turned the corner of the square. It was the last time they saw him.

Cristo Bedoya only took the time to grasp Yamil Shaium's information before he ran out of the store to catch Santiago Nasar. He'd seen him turn the corner, but he couldn't find him among the groups that were beginning to break up on the square. Several people he asked gave him the same answer.

"I just saw him with you."

It seemed impossible that he could have reached home in such a short time, but just in case, he went in to ask about him since he found the front door unbarred and ajar. He went in without seeing the paper on the floor. He passed through the shadowy living room, trying not to make any noise, because it was still too early for visitors, but the dogs became aroused at the back of the house and came out to meet him. He calmed them down with his keys as he'd learned from their master, and went on toward the kitchen, with them following. On the veranda he came upon Divina Flor, who was carrying a pail of water and a rag to clean the floor in the living room. She assured him that Santiago Nasar hadn't returned. Victoria Guzmán had just put the rabbit stew on the stove when he entered the kitchen. She understood immediately. "His heart was in his mouth," she told me. Cristo Bedoya asked her if Santiago Nasar was home, and she answered him with feigned innocence that he still hadn't come in to go to sleep.

"It's serious," Cristo Bedoya told her. "They're looking for him to kill him."

Victoria Guzmán forgot her innocence.

"Those poor boys won't kill anybody," she said.

"They've been drinking since Saturday," Cristo Bedoya said.

"That's just it," she replied. "There's no drunk in the world who'll eat his own crap."

Cristo Bedoya went back to the living room, where Divina Flor had just opened the windows. "Of course it wasn't raining," Cristo Bedoya told me. "It was just going on seven and a golden sun was already coming through the windows." He asked Divina Flor again if she was sure that Santiago Nasar hadn't come in through the living room door. She wasn't as sure then as the first time. He asked her about Plácida Linero, and she answered that just a moment before she'd put her coffee on the night table, but she hadn't awakened her. That's the way it always was: Plácida Linero would wake up at seven, have her coffee, and come down to give instructions for lunch. Cristo Bedoya looked at the clock: it was six fifty-six. Then he climbed up to the second floor to make sure that Santiago Nasar hadn't come in.

The bedroom was locked from the inside, because Santiago Nasar had gone out through his mother's bedroom. Cristo Bedoya not only knew the house as well as his own, but was so much at home with the family that he pushed open the door to Plácida Linero's bedroom and went from there into the adjoining one. A beam of dusty light was coming in through the skylight, and the beautiful woman asleep on her side in the hammock, her bride's hand on her cheek, had an unreal look. "It was like an apparition," Cristo Bedoya told me. He looked at her for an instant, fascinated by her beauty, and then he crossed the room in silence, passed by the bathroom, and proceeded into Santiago Nasar's bedroom. The bed was still made, and on the chair, well-pressed, were his riding clothes, and on top of the clothes his horseman's hat, and on the floor his boots beside their spurs. On the night table, Santiago Nasar's wristwatch said six fifty-eight. "Suddenly I thought that he'd come back so that he could go out armed," Cristo Bedoya told me. But he found the Magnum in the drawer of the night table. "I'd never shot a gun," Cristo Bedoya told me, "but I decided to take the revolver and bring it to Santiago Nasar." He stuck it in his belt, under his shirt, and only after the crime did he realize that it was unloaded. Plácida Linero appeared in the doorway with her mug of coffee just as he was closing the drawer.

"Good heavens!" she exclaimed. "You gave me a start!"

Cristo Bedoya was also startled. He saw her in the full light, wearing a dressing gown with golden larks, her hair loose, and the charm had vanished. He explained, somewhat confused, that he was looking for Santiago Nasar.

"He went to receive the bishop," Plácida Linero said.

"The bishop went right through," he said.

"I thought so," she said. "He's the son of the worst kind of mother."

She didn't go on because at that moment she realized that Cristo Bedoya didn't know what to do with his body. "I hope that God has forgiven me," Plácida Linero told me, "but he seemed so confused that it suddenly occurred to me that he'd come to rob us." She asked him what was wrong. Cristo Bedoya was aware that he was in a suspicious situation, but he didn't have the courage to reveal the truth.

"It's just that I haven't had a minute's sleep," he told her.

He left without any further explanations. "In any case," he told me, "she was always imagining that she was being robbed." In the square he ran into Father Amador, who was returning to the church with the vestments for the frustrated mass, but he didn't think he could do anything for Santiago Nasar except save his soul. He was heading toward the docks again when he heard them calling him from the door of Clotilde Armenta's store. Pedro Vicario was in the doorway, pale and haggard, his shirt open and his sleeves rolled up to the elbows, and with the naked knife in his hand. His manner was too insolent to be natural, and yet it wasn't the only final or the most visible pose that he'd assumed in the last moments so they would stop him from committing the crime.

"Cristóbal," he shouted, "tell Santiago Nasar that we're waiting for him here to kill him."

Cristo Bedoya could have done him the favor of stopping him. "If I'd known how to shoot a revolver, Santiago Nasar would be alive today," he told me. But the idea did impress him, after all he'd heard about the devastating power of an armor-plated bullet.

"I warn you. He's armed with a Magnum that can go through an engine block," he shouted.

Pedro Vicario knew it wasn't true. "He never went armed except when he wore riding clothes," he told me. But in any case, he'd foreseen the possibility that he might be armed when he made the decision to wipe his sister's honor clean.

"Dead men can't shoot," he shouted.

Then Pablo Vicario appeared in the doorway. He was as pale as his brother and he was wearing his wedding jacket and carrying his knife wrapped in the newspaper. "If it hadn't been for that," Cristo Bedoya told me, "I never would have known which of the two was which." Clotilde Armenta then appeared behind Pablo Vicario and shouted to Cristo Bedoya to hurry up, because in that faggot town only a man like him could prevent the tragedy.

Everything that happened after that is in the public domain. The people who were coming back from the docks, alerted by the shouts, began to take up positions around the square to witness the crime. Cristo Bedoya asked several people he knew if they'd seen Santiago Nasar, but no one had. At the door of the social club he ran into Colonel Lázaro Aponte and he told him what had just happened in front of Clotilde Armenta's store.

"It can't be," Colonel Aponte said "because I told them to go home to bed."

"I just saw them with pig-killing knives," Cristo Bedoya said.

"It can't be, because I took them away from them before sending them home to bed," said the mayor. "It must be that you saw them before that."

"I saw them two minutes ago and they both had pig-killing knives," Cristo Bedoya said.

"Oh, shit," the mayor said. "Then they must have come back with two new ones."

He promised to take care of it at once, but he went into the social club to check on a date for dominoes that night, and when he came out again the crime had already been committed. Cristo Bedoya then made his only mortal mistake: he thought that Santiago Nasar had decided at the last moment to have breakfast at our house before changing his clothes, and he went to look for him there. He hurried along the riverbank, asking everyone he passed if they'd seen him go by, but no one said he had. He wasn't alarmed, because there were other ways to get to our house. Próspera Arango, the uplander, begged him to do something for her father, who was in his death throes on the stoop of his house, immune to the bishop's fleeting blessing. "I'd seen him when I passed," my sister Margot told me, "and he already had the face of a dead man." Cristo Bedoya delayed four minutes to ascertain the sick man's condition, and promised to come back later for some emergency treatment, but he lost three minutes more helping

Próspera Arango carry him into the bedroom. When he came out again he heard distant shouts and it seemed to him that rockets were being fired in the direction of the square. He tried to run but was hindered by the revolver, which was clumsily stuck in his belt. As he turned the last corner he recognized my mother from the rear as she was practically dragging her youngest son along.

"Luisa Santiaga," he shouted to her, "where's your godson?"

My mother barely turned, her face bathed in tears.

"Oh, my son," she answered, "they say he's been killed!"

That's how it was. While Cristo Bedoya had been looking for him, Santiago Nasar had gone into the house of Flora Miguel, his fiancée, just around the corner from where he'd seen him for the last time. "It didn't occur to me that he could be there," he told me, "because those people never got up before noon." The version that went around was that the whole family slept until twelve o'clock on orders from Nahir Miguel, the wise man of the community. "That's why Flora Miguel, who wasn't that young anymore, was preserved like a rose," Mercedes says. The truth is that they kept the house locked up until very late, like so many others, but they were early-rising and hardworking people. The parents of Santiago Nasar and Flora Miguel had agreed that they should get married. Santiago Nasar accepted the engagement in the bloom of his adolescence, and he was determined to fulfill it, perhaps because he had the same utilitarian concept of matrimony as his father. Flora Miguel, for her part, enjoyed a certain floral quality, but she lacked wit and judgment and had served as bridesmaid for her whole generation, so the agreement was a providential solution for her. They had an easy engagement, without formal visits or restless hearts. The wedding, postponed several times, was finally set for the following Christmas.

Flora Miguel awoke that Monday with the first bellows of the bishop's boat, and shortly thereafter she found out that the Vicario twins were waiting for Santiago Nasar to kill him.

She informed my sister the nun, the only one she spoke to after the misfortune, that she didn't ever remember who'd told her. "I only know that at six o'clock in the morning everybody knew it," she told her. Nevertheless, it seemed inconceivable to her that they were going to kill Santiago Nasar, but on the other hand, it occurred to her that they would force him to marry Angela Vicario in order to give her back her honor. She went through a crisis of humiliation. While half the town was waiting for the bishop, she was in her bedroom weeping with rage, and putting in order the chestful of letters that Santiago Nasar had sent her from school.

Whenever he passed by Flora Miguel's house, even if nobody was home, Santiago Nasar would scratch his keys across the window screens. That Monday she was waiting with the chest of letters in her lap. Santiago Nasar couldn't see her from the street, but she, however, saw him approaching through the screen before he scratched it with his keys.

"Come in," she told him.

No one, not even a doctor, had entered that house at six forty-five in the morning. Santiago Nasar had just left Cristo Bedoya at Yamil Shaium's store, and there were so many people hanging on his movements in the square that it was difficult to believe that no one saw him go into his fiancée's house. The investigating magistrate looked for a single person who'd seen him, and he did so with as much persistence as I, but it was impossible to find one. In folio 382 of the brief, he wrote another marginal pronouncement in red ink: *Fatality makes us invisible*. The fact is that Santiago Nasar went in through the main door, in full view of everyone, and without doing anything not to be seen. Flora Miguel was waiting for him in the parlor, green with rage, wearing one of the dresses with unfortunate ruffles that she was in the habit of putting on for memorable occasions, and she placed the chest in his hands.

"Here you are," she told him. "And I hope they kill you!"

Santiago Nasar was so perplexed that he dropped the chest and his loveless letters poured out onto the floor. He tried to catch Flora Miguel in the bedroom, but she closed the door and threw the bolt. He knocked several times, and called her in too pressing a voice for the time of day, so the whole family came in, all alarmed. Counting relatives by blood and by marriage, adults and minors, there were more than fourteen of them. The last to come was Nahir Miguel, the father, with his red beard and the Bedouin caftan he had brought from his homeland and which he always wore at home. I saw him many times and he was immense and spare, but what most impressed me was the glow of his authority.

"Flora," he called in his language. "Open the door."

He went into his daughter's bedroom while the family stared at Santiago Nasar. He was kneeling in the parlor, picking up the letters and putting them into the chest. "It looked like a penance," they told me. Nahir Miguel came out of the bedroom after a few minutes, made a signal with his hand, and the whole family disappeared.

He continued talking in Arabic to Santiago Nasar. "From the first moment I understood that he didn't have the slightest idea of what I was saying," he told me. Then he asked him outright if he knew that the Vicario brothers were looking for him to kill him. "He turned pale and lost control in such a way that it was impossible to think that he was pretending," he told me. He agreed that his manner reflected not so much fear as confusion.

"Only you can know if they're right or not," he told him. "But in any case, you've only got two paths to follow now: either you hide here, in this house which is yours, or you go out with my rifle."

"I don't understand a God-damned thing," Santiago Nasar said.

It was the only thing he managed to say, and he said it in Spanish. "He looked like a little wet bird," Nahir Miguel told me. He had to take the chest from his hands because he didn't know where to put it in order to open the door.

"It'll be two against one," he told him.

Santiago Nasar left. The people had stationed themselves on the square the way they did on parade days. They all saw him come out, and they all understood that now he knew they were going to kill him, and that he was so confused he couldn't find his way home. They say that someone shouted from a balcony: "Not that way, Turk; by the old dock." Santiago Nasar sought out the voice. Yamil Shaium shouted for him to get into his store and went to get his hunting gun, but he couldn't remember where he'd put the cartridges. They began to shout at him from every side, and Santiago Nasar went backward and forward several times, baffled by hearing so many voices at the same time. It was obvious that he was heading toward his house as if to enter through the kitchen door, but suddenly he must have realized that the main door was open.

"There he comes," said Pedro Vicario.

They'd both seen him at the same time. Pablo Vicario took off his jacket, put it on the bench, and unwrapped his knife, holding it like a scimitar. Before leaving the store, without any agreement, they both crossed themselves. Then Clotilde Armenta grabbed Pedro Vicario by the shirt and shouted to Santiago Nasar to run because they were going to kill him. It was such an urgent shout that it drowned out all the others. "At first he was startled," Clotilde Armenta told me, "because he didn't know who was shouting at him or from where." But when he saw her, he also saw Pedro Vicario, who threw her to the ground and caught up with his brother. Santiago Nasar was less than fifty yards from his house and he ran to the main door.

Five minutes before, in the kitchen, Victoria Guzmán had told Plácida Linero what everybody already knew. Plácida Linero was a woman of steady nerves, so she didn't let any sign of alarm show through. She asked Victoria Guzmán if she'd said anything to her son, and she lied honestly, since she answered that she still hadn't known anything when he came down for coffee. In the living room, where she was still scrubbing the floor, Divina Flor at the same time saw Santiago Nasar come in through the door on the square and go up the open stairs to the bedrooms. "It was a very clear vision," Divina Flor told me. "He was wearing his white suit and carrying something that I couldn't make out well in his hand, but it looked like a bouquet of roses." So when Plácida Linero asked about him, Divina Flor calmed her down.

"He went up to his room a minute ago," she told her.

Plácida Linero then saw the paper on the floor, but she didn't think to pick it up, and she only found out what it said when someone showed it to her later on during the confusion of the tragedy. Through the door she saw the Vicario brothers running toward the house with their knives out. From the place where she was standing she could see them but she couldn't see her son, who was running toward the door from a different angle. "I thought they wanted to get in to kill him inside the house," she told me. Then she ran to the door and slammed it shut. She was putting up the bar when she heard Santiago Nasar's shouts, and she heard the terrified pounding on the door, but she thought he was upstairs, insulting the Vicario brothers from the balcony in his room. She went up to help him.

Santiago Nasar only needed a few seconds to get in when the door closed. He managed to pound with his fists several times, and he turned at once to face his enemies with his bare hands. "I was scared when I saw him face on," Pablo Vicario told me, "because he looked twice as big as he was." Santiago Nasar raised his hand to stop the first strike from Pedro Vicario, who attacked him on the right side with his knife pointed straight in.

"Sons of bitches!" he shouted.

The knife went through the palm of his right hand and then sank into his side up to the hilt. Everybody heard his cry of pain.

"Oh, mother of mine!"

Pedro Vicario pulled out his knife with his slaughterer's iron wrist and dealt him a second thrust almost in the same place. "The strange thing is that the knife kept coming out clean," Pedro Vicario declared to the investigator. "I'd given it to him at least three times and there wasn't a drop of blood." Santiago Nasar twisted after the third stab, his arms crossed over his stomach, let out the moan of a calf, and tried to turn his back to them. Pablo Vicario, who was on his left, then gave him the only stab in the back and a spurt of blood under high pressure soaked his shirt. "It smelled like him," he told me. Mortally wounded three times, Santiago Nasar turned frontward again and leaned his back against his mother's door, without the slightest resistance, as if he only wanted to help them finish killing him by his own contribution. "He didn't cry out again," Pedro Vicario told the investigator. "Just the opposite: it looked to me as if he was laughing." Then they both kept on knifing him against the door with alternate and easy stabs, floating in the dazzling backwater they had found on the other side of fear. They didn't hear the shouts of the whole town, frightened by its own crime. "I felt the way you do when you're galloping on horseback," Pablo Vicario declared. But they both suddenly woke up to reality, because they were exhausted, and yet they thought that Santiago Nasar would never fall. "Shit, cousin," Pablo Vicario told me, "you can't imagine how hard it is to kill a man!" Trying to finish it once and for all, Pedro Vicario sought his heart, but he looked for it almost in the armpit, where pigs have it. Actually, Santiago Nasar wasn't falling because they themselves were holding him up with stabs against the door. Desperate, Pablo Vicario gave him a horizontal slash on the stomach, and all his intestines exploded out. Pedro Vicario was about to do the same, but his wrist twisted with horror and he gave him a wild cut on the thigh. Santiago Nasar was still for an instant, leaning against the door, until he saw his own viscera in the sunlight, clean and blue, and he fell on his knees.

After looking and shouting for him in the bedroom, hearing other shouts that weren't hers and not knowing where they were coming from, Plácida Linero went to the window facing the square and saw the Vicario twins running toward the church. Hot in pursuit was Yamil Shaium with his jaguar gun and some other unarmed Arabs, and Plácida Linero thought the danger had passed. Then she went out onto the bedroom balcony and saw Santiago Nasar in front of the door, face down in the dust, trying to rise up out of his own blood. He stood up, leaning to one side, and started to walk in a state of hallucination, holding his hanging intestines in his hands.

He walked more than a hundred yards, completely around the house, and went in through the kitchen door. He still had enough lucidity not to go along the street, it was the longest way, but by way of the house next door. Poncho Lanao, his wife, and their five children hadn't known what had just happened twenty paces from their door. "We heard the shouting," the wife told me, "but we thought it was part of the bishop's festival." They were sitting down to breakfast when they saw Santiago Nasar enter, soaked in blood and carrying the roots of his entrails in his hands. Poncho Lanao told me: "What I'll never forget was the terrible smell of shit." But Argénida Lanao, the oldest daughter, said that Santiago Nasar walked with his usual good bearing, measuring his steps well, and that his Saracen face with its dashing ringlets was handsomer than ever. As he passed by the table he smiled at them and continued through the bedrooms to the rear door of the house. "We were paralyzed with fright," Argénida Lanao told me. My aunt, Wenefrida Márquez, was scaling a shad in her yard on the other side of the river when she saw him go down the steps of the old dock, looking for his way home with a firm step.

"Santiago, my son," she shouted to him, "what has happened to you?"

"They've killed me, Wene child," he said.

He stumbled on the last step, but he got up at once. "He even took care to brush off the dirt that was stuck to his guts," my Aunt Wene told me. Then he went into his house through the back door that had been open since six and fell on his face in the kitchen.